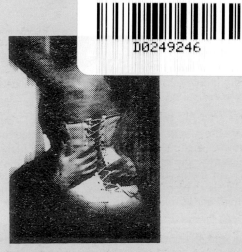

Unlaced, Undressed... UNDONE!

Five delicious stories to seduce your senses...

Short, sexy, scandalous!

An intense encounter with the passionate past.

History has never been this hot!

This is a collection of sexy, scandalous stories drawn from Harlequin Historical Undone eBooks

Whatever your favorite kind of hero—
disreputable rake or Viking warrior—
get ready to be seduced!

First time in print.

**Visit Harlequin Historical Undone at
www.eHarlequin.com**

CHRISTINE MERRILL lives on a farm in Wisconsin, U.S.A., with her husband, two sons and too many pets. She has worked by turns in theater costuming and as a librarian. Writing historical romance combines her love of good stories and fancy dress with her ability to stare out the window and make stuff up. Please visit her Web site at www.christine-merrill.com.

MICHELLE WILLINGHAM grew up living in places all over the world. When her parents hauled her to antiques shows, Michelle entertained herself by making up stories. Currently she teaches American history and English, and lives in southeastern Virginia with her husband and children. Visit her Web site at www.michellewillingham.com or e-mail her at michelle@michellewillingham.com.

LOUISE ALLEN has been immersing herself in history, real and fictional, for as long as she can remember. Louise lives in Bedfordshire and works as a property manager, but spends as much time as possible with her husband or traveling abroad. Venice, Burgundy and the Greek islands are favorite atmospheric destinations. Please visit Louise's Web site, www.louiseallenregency.co.uk, for the latest news!

TERRI BRISBIN is wife to one, mother of three and dental hygienist to hundreds when not living the life of a glamorous romance author. She was born, raised and is still living in the southern New Jersey suburbs. Terri's love of history led her to write time-travel romances and historical romances set in Scotland and England. For more information readers are invited to visit her Web site, www.terribrisbin.com, or contact her at P.O. Box 41, Berlin, NJ 08009-0041, U.S.A.

DIANE GASTON As a psychiatric social worker, Diane spent years helping others create real-life happy endings. Now she crafts fictional ones. The daughter of a U.S. Army colonel, Diane moved frequently during her childhood. It continues to amaze her that her own son and daughter grew up in one house in northern Virginia. Diane still lives in that house, with her husband and three very ordinary house cats. Visit Diane's Web site at dianegaston.com.

Pleasurably Undone!

Christine Merrill
Michelle Willingham
Louise Allen
Terri Brisbin
Diane Gaston

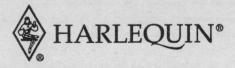

HARLEQUIN®

TORONTO • NEW YORK • LONDON
AMSTERDAM • PARIS • SYDNEY • HAMBURG
STOCKHOLM • ATHENS • TOKYO • MILAN • MADRID
PRAGUE • WARSAW • BUDAPEST • AUCKLAND

If you purchased this book without a cover you should be aware that this book is stolen property. It was reported as "unsold and destroyed" to the publisher, and neither the author nor the publisher has received any payment for this "stripped book."

ISBN-13: 978-0-373-29590-6

PLEASURABLY UNDONE!
Copyright © 2010 by Harlequin Books S.A.

The publisher acknowledges the copyright holders of the individual works as follows:

SEDUCING A STRANGER
Copyright © 2009 by Christine Merrill

THE VIKING'S FORBIDDEN LOVE-SLAVE
Copyright © 2008 by Michelle Willingham

DISROBED AND DISHONORED
Copyright © 2009 by Melanie Hilton

A NIGHT FOR HER PLEASURE
Copyright © 2009 by Theresa S. Brisbin

THE UNLACING OF MISS LEIGH
Copyright © 2009 by Diane Perkins

Recycling programs for this product may not exist in your area.

All rights reserved. Except for use in any review, the reproduction or utilization of this work in whole or in part in any form by any electronic, mechanical or other means, now known or hereafter invented, including xerography, photocopying and recording, or in any information storage or retrieval system, is forbidden without the written permission of the publisher, Harlequin Enterprises Limited, 225 Duncan Mill Road, Don Mills, Ontario, Canada M3B 3K9.

This is a work of fiction. Names, characters, places and incidents are either the product of the author's imagination or are used fictitiously, and any resemblance to actual persons, living or dead, business establishments, events or locales is entirely coincidental.

This edition published by arrangement with Harlequin Books S.A.

For questions and comments about the quality of this book please contact us at Customer_eCare@Harlequin.ca.

® and TM are trademarks of the publisher. Trademarks indicated with ® are registered in the United States Patent and Trademark Office, the Canadian Trade Marks Office and in other countries.

www.eHarlequin.com

Printed in U.S.A.

CONTENTS

SEDUCING A STRANGER

Christine Merrill

Author Note

Since I like to think every new project is an adventure, it was a real treat to do my first Harlequin Historical Undone story. My goal was to see how much story I could fit into a few thousand words, while keeping the relationship hot and still getting to the happy ending that we all love. It was a chance to take a break from plotting a full book, to let both my imagination and my characters run wild.

I hope you have as much fun with it as I did.
Happy reading!

To Mohawk the cat, who gave selflessly of his time
by teasing the dog to hysteria and sleeping
on my keyboard. Without his help, I would never
have been able to finish this story.

Look for Christine Merrill's
Paying the Virgin's Price—part of the
Regency Silk & Scandal miniseries—
in July 2010 and her linked Undone eBook
in May 2010

Chapter 1

The abbess met Victoria Paget at the door of the brothel, welcoming her in without a word. She did not ask Victoria's name or her reason for seeking out a specific man. She showed no loyalty to her customer, nor did she seem to care overmuch what the strange lady on her doorstep wished to do with her time or her reputation. Victoria suspected that the Earl of Stanton had paid the woman well to insure her lack of curiosity.

And what did it matter, if she was forced to play the whore to discover the truth? It would be worth any sacrifice, if it meant that she could put her husband's death behind her. If a subordinate's betrayal had brought about his end and she knew, and yet she did nothing? Then she failed him as a widow, just as she feared she had as a wife. Until she was sure that poor Charles rested easy, she would have no peace herself.

The woman led her through the main salon and down a hall hung with red curtains and bawdy art, and opened one of the many rooms for her. "I know the man you seek, and I know his tastes." She turned a critical gaze on Victoria, as though she were inspecting merchandise before displaying it. "There will be no difficulty in getting him to come to you, if you have the nerve to meet him." She waited to see if Victoria expressed shock or hesitation. When she saw none, she said, "Tom Godfrey is known by the girls here to be clean and gentlemanly. You are in no danger, spending an evening in his company." The woman gave a small satisfied smile. "In fact, there are those who would be jealous of your good fortune."

Victoria sincerely doubted it, but said nothing.

The abbess gestured her into the small bedroom before them. Then she turned to a silk curtain next to the door and pulled it aside to reveal a brass-bound peephole. The woman offered no further explanation, but Victoria could guess what was expected of her. Lieutenant Godfrey would be led down the hall, toward this room. The abbess would pull aside a portrait or a drapery to give him his first glimpse of the woman who awaited. She was to beguile him with her movements, allowing them both to pretend that she was unaware. She nodded to the abbess.

The woman nodded back. "Wait here and I will see to it that he finds you." Then she departed, closing the door behind her.

Victoria examined her surroundings, surprised that it was no different than a common bedroom. The walls were covered in cream silk, but there were no paintings or any sort of ornament. The room was empty but for a wardrobe, a small dressing table and mirror, and a great soft bed with virginal white sheets.

She wondered if this room had a specialized purpose: the loss of innocence. Surely this was not the place for her. She had lost that, long ago. And yet? As she hung up her cloak, a shiver went through her that had nothing to do with the temperature of the air.

When she had gone to see her husband's friend, the Earl of Stanton, with her unusual request, he had first dismissed her as foolish. Perhaps her husband had suspected that there was a spy in the midst of his company. His death did not prove the fact. Soldiers died. Surely she knew that. She had followed her husband to the Peninsula and seen the results of battle, had she not?

She had argued that her Charles had died not in battle as he should but because of false intelligence. His men had been unprepared when they were ambushed on the road. Her husband had often remarked about the strange behavior of Lieutenant Godfrey and insisted there was something not quite right about him. It must be more than coincidence that the man who her husband suspected was the only one to escape unscathed from the massacre.

Stanton had argued that she had no real proof. That the man's reputation had been sterling, right up to that moment. And in any case, he was no longer the army's concern. He had been badly wounded in another engagement, retired from the service and returned to London. Then he had thought to tease her, and made the outrageous suggestion that she find the man and ask him herself.

When she had eagerly agreed to this, he had changed his tune and tried to frighten her. Godfrey did not inhabit the sorts of places that a respectable lady might go. Did she mean to frequent bawdy houses, looking for him?

She had squared her shoulders and said, "If necessary."

And necessity had brought her here.

Victoria reached behind her to undo the modest gown she wore. She had cast off her mourning before coming here. Though black might suit her mood, it did not fit her disguise. Red had seemed too obvious. So she had chosen a green dress. She favored the color, although she had worn nothing so frivolous since before her marriage. Now she removed it and hung it on a hook at the back of the wardrobe.

She stood in petticoats and shift, staring at her own white face in the little mirror. It could not do to look frightened, when he came for her. Stanton had argued that she would be horrified at what was expected from a woman in such a place.

She lifted her chin, examining her reflection and pinching her cheeks to get some color back into them. She had informed Stanton that she was no longer a schoolgirl, and was not in the least frightened of a thing that she had done many times before.

Her frankness had made the poor man blush, and he'd pleaded with her to cry off and to forget everything he had said on the matter.

Of course, she had refused. Given the suspicious nature of his death, her husband would have expected her to act on what he had told her. Although Charles had been a good man, sometimes he had treated her no different than he treated his soldiers. He expected loyalty, obedience and courage, as well as her devotion. If the Earl of Stanton did not mean to pursue the matter, then she must. And she would be better off under his guidance than acting on her own.

When he had seen that she would not be swayed, he had shaken his head and given her the address of this place. He had promised that although it was against his better judgment, all would be arranged.

She froze. There was a whisper of air against her bare arms. It seemed to come from behind the draperies on the wall behind her. He was there, watching her.

She turned so that her back was to her supposed observer and touched her own neck, running a finger along the skin, and up to remove the pins from her hair. Then she took up the brush from the dressing table, combing out the curls as though she were preparing for bed.

Her hair was her pride and joy, now that she was back in London. She'd cried when Charles had made her cut it, saying that if she was to follow him to Portugal there would be no time for feminine nonsense. But it had grown back as full and lustrous as it had been before her marriage. She wondered if the man who watched cared for it, or if he thought her foolish as well. She twisted the locks in her hands, spread them and let them fall down her back.

Victoria stared into the mirror again. If she took too much time with her clothes, he would know that she dawdled. She took a deep breath and undid her petticoats, letting them drop to the floor, stepping free of them and taking the time to brush away the wrinkles before hanging them beside her gown. She had not bothered with stays. They hardly seemed necessary, considering what she was likely to do tonight. Now, she wondered if they should have been present as part of the ceremony of undressing, or if he preferred the glimpses of her body through the thin shift she wore. The knowledge of an anonymous watcher and his opinion of her was like a bit of ice drawn slowly over her heated skin, bringing sensitivity wherever it touched.

She sat down upon the bed, ignoring the way the shift's hem rode high to reveal her legs. She removed her slippers, dropping them on the floor. And then she undid her garters and rolled her stockings down, pointing her toe and flexing her bare legs. She shifted on the mattress until her back was against the wall at the head of the bed and felt the hem creep almost to her waist as she did so. And for the first time that evening, real fear took hold of her. She felt exposed, vulnerable.

Then she banished the feeling with a false smile. She knew what she might have to do, when her quarry entered the room. In comparison, the task of the moment could hardly be considered frightening. She was still alone.

It was not as if, even when alone, she had allowed herself to behave with abandon. It was not proper. But she was in the last place in the world where she would have to concern herself with propriety.

She reached up, tentatively at first, and touched her own breasts through the lawn shift that covered them, shocked at how sensitive they felt. Her nipples tightened in response to the pleasure and the coldness of the room. She closed her eyes to hide herself from her circumstances and cupped her hands under them, pushing them tight to her body so that they almost spilled from the neckline of the shift, enjoying the weight of them.

She let her hands drift lower, to catch the hem of the shift and draw it completely out of the way. She bit her lip as though in desire, and blocked the last of her fear in her mind. Then she let her legs fall open, exposing herself to anyone who might be watching from the hall.

From some hidden place, there was a sharp intake of breath, and the slow hiss as it was released again.

The sound sent a tremor of awareness through her. Was the man on the other side of the curtain the man she sought? Perhaps it was some other stranger. Whoever her audience might be, they were expecting her to continue.

And suddenly, her body trembled again, and she wished it as well. She spread herself with her fingers, and began to play.

Tom Godfrey looked at the woman sitting on the bed and tried to disguise his shock into something within the realm of expectation or eagerness.

The abbess touched his arm, to silently ask if this was the sort of woman he had been looking for.

He placed a hand over hers and nodded. Not only was the

chestnut hair just as he had wished, and the eyes bright green, but the shape of the face was the same as well. There was the short nose, the gently rounded cheeks and the small dimple in the chin.

He had not seen her body in the little miniature his captain had carried. But he had imagined it: the pale skin dusted with gold from the sun of Portugal, with long legs, high breasts and a trim waist flaring into soft round hips. His imagination did not do this woman justice.

The madam smiled and nodded, gesturing to the door at her right and pressing a key into his hand. He pressed a coin into hers in return. Then, she retreated.

He stood there for a while, staring into the little window, enjoying the clandestine view it provided. The woman was very like the one he longed for. And with his desire came the faint feeling of guilt.

Though why he should feel guilty about thoughts not expressed, he did not know. It was not as if he had ever bothered Victoria Paget with his opinions of her. He had never even met her. He had not even sent the briefest of condolences along with her husband's personal effects, fearing that some stray comment in it would lead her to guess the truth. He had done nothing to be ashamed of.

But while his actions had been blameless, he regretted his uncontrollable thoughts. Captain Paget's descriptions of his wife's spirit, and her unfailing loyalty and courage, had moved him to envy. The devotion of his own fiancée waiting in London for him had seemed ambivalent in comparison. And then, Paget had shared a glimpse of the little portrait that he had so often admired himself.

Tom had felt the first stirrings of jealousy. Perhaps it was because he doubted that Paget deserved such a wife as the one he'd described. At times, he had spoken of her as he might of a particularly good soldier, and not a woman who was worthy of respect and tenderness. And though the captain had claimed to have a great fondness for her, when the war parted them he had shown no particular desire to be faithful to her in the way he swore she was to him.

Perhaps it was merely covetousness on Tom's part. He had seen the peace it brought Paget to look on the picture before a battle. And he had wanted some bit of that peace for himself. He had longed for reassurance that someone waited for him and cared for his survival. The few pitiful letters he'd received from his supposed love filled him with doubts about their future. And his fears had been proven true soon after his return to England.

But worst of all, there was lust. He had seen the picture, and wanted the woman in it. When the captain had died, Tom had searched his pockets for it, out of a sudden shameful desire to keep it for his own. That he could have it to gaze on each night, before he slept. And to imagine…

It had repelled him that he could have such thoughts about the widow, with the husband barely cool on the ground before him. So he had bundled the miniature up with the captain's few personal effects, tucked the lot into his haversack to keep it safe from the soldiers who were looting the battlefield, and sent it back to camp with the next courier.

When he had arrived there on a stretcher almost a month later after another skirmish had shattered his leg and his career, he had wanted to meet with her and to explain the circumstances of her husband's death. But she was already gone back to London. Disappointment and relief had mingled with the pain of his wound.

Grief was an indulgence not always followed by the women in the camps. Although it was rare in officer's wives, there were some women who put greater store in being married then they did in the identity of their husband. An unfortunate death in battle meant that there would be a drumhead wedding to someone when the company returned.

If the opportunity presented itself, how would he have been able to resist an inquiry? He was not even free to make the offer. And worse yet, suppose she'd married someone else?

But, no. She would be brokenhearted, he was sure. She would have thought him coarse beyond words to suggest that she wed again so quickly. Now that he was free, perhaps he would seek her out, after a respectable period of time.

In the waiting for the opportunity, the desire for her had only grown in him. He had come to a brothel for relief. And now, he found himself peering into the boudoir of a woman who could easily be the double of the girl in the portrait.

But not in nature. Even in his wildest imaginings he had not dreamed of seeing her like this. She was touching herself. She cupped her breasts, and then sat back upon the bed and spread herself wide before him, letting her fingers sink into the curls of hair between her legs before settling into a rhythm against her own body.

Tom swallowed and tried to still his breathing. She must know that he watched. There was a sly smile upon her lips as though she could imagine the effect that her play was having upon him. And then it was forgotten in a gasp as she shuddered and made a faint noise of pleasure released.

The effect was exquisite. He was hard for her, almost to the point of pain. He fingered the key in his hands for a moment, watching as she arched her neck and gave another shudder of satisfaction from her own touch.

Then he went to the door, opening it hurriedly, entering and locking it behind him again.

Chapter 2

Victoria smiled in triumph as a man limped into the room, for it was obvious that she had been right. He had watched. She could see it in his eyes. And it was plain that she had aroused him with her behavior.

His cheeks were flushed as though from too much wine. But it was not drunkenness. Desire, of course. She had expected that. But embarrassment? Watching and knowing that she knew. She had been told he was no stranger to houses of ill fame. But perhaps he was not usually a voyeur. He was younger than she had expected, little older than herself, but ten years younger than Charles. And though the sight of him locking the door should have scared her, his appearance did not match the dark villain she had expected. Tom Godfrey's hair was brown, touched with gold from too much sun, and it fell in his eyes as he looked at her. He reached up and brushed it away.

"Do you fear interruption?" she asked, glancing at the locked door.

He dropped the key into his pocket. "I certainly do not wish it." His voice was pleasant, almost defying her to enjoy the sound of it. He approached the bed, and she resisted the urge to close her legs. Instead, she leaned back against the pillows, stretching her arms over her head and clasping her hands together. She could feel her breasts draw tight, straining against the chemise as she moved.

He shed his clothing quickly, as though there were little time to waste. And judging by the state of him, perhaps there was not. She felt an inappropriate frisson of desire at the sight of him. He was a soldier, body hardened and marked by battle. There was an angry red scar high on one leg, which explained the hitch in his gait as he walked.

But he seemed healthy enough. And aroused he was almost frighteningly large.

It had been a long time since she had been with a man, she reminded herself, trying not to stare. And while she had no reason to want this particular man, her body's reaction to his was normal, and not the least bit traitorous to her husband's memory. As long as she did not dwell on it.

He smiled at her, and climbed on to the bed, reaching for her. As he took her into his arms, she felt the tingling friction of his bare skin against hers, and dropped her arms to circle his neck. Heat rose in her at the contact, and she fought down her guilt. What was about to happen meant nothing. She must separate physical response from more tender emotions. She would lie back and close her eyes and it would be over in no time.

And then, his lips touched hers.

She shied away from his kiss, turning her head. The man might expect no more than a lack of struggle in the actual act, but there would be no way to hide what she felt for him if they kissed.

He pulled away as well. "I'm sorry." He glanced around the room. "Have I misunderstood? Because if you are unwilling…" He was hard against her leg, but very still, as though he awaited her permission to proceed.

The reaction surprised her. He was strong, and she'd been afraid he would force her cooperation if she did not give it. "I am willing," she said softly. "But not to kiss. Not upon the lips, at least."

He smiled. "Why ever not?"

Why indeed? "There are some things best shared between true lovers. And I wish to save some small part of me, for that."

He seemed puzzled. And she wondered, did he need to fool himself that an encounter in such a place meant something more than it actually did? It was a sign of a romantic nature, a weakness that she had put long behind her after the hardships of even the happiest moments of the last few years. To reassure him, she said, "There are other things, very pleasant, I assure you, that I am quite willing to do." She ran a hand down his body, slowly over the chest, and followed the trail of hair on his belly lower, until she could take him in her hand.

The act was all it took to render him incapable of further questions. The confusion on his face was replaced with a dazed smile and he closed his eyes and sighed. She had imagined a coupling almost brutal in its suddenness. But it appeared that he was content to let her be the aggressor.

It was strange and exciting to have such power. She could set the pace, and the action, and perhaps she could avoid joining with him at all.

Victoria pushed lightly upon his shoulder, rolling him onto his back. Then she knelt between his legs and slowly massaged his member, from shaft to tip and back, spreading his own moisture upon him, feeling him pulse beneath her hand, and an answering pulse in her own body.

He groaned, and covered her hand with his own. "Darling, your touch is heaven."

A wicked thought occurred to her. And as she stroked him, her curiosity grew to insatiability. What better place to give over to such a whim than here? She bent over him. "Then what shall you think of this?" And she gave him the kiss that no man could resist, taking him gently into her mouth, surrounding him with her lips and running her tongue along the tip of him, feeling smoothness, tasting salt.

His hands clutched the sheets on either side of her head, as though he were afraid to reach for her, lest she stop. She moved her mouth over him, taking him deeper, and his back arched as muscles tightened in growing excitement. His moan stopped suddenly, his teeth closing with a snap. "Please." The word was shaky, little more than a gasp. "Oh, yes." He trembled. She could feel his control slipping, and it caused an answering tremor in her own body, before she reminded herself that what was happening between them had no meaning.

"We have not been introduced," he ground out, with a desperate laugh. "My name is Tom Godfrey."

She withdrew slightly, and purred against his skin. "Thomas."

He groaned as though the sound of his own name was as exciting as her kiss. Then, he reached out a hand and stroked her hair. The gesture was strangely tender. "Your name. Please. I must know…"

She gave one last whirl of her tongue against him, and said, "Victoria."

He gave an almost convulsive shudder and rolled away from her, spilling his seed into the sheet beside them.

For a moment, she felt strangely bereft. She missed the feel of him against her cheek and in her mouth, and the warmth of his body close to his. Had she really been alone so long that even the touch of an enemy was welcome?

He was curled over with his back to her. And his shoulders were shaking with what looked to be silent laughter.

It angered her to think that he found her performance so amusing. Was she really so unskilled that her actions were laughable? She buried the feeling, and reached out a hesitant hand to his shoulder, as though from concern. "Is something the matter?"

He was definitely laughing, for his words escaped after a chuckle. "An old gun does not usually have a hair trigger."

"Old?" At first it made no sense. Then, she realized he spoke of himself. "You are hardly thirty."

He rolled back to her, still smiling, and touched her cheek. "That is old enough to have learned control. But you quite overcame me. I embarrassed myself like a greenling on his first trip to a brothel. Unlike some, you are too kind to comment upon it."

Perhaps, if she had truly been a whore, she would have known the correct response to what had just happened. Should she have laughed at his joke, to put him at ease? She must do something quickly. If she wished information, she could not have him pulling on his boots and leaving her. "We could try again."

"My thoughts exactly." He leaned forward to kiss her.

Without thinking, she turned her head from him again, causing him to draw back.

"You are a most curious woman, Victoria." He was staring at her as though he was the one who had come to search for truths. "I cannot decide what arouses me more, what you will do, or what you won't."

"That was not my intent."

He ran a thumb from her cheek to touch her lower lip, and

then drew it slowly down to stroke her throat. "Liar. I think it is in your nature to drive men mad." He leaned forward to kiss her throat at the spot where his thumb rested, and she felt a jolt of excitement.

"Please, do not."

"You do not like it?"

It would do no good to lie. "Of course. But…"

He kissed her again. "It will be some few moments before I am ready again. If you will not spend it in kissing, then I must find another way to pass the time."

Now he was ringing her throat with love bites, as though tracing the path of a necklace as his hands roamed over her breasts. His touch was hard, possessive, just as his kisses were. And it was not the only thing hardened, for she could feel his body growing eager to join with hers. She gave a weak laugh. "Dear sir, I think you are quite ready enough, now."

"Do you?" He dipped his head to take the tip of her breast in his mouth through the cotton shift. "But I wish for you to be ready as well."

"I do not require satisfaction." She gasped, for his hands were between her legs, tugging at the curls there. "At least, not in that way."

"You hurt me, darling, to make me think that it is my money that matters to you. You might not require this. But you certainly deserve it, after what you just did to me." As his mouth slid down her body she had a fleeting fear that his actions were as much about control as hers had been.

And she could feel it slipping away as he moved closer and closer to where her body wanted him. She tried to pull away, but he wrapped his arms around her waist, holding her fast. "Please, sir, no."

"You will not let me kiss you on the lips." He sighed, but

did not release her. "So you must allow me to imagine what it might be like." He dipped his tongue into her navel. "To whisper into your ear and touch it like so. To kiss my way along your cheek." He trailed the kisses along her belly. "Until my lips find yours." He settled himself carefully between her legs and barely touched her with his mouth. "Gently at first. Ever so gently. Just a touch."

The shock of it was too much, and she gave another shudder. What had the abbess said, about the jealousy of others working here? If this was how he was in the habit of treating them, then she understood. His kiss was rougher now. And as he thrust his tongue into her, his fingers crept up to stroke.

Victoria put her own fingers into her mouth and bit down, trying to stop the scream of pleasure that she knew was coming. But the feel of them, the intrusion and the sharp pain of her bite along with his repeated invasion of her body tipped her over the edge into another cascade of pleasure.

Yet, his kiss did not cease. She struggled against it for a moment. But it was all too much, too good, and she was unable to think for wanting more.

Only when she was sure that she must be spent did he obey and release her, to slide his body up hers. "And now, I think you are ready, are you not?" He hovered for a moment at the entrance to her body, before beginning a slow thrust into her. He stopped. "Unless you do not wish it."

His hesitation was almost painful, for she longed to be filled. "Please." Later, she could regret asking him. But now she was so close to coming again that it was impossible to do other than beg for more. "Please. Oh, yes. Please."

He pushed into her with a sudden, hard thrust and she gasped. She had not expected it to be so...

He withdrew and thrust again.

…different. The act was familiar and yet new, because her lover was different. The intense pleasure she felt was from the novelty, nothing more. Or so she told herself, as she dug her fingers into the muscles of his shoulders and moved her hips to match the strength of his thrusts, eager to feel him deep inside.

Sensing her need, he was not gentle. He raked his fingers down her back to clutch her bottom and pounded into her with a strength that demanded nothing less than her total surrender. Then he buried his face into the side of her neck, his teeth grazing her skin, and he licked hard at the muscle on her shoulder until she moaned in response.

At the sound, he rolled so that she could be on top of him and squeezed her hips to urge her on.

And she rode him, squeezing her legs together around him, tightening her muscles about him to feel how impossibly hard he was until she heard his answering groan and his body began to arch. As he lost control, he reached to the front of her, rubbing her with his thumb to bring her over the edge with him, shattering.

She collapsed on top of him, sprawling across his body, her cheek against his chest. It made her feel alive again to lie still for a moment, as passion receded and sense returned. He was taller than she had expected. His body big and solid under her, and still inside of her, undeniably male.

It felt good to be wanted. To be desired. And not to be alone.

He wrapped a hand around her waist. His grip was weak at first, little more than the weight of his own arm, as though exhausted by his own climax. Then slowly, he curled it possessively around her, the hand angling up toward her shoulders in a caress.

She could not see his face, but could tell his smile was gone by the tone of his voice. "I know who you are," he said.

Chapter 3

Victoria Paget was lying in his arms, spent from lovemaking, just as he had always imagined her. It should be a dream, but now that the act was done, it was set to turn to nightmare.

Why had he asked her name? The question tortured him. He should have remained in ignorance, convinced that he was with some nameless bit of muslin. Or perhaps he should have left at the first moment of suspicion, when he'd stood outside the room.

Of course, that would have left her at the mercy of the next man to come along, and the thought of that haunted him even more. She was the object of his desire. A desire that had bordered almost on obsession in the months he had spent recuperating from his injury. He had hoped to exorcise the demon of her memory in a harmless game of pretend. A woman of experience would have him without complaint, scars and all. And the madam had assured him that in dim light, the girl she'd found would pass for the one he dreamed of.

She lay still against him, as though waiting for him to speak. "I know who you are." There. It was out and said.

"Wh-what do you mean?" There was the barest hesitation

in her words, before her face returned to tranquility. He had startled her, but she was pretending ignorance.

It angered him that she thought she could still fool him with lies. "You are the widow of Captain Charles Paget, are you not?"

She said nothing, but glanced quickly toward the door and back. Did she fear him enough to run?

"I recognized your name," he said, not caring about her fears. He tightened his hand on her back, still gentle, but enough to forestall an escape.

"It is a common name," she argued, making no move to leave. "And I gave you no surname."

"Perhaps. But it does not signify. You are Victoria Paget."

"I did not think that you…that anyone would realize." He could feel her budding resistance fade. Her eyes dropped, probably in shame of what she had become.

"I served under him. He spoke of you often, with much pride and affection." And yet, she had come to this. He made no attempt to hide his disappointment. "He showed me the miniature he kept with him. I was there on the road with him, when he died. It was I who gathered his effects and returned them to you."

"Why did you bother?" There was bitterness in her tone as well, to answer his.

"It was the least I could do. Not enough, I know. I could not save him. Nor could I help the others." And now, he was the one who felt shame. What sort of monster was he, to offer words of condolence on a brothel bed? He rolled to the side, so their bodies could part from each other. "If it gives you comfort to know it, his death was sudden. The pain was brief. If he had time for a final thought, it was of you. But I did not want to see his possessions taken by looters. They were rightfully yours."

"And much good they did me." She drew even farther from him, fumbling for the sheet as though it would be possible to hide from him, after what they had done.

"What brings you here?" Had Paget left her nothing but that damned picture, that she had been driven to this on her return to London? "The abbess said you were new to this place. But that is a common lie."

"In this case, it is true. Just this night. For money," she said simply, as though it explained all. And it did. After all his fine talk of his stalwart wife, he'd thought the captain would know enough to set a portion aside for his widow. But some men expected to live forever and sort out the finances after the war.

He reached out and clasped her hand. "I could not save Charles. But I will save you from this, if you let me."

"How would you do that?" She looked at him with a slanted cat's gaze, as though weighing his intentions.

"Come away with me. Now. Tonight. You need have no fear of the mistress of this house. She will not dare to cross me. Once you are settled in my rooms, you can send for anything you wish. Or I will purchase what you need."

God knew how. He could little afford a ladybird, should her tastes prove extravagant.

She thought for a moment, and then nodded. "I have nothing but the clothes I came with. I will dress, and then we may go." Her lack of expression surprised him. He had expected some display of emotion, either enthusiasm or argument, or perhaps an embarrassed speech about how this was not normally her way. But she did not seem overly bothered by what had happened between them. Nor was she relieved or upset by his offer, just as she'd not been bothered by the knowledge that a stranger had watched as she'd touched herself. Perhaps she had been seeking a protector, all along.

Fool that he was, he had imagined the captain's widow wrapping herself in grief and propriety. But the true Victoria Paget was mercenary, to an almost military degree. Her cold blood was almost as disturbing as the truth of her identity had been.

She was dressing as he waited. Strangely, the sight of her becoming clothed was more arousing than the sight of her naked had been. He wanted to peel the clothes away again, and touch her skin to assure himself that the event of the evening had truly happened. He turned his head, trying not to look at her. "You are sure you have no possessions?"

"There is nothing for me here." Her cloak hung on a peg in the corner of the room, and he reached out for it, dropping it over her shoulders, then he escorted her from the room. As they left, she did not look back.

They rode in silence toward his flat, and he wondered if her feelings toward him would warm, given time. Would her opinion change in regard to kissing him? It did not seem so. When the carriage door was closed he had touched her chin as a prelude to turning her mouth to his. And she had looked away again.

What did it matter that she felt no tenderness for him? She had agreed to come with him, knowing what it would mean. He could have her again, soon. Tonight perhaps. And as often as he liked hereafter.

Bought and paid for.

The words echoed in Tom's mind as the carriage stopped and he helped her from it and up the few steps to his apartment. His manservant looked up as he entered, with some small surprise that he was not alone. Tom gave the smallest shake of his head to indicate that he would explain in time, and the man went about his business as though there was nothing strange.

Then he said with some embarrassment, "I am sorry that my quarters are so small. Just the sitting room and the bedroom. My servant, Toby, sleeps by the kitchen fire. I do not have even a cot to offer you. In time, you shall have your own room. Or an apartment, if you wish it."

How silly. Of course she would wish. What sort of idiot offered a carte blanche to a woman he could not afford to keep?

"You shall have a maid. Dresses. Anything you wish. But it is rather late. In the morning…" They were rash promises, and he had no idea how he would manage, but he would give her anything she desired, if it meant he could touch her again.

"Of course," she said. "I understand." And then she fell silent.

It worried him that he did not know what to say next, other than to repeat the pathetic offers he had just made. There was so much more to be said, so much that he wanted her to understand. And in turn, there was much he wanted her to answer for. But he doubted that either of them wanted to hear the truth. For now, he would let his body speak for him. He stepped forward and reached for her.

She took the slightest move away, as though his touch was unwelcome, now that she had what she wanted. And then she said, "When did you recognize me?"

The suddenness of it stunned him. Perhaps she wished to defend what was left of her honor, now that she had seen the humbleness of his quarters. It was a harsh thought, and he did not wish to believe it of her. But better not to act like a besotted fool, lest she announce that she had no wish to lie with a cripple if they would be forced to share the bed after.

He retreated to neutral hospitality, taking her cloak and leading her to a chair by the fire, then signaling his man to bring them a brandy. Once the servant had retired to the kitchen he said, "I did not know you at first. Not until you said your name. If I had known, I would not have allowed you to do what you did."

Liar. He'd known in his heart exactly who she was from the moment he had laid eyes on her. But he had not been able to resist having her.

"Once I realized the truth, I could not stand by and leave you in that place, to God knows what fate. I owe it to a brother officer, to see to it that his family does not suffer. And that is why I brought you here."

"After the fact," she said, bluntly. And for a moment, there was a light in her eye that made him wonder if she sensed the truth of what had happened the day her husband died, and had come to him to exact punishment for it.

Or she might simply be expressing the obvious. His own guilt pricked sharp, like needles inside him. It had been so much easier to be angry and to blame her loose morals for what had happened tonight. But he had wanted her long before he had any right to, and he had taken her the first chance he'd got. Then he'd convinced himself that her desperation was a sign of unworthiness, and that his lust was somehow her fault. No wonder she was cold to him. He sighed. "What I did was unconscionable. But once things were begun, I did not know how to stop them, or how to explain myself." He bit his tongue, and began again. "That is not true. Once we had begun, I did not wish to stop. I was selfish, and thoughtless of all but my own needs. Because of my injury, pleasure has been infrequent, and to find myself in the company of such a beautiful woman?"

He shrugged as though it were possible to minimize his attraction to her. "But that is no excuse. Although it is too late to take back what I have done, I will not trouble you further with my attentions. I only wish to know that you are safe, and that you are not forced to debase yourself further because of misfortune."

"Oh." There was a crease in her forehead, as though she were puzzled. Or perhaps she was disappointed, although that hardly seemed likely. "Thank you for your kindness." She sipped from the drink she had been offered.

He thought for a moment that she meant to explain how she had come to the state she was in. But she said nothing and he had no right to inquire. Perhaps there was something even more horrible than what she currently experienced.

Then she looked up at him from over the rim of her glass. "But I cannot accept the terms you offer. If you wish to give me your protection, then I must give you something in return. It makes no sense to pretend modesty, and refuse you companionship." She touched the neckline of her gown.

He was mesmerized by her hands. How graceful they were. Long fingered. Supple. His body remembered how it had felt to be touched by them, and grew hard in response. And he knew that his attempt at nobility was for naught. She had offered. And he would take from her again.

It hurt him to know that what was about to happen would mean nothing to her, other than a bartering of services. She was not the woman he imagined her to be, and her husband's shining description was little more than the fondness of long association.

He set his drink aside and reached out to take her by the wrist, drawing her to her feet and toward the door to the bedroom. And as he did so, the glass shook in her hand, and spilled a few drops of brandy onto the silken flesh above her breasts. He took the glass from her and threw it onto the hearth, listening to the crystal shatter as he pulled her into his arms, burying his face against her throat, chasing the drop of liquor down to catch it on his tongue. When the bodice of her dress blocked him, he reached behind her and undid the fastenings, pushing it and her chemise out of the way until he could reach her breasts, taking the nipples by turn into his mouth to suckle them until the skin puckered and the tips grew hard.

He felt her fingers in his hair, a gentle, almost fearful touch holding his mouth against her body. And then she pulled her hands away, and he could feel her arms go rigid at her sides.

He lifted his head and put his arms on her shoulders, pushing gently until her back was to the wall. Then he dropped his hands to cover her, rubbing his thumbs against the sensitive tips and watching her eyes widen in response. Perhaps she was not such a dispassionate schemer after all. Was it fear he saw on her face? Or could it be desire? He gave the flesh beneath his fingers a gentle pinch, and she gasped and bit her lower lip as though she could bite back the response.

He smiled and stared at her mouth. "If you truly do not wish me to kiss you, you must stop that immediately. You are tempting me beyond endurance."

"I did not mean to," she whispered.

He laughed and leaned forward to catch the lobe of her ear between his teeth, nipping it as she had her own lip. "Of course you did. From the first moment. Lying on that bed, offering yourself to me. You are temptation itself."

"No. Not that. I did not…" She gasped again as he bit harder, and wrenched the truth from her. "I did not mean to enjoy this."

He could feel his body straining to pleasure her, just as hers strained to resist him. "Is that so?" He released her breasts and fumbled with the buttons on his trousers.

She glanced down, and then over her shoulder at the door behind them. Her mouth was a perfect O of shock. "The bedroom?"

He shook his head. "Here. Now. You do not wish to enjoy this. And I do not wish to wait." He could see by the eager way that she lifted her skirt that his pretense at brutish behavior was as exciting to her as anything else they had tried. He touched her between her legs, spreading her with his fingers, stroking for a moment before pushing one inside of her. She was wet and ready, bracing her back against the wall, bearing down on his hand and shuddering with delight. He pulled his hand away and fitted his body to hers, pausing for just a moment before pushing slowly into that wonderful tightness.

The fear disappeared from her face. Now it shone with the light of pure bliss. And then she shut her eyes, as though she thought she could hide it from him.

He withdrew and thrust again, even slower than before, trying to ignore the dizzying rightness of being inside her. He pressed his body tight to hers, one of his hands trapped between them so that he could clutch her breast. With the other hand, he touched her face, running a thumb along her jawline to tip her face toward his. "Open your eyes."

She blinked up at him, looking as dazed by what was happening as he felt. Her lips were parted, swollen and red, and he longed to kiss them as he thrust again. "Tell me what you are feeling," he said, and rubbed his knuckles against them.

She touched his hand with her tongue, and he sucked in a breath, not wanting to lose control too quickly. She hesitated, and he thrust again.

She let out a little squeak of surprise that made him smile. So he kissed her cheek, tantalizingly close to those lovely lips, and said again, "Tell me."

At last, she murmured, "It has never been like this." And as he moved in her, her breathing became irregular, muddling her words. "I have never…more than once…and the way you look at me…and your body…it makes me…every time."

He could feel her losing control again, her body tightening on his. He squeezed her breast and felt her back arch, her hips rock forward into his, her arms wrap around to hold him as she began to tremble. So he enjoyed her perfect body and imagined her perfect lips, and spent himself in her again.

How many times had that been tonight? He smiled to himself, hugging her to him, trying not to lean too obviously upon her. Damn, but he was weak as a kitten. Standing had been a mistake. His leg was aching, and he must get the weight off it, or he would be too stiff to rise in the morning.

From his shoulder came a soft sob.

He lifted his head to find her face wet with tears. He reached to stroke her hair, wondering how he had ever thought her cold. "What is it, love? Tell me."

"I am a terrible wife," she whispered back.

He almost laughed. "Right now, you are no wife at all." Although perhaps she ought to be. At the rate they were going, there would be a babe soon. Surely a wife was easier to keep than a mistress.

And then the weight of her words hit him, and with it, the old guilt. He held her close, not wanting to let a ghost come between them. "He is gone. You are free."

"But I should not behave in this way. And with a man I barely know. With you, of all people."

So that was it. She'd given herself to a lesser man. He focused on the ache in his leg, for it was easier to deal with the physical hurt than the pain her words had caused. He straightened, taking back his own weight, pulling her gown up to shield her body, and offering her his arm.

"How you behaved this evening was little fault of your

own. It is I who should be ashamed. I owe you reparation for my base behavior. You honor me by accepting my protection." He swallowed his nerves, for he knew what he truly owed to a lady, even if his words were met with scorn. "And you would honor me still further, if you would agree to wed me."

Chapter 4

Victoria gave a small, surprised laugh to cover her confusion, putting a hand to her throat to keep her gown from slipping again. "Marriage?"

"I dishonored you by my actions. As a gentleman, I wish to make it right again," he said, as though it were the most reasonable thing in the world to marry a woman that he had met in a brothel.

"But between us?" She had convinced herself that she should come home with him to gain time to search his possessions and question his servants. But he had so little. Suppose there was nothing to find?

What if Tom Godfrey was innocent? A part of her dearly wanted that to be true. If he was not, how was she to reconcile her feelings when he touched her with the suspicions she had held for so long? She stalled. "How shall I explain the suddenness of it to my friends?" And how would she explain to Lord Stanton? He thought her mad already. What would he think of this turn of events?

Tom smiled. "It will hardly be seen as a nine day's wonder if you marry a soldier. I am a cripple and of inferior rank to your late husband. But we share a common past, we have mutual friends, and I am sympathetic to your plight. Tell anyone who cares that we met in London. Our previous acquaintance led me to offer for you out of concern for your safety and a desire to know that you are well provided for."

"But marriage?" It did make sense, as he described it. But suppose she had been right, and her second husband was hanged for the murder of her first?

"For my part, my friends will congratulate me on my extreme good fortune in catching you. You are a very attractive woman, Victoria. And…" He seemed about to say something, and then muttered, "We do share a certain physical compatibility."

He grinned at her. And the grin widened as he saw her blush. Then he grew serious again. "I understand that you do not love me, and that what I suggest will seem as sudden to some as it does to you. But I would do everything in my power to bring you pleasure by night, and to make you happy by day. Please allow me to help you."

Her intended victim was all but begging that she come close enough to betray him. But if she had been wrong, how could she ever explain to him? Or was there some way that she could avoid the truth? At last she said, "It is all too much for my poor mind to grasp. May I decide tomorrow? I am quite tired." Perhaps in the morning, she could come up with an answer. She let her voice trail off as if to confirm her words, and glanced toward the bedroom door.

"Of course. It is late. Until then, will you accept my hospitality?"

She gave a slight nod, and he led her into the other room. He turned back the covers on his bed, offering his place to her. Then he went to sit on a small couch in the corner of the room. "Until you decide, I think it best that I sleep here." He smiled and added, "To avoid temptation." He took off his coat and boots, lay down and rolled his face to the wall.

As she prepared for bed, she stared across the room at him. Despite her doubts, she could feel her body longing for his. She could not fool herself into thinking that her enthusiastic response to him had been caused by loneliness, or because she had forgotten how wonderful it felt to be with a man.

It had not been like this with Charles. Not ever. Her father had assured her that it was a good match, and that she had nothing to complain about. And he had been right. Charles Paget had been a good husband to her. And she had loved and respected him, and wished always to make him happy.

But he had never looked at her with the hungry intensity that Tom Godfrey did. She had certainly never been loved to completion multiple times in a night. And Charles, God rest his soul, would have told her to leave off with her nonsense and obey him immediately, had she ever dared to refuse him a kiss. From the moment she had said her vows, she had known that while it was important to love one's husband, to honor him was more so. And total obedience trumped them both.

But Tom had taken her refusal to kiss as a challenge. Her body burned hot at the memory of it. He had been a generous lover, more concerned with her pleasure than his own.

She could not remember the last time that her pleasure, her wants or her desires had been important to anyone. Not even herself. She had learned to ignore them, to postpone them or to do without. Perhaps that explained her sudden and extreme attraction to Tom Godfrey.

And with that, she felt an unexpected pang of guilt. She had insinuated herself into his life to spy upon him. Perhaps she was in the right, for she had done it for England and her husband's memory, instead of for French gold.

But if she had accused an innocent man?

And there was the rub. His behavior toward her was—she struggled to find a word. It was gallant. She felt safe in his company, from the way he wished to rescue her from the brothel, to the foolish gesture of sleeping on a bench, when his own bed was just across the room. Would it not pain the wound in his leg and side to sleep in such a cramped way?

The Tom Godfrey she had imagined was a coward who had sacrificed all around him for personal gain. But from the first moment this stranger had touched her, she'd trusted him. She had given of herself and in ways that were new to her, sure that no matter what they tried, he would not hurt her. That trust had been at the heart of their lovemaking, and her response to it.

On the other side of the room, Tom let out a sigh, and rolled again, to face her. And in the barest whisper he said, "You are awake, aren't you?"

"Yes." She sat up in bed and stared across the room.

He sat up as well. "It is quite hopeless. I meant to bring you here, and to care for you, hoping that I could avoid what I must say. But I will not get a moment's sleep if I do not just admit the truth."

She bit her lip and gave a little nod, suddenly afraid that she might hear the very thing she had expected.

He took a deep breath. "The day Captain Paget died my horse was losing a shoe. He favored a leg, and I was lagging behind, trying to nurse him along. If I had been ahead on the road, as I should have been, they would have had warning. It would have been I and not he." His eyes grew vacant for a moment as he remembered it.

There had been no mention of this in any of the accounts

she had heard. But it explained how he had come to retreat, as the rest advanced to their doom. "What became of the horse?"

He looked at her as though it were the maddest question in the world. "Shot in the battle. Poor dumb beast. It was all for naught. In the end, I spared him nothing. I should have ridden forward with the rest and died."

He touched his wounded leg. "Until I met you, this wound seemed a sufficient punishment for any wrong I committed. But now?" He shook his head. "That day, I took your husband from you with my carelessness. And I took your honor tonight. If you will have me, I will do everything in my power to make this right."

Something inside her eased, as though a weight had been lifted from her shoulders. And without thinking of what had brought her to this place and this moment, she let out a sigh of relief. Then she patted the mattress beside her. "I do not think I need 'til dawn to make a decision, after all. Come to bed, Thomas."

Chapter 5

He reached for her again in the night, touching her skin and smiling in wonder as though her presence beside him was miraculous. She touched him in return, laying her hand against his cheek, tracing the planes of his shoulders and back, learning him in a way that was quite innocent, compared to their earlier coupling.

He paid attention to the details of her body, kissing the hollow of her shoulder, the crease of her elbow, her finger tips, and running his thumb along her spine to find a place on her back that was surprisingly sensitive. It made her gasp, and he smiled, continuing to stroke the spot as he bent his head forward to nip her throat and her breasts. Tom was setting a leisurely pace, as though they had all night to pleasure each other. He gave another flick of his finger, which he combined with a slow pull on her nipple that made her arch against him, clutching his hair to hold him tight to her, clawing with her other hand, down his side to search for him, stroke him and spread her legs for him. Her need grew more urgent the slower he moved. She could feel him laughing in triumph as she shuddered against him, so she pushed him onto his back and straddled him, impaling herself upon him, pressing his hand against her most sensitive place, forcing him to give her more pleasure as she bucked against him, her body clenching and releasing him, as she squeezed his hips between her thighs. She heard the moment when his laughter stopped and he relinquished control to her. His breathing quickened, his body thrusting in response, until he whispered her name and lost control inside her again. The sensation was rare, and she closed her eyes as she savored it. The risk of children born while on campaign had been too great to allow such completion. Now, she might have it whenever she liked, and the children as well.

But when she looked into her lover's eyes, she saw pain as well as pleasure. "Your leg?" She pulled away so that he could withdraw.

He nodded, but laid a steadying hand on her arm. "It is all right." His eyes seemed to glaze for a moment, and then he smiled, and said through clenched teeth, "No. It was marvelous. Well worth a twinge or two."

But all the same, she disentangled herself carefully to lie beside him, careful not to stress the wound.

He put his arm around her shoulders, and kissed the top of her head. "That you would be willing to lie with me at all is pleasure enough. But that you have accepted my offer is quite amazing as well. There have been others who were not so generous."

She frowned. "How strange."

He laughed at her confusion. "My dear, I am not whole. It is quite obvious to you."

"But for the pain in your leg, you seem well enough." She had the temerity to blush, and he laughed again.

"In our case, perhaps it is better that you lie with me before you wed me. The woman I expected to take to wife on my return from the war was none too sure about me. Her father told her that the location of the wound might have rendered me unfit as a husband. And while his daughter had no qualms about my entering the military and was quite taken with the sight of the braid on my uniform, there was something less than heroic about my homecoming, when it could not be made on two good legs."

"But that is horrible. To have served your country is an honorable thing. And to have suffered as you did is a cause for increased respect and not rejection."

"I knew you would understand. You of all women…" He said it reverently, as though she were precious beyond words to him. Tom reached out and touched her lips with his fingers with such gentleness that it startled her. If her eyes hadn't been open, she'd have sworn that he'd kissed her.

And then, with a smile, he closed his eyes and fell asleep.

Victoria wrapped her arms around him and laid her head close against his side, wishing she could take the pain away. She had been so very wrong about Thomas Godfrey. He had suffered at the hands of the French and from the faithless woman who would not take him back.

And he had suffered from her actions as well. She had defamed him to the Earl of Stanton, putting doubts in the man's head that had no place there. Tomorrow, she would write a letter to Stanton, explaining what she had found, and the strange turn of events that things had taken.

And she would never speak of it again. For much as Tom Godfrey seemed to think he owed her happiness, she owed him a similar debt. She would make up for her lack of faith by being the wife that he longed for her to be.

* * *

When she awoke the next morning, Tom was already out of bed, washed and preparing to go out. As though he sensed her return to consciousness, he turned to look at her with an encouraging smile. "Did you sleep well?"

"Yes." Surprisingly, she had. Her decision had given her an easy rest.

"I have no female servant to assist you. If you wish to wait, I can have my valet send for someone. Perhaps there is a girl in a neighboring flat. Or I…" He broke off shyly, holding his open hands in front of him, to show that he was at her service.

"That is all right. I have learned to manage." Her clothing was simple for just this reason. And compared to some of the places she'd stayed with Charles, this meager room was a luxury.

He nodded. "I must go out. And until more things are settled, it is hardly proper for us to be seen too much together. We will see if there is a way for your things to be sent for, discreetly."

"No!" She had forgotten that there were details of her life that could not be filed away and forgotten. It would not do for him to see how she lived. At least not just yet. How could she explain her presence, apparently downcast in a house of ill fame, once he saw that she lived better than he, with more space, more comfort and more servants? "I will take care of sending for what I need. I need no help."

He looked surprised at her sudden denial. But then he shrugged as though he did not want to broach a topic that she might find embarrassing or painful. "Very well. I will trust to your own judgment in such matters. But be mindful of appearances, and take care not to be seen, should you leave."

"Why is that?"

He raised an eyebrow, and smiled. "I should think it would be obvious. Your reputation is as precious to me as it is to you.

I should hate to have to challenge some young buck to a duel, should he see you creeping from my rooms with the dawn."

She colored. She had been so long married, and out of London society, that she had almost forgotten that anyone might care.

He grew serious again. "You do still wish to wed, do you not? For if you have had a change of heart?" He ran a hand through his tousled hair. "It quite changes my plans for the day. I had meant to procure a special license."

Again she felt the unfamiliar ripple of pleasure, to see him so eager to wed that he could not wait for the banns. "No, I have not changed my mind."

And now, he was smiling broadly at her, as though the reassurance had brought him immeasurable pleasure. He stepped forward, drew her up to sit, and kissed her on top of the head. "I am glad. And I will work to make you comfortable. And happy again, if you will let me."

Happy. What a curious idea. In her old life, she had been content, certainly. But had she been happy, traipsing about the Continent after Charles? Not really. She would have preferred her townhouse, the company of friends. A regular bed and regular meals. And perhaps a regular husband. "That would be nice. Thank you." She hoped he had not been expecting some declaration of love, for it seemed too soon to use that word. But to have a man to love, just an ordinary man, and not a soldier? And to have that man be as devoted to her as Tom Godfrey was? The possibility shimmered before her for a moment, like a beautiful dream.

"I had best get to it. If you are sure that you can manage?"

She gave him an encouraging smile in return. "I will be fine."

"Then I will go and make arrangements. And in no time at all, you will be Mrs. Godfrey."

Chapter 6

Tom smiled through clenched teeth as he climbed the steps to his final destination. The pain in his leg had not been so very bad as he had gone about the tortuous process of applying for the special license. But he did not wish to show weakness before the Earl of Stanton at the Home Office. He tried not to lean too heavily on his cane as he spoke to the clerk in the front room, and politely insisted that he had served under the earl when he had been simple Captain St John Radwell. Surely, a brief visit from an old comrade would not be unwelcome.

He heard a bark of affirmation from the door behind him, and words of welcome. But when he turned to face his old superior, the look in the man's eyes was wary. It seemed, after the disaster that had befallen his last captain, Tom would have to prove himself again to this one.

Stanton reached out and grasped his hand, pulling him into the office, but did not bother to shut the door behind him. "What brings you here, Tom? Are you doing well since your return? How is the leg, man?"

He shifted his weight to prove its strength. "As well as can be expected. It will never be right. But slowly, it improves. But other things?" He could not help the grin that spread on his face. "I suppose they are both very good, and most difficult."

"How so?"

"I have it in my mind to marry."

The earl looked startled quite beyond what he'd expected. "Marry? I had not heard…"

"That is because the decision is sudden. Fast as lightning, some might think."

"Do I…know the woman involved?"

The question stopped him. Perhaps Victoria's fears were justified. "I do not see why you should. She is the widow of a friend of mine. I hesitate to mention the name until the announcement is made. It is as sudden for her as it is for me. If she has people, they should hear of it before I go trumpeting my good fortune about the town, tempting though it may be to brag."

Stanton nodded, although there was strange hesitation in his reply. "That is probably wise. If there is a reason to cry off, it will save embarrassment."

And how little confidence in him did such a strange comment betray? "I am not worried on that account. We are in total agreement."

"But you spoke of a difficulty?"

"Simply that I had not thought to marry so soon. While I can manage to provide for her, it will not be as easy as I might like. I seek employment. I wondered if perhaps there might be some use you could find for a man who has already proven his loyalty to the crown."

And just as he feared it might, a shadow flickered behind the other man's eyes. He must have heard the rumors. Tom had no wish to deny the charges before they were spoken. When half a company died around a man, there were bound to be those who thought him responsible, through negligence or connivance.

Stanton shook his head. "I am sorry, Tom. But I have nothing to offer you. I will keep you in mind, of course. And if the occasion arises, I will be in touch. Leave your direction with my man. But now, there is simply no need of another body."

Tom nodded, and tried to keep the bitterness from his voice. "I understand. Better than you think, perhaps. What you believe about me is not true. If I can find a way to prove it to you, I shall. And then, God help whoever has put these foul rumors in your head. I shall see they pay for their lies."

The earl shook his head. "Then God help you, Tom. For I cannot. Good day to you."

With that dismissal, Tom exited the office, back stiff with shame and the pain of fruitless exertion. Stanton shut the door behind him with a snap. And as he proceeded to the outer room, the little man who had tried to prevent his entrance now moved to block his exit. Tom raised his head to look and the clerk gestured to him, with a barest crook of the finger. "You seek employment?"

Tom nodded.

"And he turned you away, did he not?"

Tom nodded again.

The clerk gave a grim smile and whispered, "There is work enough here, should he choose to take you on. But he does not trust you. It is a shame. But I know of someone who is seeking men with knowledge that they would share. And although you are not as valuable as you might be, if you could return quietly to this office while still in his service, there are some tasks that would suit your abilities."

"Might suit me?" Tom said, a little dumbly.

"I heard, just now, that you wished to take back some of your own against those who have put you in this unenviable position. You are crippled for doing what you thought was right. And now you have been discarded by those in whom you put your trust. I offer you the opportunity for revenge." The man smiled. "And profit as well." He scribbled a few words on paper and pushed them hurriedly into Tom's hand just as the door to the earl's office opened again. Stanton looked at him with only the mildest curiosity, and turned his attention to the clerk.

While they were both distracted, Tom slipped quietly from the room.

Victoria sat in the little chair by the fire, awaiting her lover's return. Tom's manservant would not leave her alone, since he'd caught her going through the drawers of the little desk in the front room. He'd enquired if there was anything he might get for her. And asked again if she wished to send for her possessions.

She'd shaken her head, smiled and assured him that there was nothing she needed. And still, he watched her with sharp, dark eyes that said his master might be easily gulled by his feelings for a beautiful woman, but the servant was nobody's fool.

She had wanted pen and ink to write to Stanton, and enough privacy to do it unobserved. With the servant hovering behind her, how would that be possible? And she could still find no way to explain the comfortable life she had been leading just a few short miles across town.

The more she had seen of Tom's civilian life the more guilty she felt for suspecting him. He lived simply, just short of poverty. If he had turned coat for the French, then they would have rewarded him in some way. There was no sign of the zealot in him that might make her think he'd done it out of loyalty to Boney.

And now that she had seen the scars on his body, she could

not convince herself that he had staged a minor injury to disguise his perfidy. What kind of fool would come near to sacrificing his leg just to throw the hounds from his trail? It had rendered him unfit for duty, and for many forms of employment.

She had wanted to believe him innocent last night, as he'd held her and slept. But in the morning she had viewed the problem from all angles, lest her judgment had been swayed by sweet words and soft touches. As she weighed the bits of evidence against each other, no matter how she looked at it, it appeared that she had been wrong.

If only she could have come to the conclusion a few hours sooner, she might have slipped away from him last night, and avoided the painful admission she might have to make today.

But she had not left because she had not wanted to, just as he had not stopped himself in the brothel. When he learned the truth he would turn her out, and she would be well punished for her playacting and foolish suspicions, because she would never again feel as she did when he held her in his arms.

As she worried on it, Tom burst in through the door of his room, tossing his hat and gloves aside, but keeping his stick as he dropped into the chair beside hers. "Toby," he called to his servant, "paper and ink. Immediately. Sharpen a pen, and bring the writing table closer to the fire for me. Then, prepare yourself to deliver a message to the home of the Earl of Stanton. You are not to leave until you see the man. Put the paper I give you into his hands and no other's. He will hear me out on this, damn him, if he cares for his country."

"Tom, what are you about? What has happened?" The mention of the earl made her mouth go dry. But Tom seemed more elated than angry. Proof that whatever he had learned it was not the whole truth.

He flexed his bad leg and sighed. "It has been a most

curious day. I procured the license, or at least set things in motion to make the damned thing procurable. And then, I went to visit an old friend in the Home Office. The Earl of Stanton was my captain, before your husband. If we are to make a go of it, I cannot lay about here, mooning over the past. I need employment." He was grinning at her as though he thought it the most wonderful thing in the world to toil for her, and she could feel her heart breaking a little.

He shook his head. "But he would not have me. It seems I am not trusted. There were rumors, you know, after the incident. Some thought me a coward, and others a traitor for my damned luck on that day."

She cringed at his casual mention of the very thing that had preyed on her mind. "Perhaps the people who doubted did not know you as I do now." And she would find a way to make it right, now that she had seen the truth.

He smiled and gave another shake of his head, this time in amazement. "No matter. Today, I think it has all happened for a reason. Stanton's secretary was quick to take note of the cold reception, and made me a most unusual offer. I think he hoped that there was some bit of information that I might wish to sell, or that the enemy had some use for a desperate and angry man."

"No." She almost moaned the word. It would be a sad thing if her presence had made him the very traitor she hoped to catch.

He placed a hand on hers. "Do not worry. I am not tempted. But I kept mum about the fact. And now, it seems I have information that would be most valuable to Stanton, and he will be forced to apologize for turning me out." His eyes narrowed. "As if I would turn so easily to help the lot that gave me this gamey leg." His hand tightened on hers, as though he could shield her from the pain of the past. "I know we are barely met. And this all must seem most curious to you. But if asked,

I will spy for Stanton and meet with these men to divine their purpose. Perhaps I can lead them to reveal others. If I can deliver them into the very hands of those they seek to betray, it will be most satisfying. I will lie if I must, and appear to be a rogue and traitor. But you must believe that I am as true to my country as I will be to you." He brushed the hair out of her eyes. "I will make an excellent spy, since it is so easy for most to believe wrong of me."

"Don't." The proof of his innocence hurt almost as much as the fear of his guilt.

He was holding her hand almost painfully tight, as though he feared she would leave. "If we are to be together, you will hear what people say of me. But know that it is all lies. For you, I have nothing but truth. If there was any sin I was guilty of, in all the time on the Peninsula, it was of envy. For Charles told me of you, and I…" He took a breath. "I loved you long before I met you. But I never meant to act on it. At that time, I thought I had a future of my own, even if it was not so bright as his. I would never have hurt him, for doing so would hurt you. And I never could. Not in all the world."

So his last secret was that he loved her better than she knew. And he did not want her to think him dishonorable, should he resort to spying. She could feel the tears welling up behind her eyes. For how was what he was planning any different than what she had done to him?

Other than that she had been wrong.

"What is it?" The concern for her was echoed in his eyes, his voice and every line of his body, as though he strained from his very soul to put her at ease. It only made her betrayal of him worse. She could feel the sob breaking, and was powerless to stop it.

His arms were around her. "There, there. I have upset you."

"No. It is I who was false to you. You will hate me when you know."

He stroked her hair, letting her cry. "What could you ever do that would make me love you less?"

"The rumors about your disloyalty came from me. I went to the Earl of Stanton. It was I who put the doubts about you into his head. I hoped that I could trick you with my body into revealing the truth."

There was a horrible pause before he spoke. He went still and his face became blank. "And so you have. After less than a day, there is not a secret left in me that you do not know."

"I hate myself for what I have done."

"For giving yourself to me?" His hand moved ever so slightly on her.

"No. That was..." What good did it do to lie and protect the feelings of the dead, when it would further wrong the man who held her? "Perfect. When we are alone? It is unlike anything I have known and I do not regret a moment. But I wronged you with my words, and I lied to you, even after I knew I had been mistaken about your guilt."

"You never needed my help. Not even from the first?" He gave an incredulous laugh.

"I was in the brothel only to trap you. I would never... I do not need money, or the protection of any man. I could have lived out my days alone in comfort. But I had to know...."

"And now you do." His back stiffened, but he did not release her. "Charles was right. Your loyalty to him knew no bounds. Not even those of propriety, if you were willing to lie with me just to prove my guilt."

She opened her eyes and looked up into his. "All I found was that you were a better man, and more honest and noble than I could possibly imagine."

"And now, I am vindicated?" He said it as though it were a small comfort. "And when you accepted my offer of marriage?" There was no rancor in his voice, only a gentle prodding to get to the truth.

"I knew in my heart that it would all end once you realized what I had done. But I could not manage to say no."

He released her and leaned back in his chair, rubbing his hand over his eyes as though befuddled by her answer. "If I had behaved as a man of honor when we met, we would not be in this muddle. I should have walked from the room as soon as I suspected the truth of your identity. But I wanted you, even when I thought you would sell your body to any who would have it. I thought you a common whore, who would leave as soon as she saw how little I had to offer. But I could not let you go."

"You offered yourself. And it was more than I deserved."

"And what you did to me was done out of loyalty to your country, and to your husband. What sense would there be to punish you for believing what everyone else thought true?" He sighed again.

"You do not mean to cast me off, then?" she asked in a small voice, fearing what his answer would be.

He gave her a wan smile. "You must know, Victoria, that it is up to you to decide whether to keep me or cut me loose. A gentleman does not cry off of an engagement."

Without meaning to, she laughed, and then gulped to swallow the sound and covered her mouth with her hand. There was nothing funny about the predicament they were in. He had not been a gentleman, nor had she acted like a lady. She was a spy and wished she wasn't. He was ready to become one to earn money that she did not need. And nothing she'd assumed about him was true. He was sweet and kind and he had loved her before she'd even known him. And perhaps, there was a chance she might love him as well.

"Money does not matter," she whispered, afraid that she might offend him. "I have enough for both of us. But I will be happy without, if you wish me to."

He gave a dry chuckle. "I am not so great a fool as to wish for poverty to salve my pride. You may keep your money, and I will not be as useless as I have been, once Stanton gets my letter. I am sure we can find a happy medium, and live quite comfortably." He paused. "If you still wish to make a go of it."

"If I wish it?" She scarcely dared breathe. For after all she had told him, he still spoke as if a promise made in the dark was an unbreakable oath. "If I did not want to release you?" she whispered. "If I wished, with all my heart, that there was a way to take back the terrible things I said and thought?"

"Then you know what you must do." He was staring at her as though it should be perfectly obvious what he expected.

Was it an apology he wanted? It was his. "I am so sorry. So very sorry, that I hurt you. That I did not take the time to understand, or to know you for who you truly are."

Still he stared at her, unmoving and expectant. There was something else.

And then she realized. There was a way that he would know that it was truth. She leaned forward and reached for him, putting her arms about his neck and her mouth on his. "Let me begin again," she whispered against his parted lips. She slipped her tongue between them, beginning with barely a touch. It was one more thing about him that was different. He tasted…

"Mmm." She smiled to herself as her tongue touched his. For without thinking, she'd made a noise of satisfaction before delving deeper into the kiss.

Suddenly his hands caught her by the waist and dragged

her body close and into the chair with him to sit on his lap. She wrapped her arms even tighter around his neck as he kissed her in return. And she decided, if there had been a secret he was hiding from the world, it had nothing to do with loyalty and betrayal, and everything to do with the skill of his kisses.

He broke from her and muttered, "Now I know why you denied me that, when we first met. How could I leave your bed, after such a kiss?"

She laid a hand on his shoulder, tracing the seam of his coat with her finger. "It would not have been like that, at first. I did not want you to know the contents of my heart."

"But now you do?"

"I would like nothing more." And she kissed him again.

* * * * *

THE VIKING'S FORBIDDEN
LOVE-SLAVE

Michelle Willingham

Author Note

Vikings have always been notorious for being fierce warriors—sexy men who fight for what they want. The idea of being stolen away by a handsome Viking was the inspiration for this story, but what if the warrior has a sense of honor? Irish heroine Aisling Ó Brannon tries to win her freedom, but never expects to find love. This story is linked to the novel *Her Warrior Slave,* which tells the tale of Aisling's brother, Kieran. I hope you enjoy this fantasy.

I always love to hear from readers. Visit my Web site at www.michellewillingham.com or e-mail me at michelle@michellewillingham.com.

With thanks to Larissa Ione, a great friend, writer and margarita buddy. I appreciate all the support!

Look for Michelle Willingham's
Surrender to the Irish Warrior
Coming September 2010

Chapter 1

Ireland, 1102

Darkness enveloped her, thick and suffocating. Her jaw ached, and her lips were cracked from thirst. Aisling Ó Brannon shifted her wrists, but they were bound tightly with ropes.

Rising panic swelled in her veins, along with the memory of the Norse raider who had stolen her away. She vaguely recalled a wooden longboat and hours spent at sea.

Where had he taken her? And…what would become of her? She struggled against her bonds, and realized she was lying upon a bed.

No. Not that.

The taste of fear rose up in her throat, quickly replaced by determination. She wasn't going to lie there like a helpless babe. With her fingertips, she struggled to loosen the ropes.

"You're awake." A male voice filled the interior, deep and resonant. Heavily accented by the Norse language, she sensed that his grasp of the Irish tongue was not a strong one. She blinked, trying to see him, and then realized her vision was blocked by a length of cloth.

The loss of her sight made the unknown all the more frightening. Aisling rolled her body to the side, straw crackling beneath the mattress. A hand reached beneath her shoulders and eased her to sit up.

She struggled to move away, but then he pressed a cup to her lips. The instinctive need to quench her thirst overcame all else. She tasted the sweetness of mead, and unable to help herself, she drank deeply.

"Where am I?" she demanded.

"Just outside Vedrarfjord."

She recognized the *Lochlannach* name for the lands so close to her own. Thank the Blessed Virgin. She remembered little about her kidnapping, and time had blurred.

She moved her face away from the cup, trying once again to see who was holding her captive. "Why am I blindfolded?"

"It wasn't meant to be one."

She felt him touch her head, and she winced at the tender pain upon her scalp. Her jaw felt swollen, as though someone had smashed a fist against her cheek. The Norseman unwrapped a length of cloth until at last, light speared her eyes. Aisling blinked, struggling to see her captor.

He was tall enough that she had to lean back to look at him. Dark golden hair fell upon broad shoulders, while a bronze torque gleamed around his neck. The thick corded muscles of his forearms had black runes deeply tattooed into his skin. Even with her hands bound, Aisling had the urge to cross herself against the sight of the mystical lines.

He wore a gray tunic that hung below his waist and dark trews, colorless clothes that might have been suited to a peasant, were they not so well made. The fine weave of the material suggested he had chosen these shades and paid good coin for them. Only a long cloak, dyed a rich shade of burgundy, revealed any color. A gold brooch shaped like a serpent fastened the garment to his shoulders.

This man was no commoner. She could see it in the way he held his head up, in the way he stared at her, as though she were his possession. Not by half. Not if she could help it.

The way he was watching her made her skin tighten. The air inside the room suddenly grew stifling, and she reminded herself of all the lessons her brothers had taught her about defense.

If he dared to touch her, he would regret it. As soon as she could get a weapon, she would be free of him.

Her hands curled into the rough covering over the mattress. *Don't let him see your fear.* "Who are you?"

"I am Tharand Hardrata." At his penetrating stare, she offered her own name in exchange.

"Are you a *jarl*?"

"No. I am a member of the *hird*. A freeman."

It startled her to hear it. As a Norse warrior, why would he dress so plainly? And what did he want with her? She tried not to think about why she was bound upon his bed. Swallowing hard, she asked, "Why did you take me as your captive?"

Tharand made no reply. Instead, he reached for a dagger at his waist, and the blade flashed in the firelight. Aisling held herself perfectly still. *Don't breathe.*

But he only reached behind her and grasped the ropes that bound her. His hands curled around her wrists as though he could snap the bones without any effort at all. The heat of his palms penetrated her skin, chaining her in his grasp.

"I'm going to cut these." He grasped a single rope, tightening it against her skin. "Don't move."

With him so close, she could feel the muscles of his upper

arm pressing against her. The contact was accidental, but the heat of his body warmed her cool skin. Aisling took a deep breath to push back the rising panic.

The greater danger was being alone with this man. Fierce and forbidding, his strength could easily overpower her.

His thumb edged her palm, and the touch sent a rush of apprehension through her. A faint spiciness rose from his skin, a scent reminiscent of faraway lands to the East. In the firelight, his silhouette dominated her own.

"What do you want from me?" she asked. "Am I now your slave?"

His knife sliced the ropes in a swift, lethal move. Tharand sheathed the blade, never taking his eyes from her. His gaze was discerning, as though he were trying to measure her worth.

"You will be a gift to King Magnus," he said at last. "He has returned to Erin."

A gift? Her lips tightened at the thought. "And what makes you think he would want another slave?"

He reached out and took a length of her dark hair, running his fingers through it. Gooseflesh raised upon her neck, her heart hammering.

"You would not be another *ambatt*," he said. "A woman such as yourself has more value than that. If you are fortunate, you might warm his bed."

Words of outrage tempted her lips. *I am not that sort of woman*, she wanted to shout. But that was what she'd become, wasn't it? Her freedom was gone, stolen away.

She rubbed her raw wrists, trying to will sensation back into the numbness. The warrior stood before her, and she longed to cut him down for what he'd done. And for what he was about to do.

"What will you receive in exchange?" she demanded. "Gold? Thirty pieces of silver?"

His expression chilled. "You should be grateful for your life."

"Why me? Why not some other woman?" Inside, she wanted to scream. Nervous energy roiled within her skin, trying to claw its way free.

Tharand shrugged. "You are of noble Irish blood, and that will make you suitable to serve his needs."

Serve his needs? Aisling gritted her teeth. Not very likely. She wasn't about to stand meekly aside and let herself suffer such a fate.

But the winter season made an escape even more complicated. She would need shelter, as well as a horse and supplies. She couldn't simply run, not without careful planning.

Aisling rubbed her wrists again, trying to relieve the pain. Her jaw ached, the skin swelling up. But the discomfort was not only physical. Her imagination had run wild with thoughts of what this raider would do to her. Though he had not forced himself upon her yet, perhaps he was biding his time.

She needed a weapon. The gleam of steel against the back wall of the dwelling caught her eye.

"Eat," Tharand interrupted, handing her a wooden bowl. His large frame blocked her line of sight, making her scramble backwards upon the bed.

At the sight of the salted fish, her stomach rebelled. "No, thank you."

"I won't have you starving yourself." The command was lined with steel. He dropped the bowl in front of her and folded his arms across his chest. Against her will, she found herself staring at the tattooed runes that seemed to writhe against his skin.

"It isn't that." She held her breath against the offensive odor. "It's that I don't care for fish. Or anything from the sea."

And right now, the idea of eating made her stomach twist. She was long past hunger, hardly remembering the last time she had eaten.

"Prisoners should be grateful for any food at all."

She drew her knees up, holding them against her chest. "If it's all the same to you, I'd rather go hungry." The soft wool of her overdress had absorbed the heat of the fire, and she tried to keep as much of her body covered as possible.

Tharand's expression held disbelief. He took the bowl away, frowning as though he didn't know what to make of her refusal.

She buried her face in her knees, breathing deeply to calm her racing heart. Where were his servants and slaves? His family? She was accustomed to the busy noises of people working, of animals penned outside, and the conversation of family.

But here, there was no one. It made her uneasy.

At last, she swung her legs over the side of the bed and tried to stand up. For the first time, she realized Tharand had taken her shoes. The cold ground chilled the soles of her bare feet before her knees buckled. He crossed the room to steady her. The touch permeated her skin, burning embarrassment into her face.

"I won't stay here." She shoved away from him and strode toward the door, wondering if Tharand would try to stop her. This was her life. Her freedom. She wouldn't cast that away without a fight.

He sat down upon the bed, seemingly unconcerned. "There is nowhere for you to run."

The room swayed, and she held onto the door to regain her footing. Defiantly, she opened it, unprepared for the freezing air. The lack of outer clothing imprisoned her as surely as ropes. Her hands and body shook, even as she tried to rub her arms for warmth.

"You're letting in the cold." Tharand's warning sounded irritated.

Her response was to walk outside, letting the door slam in his face. Outside, the winter air lashed against her *léine*, soft flurries of snow drifting. She gritted her teeth against the icy frost beneath her bare feet.

Although her brain railed at her for venturing out in such weather, this was, perhaps, her only chance to see the *Lochlannach* settlement.

Rectangular-shaped thatched houses were set within quadrants. Four homes framed a small, shared courtyard. The two-storey buildings were larger than the circular stone huts she was used to. Each of these dwellings could house two families with no lack of space.

A stone wall surrounded a ditch that was perhaps eight meters wide. It made her angry to see their defenses.

Thieving raiders. How dare they live in such luxury, when she and her family had to fight for their own survival? She'd watched them burn her home, the fire searing her possessions into ashes. The desire for vengeance took root within her, gathering strength.

Outside one of the homes, a young boy picked up a handful of wet snow and aimed the ball at one of his friends. His face was rounded and healthy, a child who had never known hunger like their tribe had endured. Unlike her younger brother.

Egan. Her heart bled at the memory of the *Lochlannach* slavers dragging him away. She clenched her fist, remembering his thin face and her eldest brother, Kieran, who had gone to try and save him. Were they even alive?

The anger returned, suffocating her with its intensity. She

flexed her fingers, wishing she had a blade to wield. Somehow, she had to leave this place. Gazing around the stone palisade, the *longphort* seemed impenetrable.

The door behind her suddenly opened, and she whirled around, half expecting her captor to drag her back inside. Instead, Tharand drew his cloak around himself, sending her a glance as if daring her to leave.

She couldn't. Not without warm clothing, a horse and supplies. None of which she was likely to gain without help.

The warmth of the house beckoned to her as the winter's ice froze her feet. With reluctance, Aisling took a step toward her captor's longhouse. He knew full well that she could go nowhere.

Tharand strode past the young boy playing in the snow. Terror transformed the child's face, and he dropped the snowball, skittering inside his home.

The warrior continued walking, as though he hadn't noticed the child's fear. Beneath her false courage, Aisling wondered if she had reason to be afraid.

Killer. Cursed son of Odin.

They had called him worse, Tharand supposed. He was accustomed to it by now. But as much as his own people shunned him, they revered him in battle. Like one of the gods, he slew anyone who threatened them. During battle, he'd killed upon his king's command, the guilty and the innocent alike. And for each life he'd taken, he'd carved a rune upon his own skin. Flesh for their flesh.

Tharand didn't bother glancing back at the longhouse where he'd left the prisoner. Beautiful, she was, filled with fire and courage. Years ago, he might have pitied her. Stolen from her family and about to be gifted to a king, her fate was one many a maiden feared.

And he felt nothing. Only a sense that he'd sunk even lower. That there could be no redemption for what he was about to do.

Sacrifices had to be made for those he loved. Even if it meant handing over an innocent.

As he continued through the *longphort*, the folk averted their gaze. They knew he had a female prisoner. Let them think what they wanted. The woman would not be his for long. After he gave her to King Magnus, she was no longer his responsibility. For now, she was the spoils of war.

And though tradition demanded that he punish her, conquer her body as any prisoner deserved, he intended to save her for the king.

When he reached a dwelling at the far side of the *longphort*, he pounded on the door. After it opened, he removed a golden band from his upper arm and handed it to Asgaut. The male warrior grunted and tested the weight.

"Prepare supplies and a horse for my journey. Send a message to Ludin that I am bringing a slave with me. We'll need shelter there."

"You're going to Magnus." It was not a question. Asgaut's face grew taut.

"I am."

"Jóra is likely dead, Tharand." The accusation in Asgaut's tone was unmistakable. "It is too late to save her."

He made no excuses. He'd been a commander for years, his sword bringing justice and death to those who had earned it.

"Send the message," he repeated. Without another word, he turned his back on Asgaut.

Aisling warmed her feet near the glowing embers upon the hearth, biting back the pain. Think, she cautioned herself. This was not a game; this was survival.

Know thine enemy, her father had always said. She shivered, remembering Tharand's wide palm against her spine. The way he'd unwrapped the linen from her head, as gentle as a lover.

The single room contained the bed where she'd been bound, and a low table. Two chests made of oak were on the opposite side of the room.

Upon the back wall, she saw weapons. So that was the gleam of steel she'd noticed earlier. Battle-axes and swords, spears and knives hung in neat rows. One small ax head, slightly larger than her hand, was inlaid with silver wire. Twisting swirls resembled a dragon, while a single row of points outlined the center. Not a speck of rust marred the iron, nor any blood. Each blade was honed and polished.

The executioner's hut, she thought dryly. But no, he was a warrior, so it made sense for him to have so many weapons.

What didn't make sense was his lack of servants or people to tend the house. Where were the women? Her memory hearkened to the young boy's terror at the sight of Tharand. Perhaps no one wanted to be near this warrior.

Herself included.

Aisling chose two blades, a small dagger and a knife the length of her hand. She contemplated tearing the hem of her gown, needing a scabbard for each blade. But then, why should she destroy her *léine*? Tharand should pay the forfeit. After searching through one of the chests, she found a man's linen tunic. Within moments, she cut a long strip of cloth and bound up the weapons, tying them to her thigh and calf.

She lowered her skirts, half expecting the warrior to stride in at any moment. When he didn't, she explored the house more. Her skin prickled with unease, for she still didn't trust him not to hurt her. But at least now she was armed.

It startled her to realize how clean his dwelling was. Nothing was out of place, not any clothing nor soiled dishes. Her own brothers, though she loved them dearly, were terrible when it came to keeping their home neat. Time and again, she'd found a tunic shoved behind a barrel or a pair of shoes in the middle of the floor. Kieran was the worst, leaving wood shavings all over the place from his carvings.

Her heart ached, the hollow feeling pushing away her sense of hope. Both of her brothers were gone. Kieran had saved her from one of the raiders before going after Egan. Afterwards, Tharand had stolen her.

She didn't know what had become of them. Or whether she would see them again. The thought made her want to rip all of the weapons off the wall, shattering anything she could get her hands on. Damn the *Lochlannachs* for what they'd done.

Aisling choked back the tears and took a deep breath. *You must leave*. She couldn't rely on anyone but herself. Her hand moved to the cool blade against her thigh, and it reassured her. Tharand would return soon, so she'd best get on with searching his belongings.

Footsteps resounded outside, and she fled toward the hearth before the door swung open. A man entered the longhouse, wearing a chain mail corselet and an iron helm. Like a god of the underworld, his gaze settled upon her as though he intended to claim her.

"I came to see Tharand," he said. "But you're his new captive, aren't you?"

Aisling reached for one of the knives, but his armor would make an attack more challenging. *Wait*, she cautioned herself. *Your time will come*.

The Norse warrior moved forward so quickly, she didn't have a chance to react. He gripped her waist, forcing her back against the wall. He used his strength to trap her there. "I could buy you from him," he whispered as his hand moved to cup her breast. "Or perhaps he'd share you."

Aisling fought to reach the blade, her wrist aching with the effort. *Almost there.*

A second later, another blast of cold air interrupted. Tharand closed the distance and hauled the attacker away from her. A sickening crunch resounded as he struck the man in the face. Fists met flesh, and a grim satisfaction filled Aisling as her captor pounded the soldier.

"No one touches her," Tharand growled.

"She is a slave," the man argued.

"She is mine." With his arm across the man's throat, Tharand dragged him toward the wall of weapons. "Look upon these blades. The next time you, or any man, comes near her, I'll let you choose the weapon that will end your life."

With that, he threw the door open and tossed the soldier into the snow. When he turned to her, his rage was not diminished. "Did he hurt you?"

"N-no," she managed. Aisling could feel his stare sliding down her body, the way the chill crept into her bones. Her earlier relief at being rescued was replaced with uneasiness. Why had he attacked one of his own men?

"I have my own purpose for you," he said, answering her unspoken question. "No man will harm you while you are under my protection."

Aisling forced herself to look at him. He unpinned the serpent brooch, removing his cloak. He didn't toss it aside the way her brothers would have. Instead, he folded it neatly and hung it upon a wooden peg. His attention moved toward the wall of weapons, and instantly his eyes narrowed at the blank spaces where the daggers had once been.

He knew the weapons were gone. But she refused to feel guilty. Everything this man possessed had been stolen from others. She would do what was necessary to survive.

Aisling's hand palmed the hilt of the dagger strapped to her thigh. Though he claimed no man would harm her, perhaps that did not include himself. Alone with him, she didn't at all like the look in his eyes.

The *Lochlannach*'s presence seemed to fill up the space, cornering her. The fire glowed upon the hearth, offering the only light inside the darkening space. Outside, she heard the faint spattering of ice crystals upon the thatch.

Run, her mind insisted, even though she knew it was futile. Tharand would allow her to go nowhere.

"Why did you come back?" she managed, her hand resting upon the dagger beneath her skirts. She didn't delude herself into believing she was safe. Whether she was meant to be a gift or not, this man would not hesitate to use her to his advantage.

His hand covered hers, pinning the dagger against her flesh. "I came to prepare you for what lies ahead."

Chapter 2

Tharand had known the weapons were missing from the moment he'd returned. The assortment of axes and swords was not decorative, unlike in other houses. He knew every blade as though it were a member of his own family. Every edge was honed until it would slice open a finger at the slightest touch.

He prided himself in caring for the tools, for his weapons protected those he loved.

Aisling had taken two daggers from the wall. He didn't know what she intended, but she did not seem like the hysterical sort. For now, he would let her keep them. Let her feel safe and in control. When she lowered her guard, he would take the daggers back.

"Let go of me," she gritted.

His hand palmed her thigh, letting her know that he was quite aware of her stolen weapon. He kept his grasp upon her skin a moment longer, just to intimidate her.

Her womanly scent caught his interest. Like a soft summer wind, it wound around him, enticing him with a sudden desire. He quelled it, for it would come to nothing. Women ran from him; he was well accustomed to it. Most avoided him whenever possible, as if afraid he'd notice them.

But there was no fear in Aisling's eyes. Anger blazed in her expression. "If you do not let go of me, you'll regret it."

He intended to. But he held her a moment longer, sliding his hand up to her waist in silent dominance. He could feel the bones of her spine beneath his palm. Terribly thin, nigh to the point of starvation.

The skin upon her forearms tightened with goose bumps. She averted her gaze, which bared her nape, the soft skin enticing. She fascinated him, though she was like all the others who hated the sight of him. With reluctance, he let his hand fall away.

"King Magnus has his eye upon your tribal lands," he said. Which was the truth. Magnus had every intention of conquering as much of Erin as he could gain.

Tharand moved closer to the hearth, holding his hands outstretched as though he needed the warmth. "If you win his favor, I imagine he would leave your family alone."

Her dark brown eyes narrowed. "I will not be a king's whore. Or any man's."

The bluntness of her words made it clear that she would accept none of his suggestions.

Tharand picked up a chunk of peat and tossed it onto the fire. Sparks glittered against the darkness before flames took hold. "We leave at first light, so long as the snows are not too deep."

"Then I'll pray for snow." She sat on the earthen floor beside the hearth, curling her knees up beneath her gown. Long black hair spilled over her shoulders, a river of ebony against her *léine* and overdress. The gown revealed the curve of her breast, but her slender waist reminded him of the winter her tribe had endured.

Some of his kinsmen were to blame for Aisling's hardship. Although he had never interfered with those who went on raids, it needled him to see a woman who had known suffering.

Why hadn't she eaten the fish, for one so hungry? Did she truly find it so distasteful?

Though he shouldn't concede to her preferences, no woman under his protection would go hungry, whether it was her will or not.

He filled an iron pot with water and set it to hang above the hearth. From the storage cairn below the longhouse, he brought out a frozen piece of meat.

"Does the taste of beef offend you also?" he asked quietly. "Or only fish?"

She raised her head up to look at him, taken aback by his offer. "I will eat meat."

"Good." He used one of his sharper knives to cut the meat into small chunks. The mindless task eased him, and he tossed them into the pot of water.

"Where are your other slaves?" Aisling asked.

"I sent them away." He preferred being alone, whenever he returned from serving the king. The *thralls* who tended his longhouse were under strict orders to remain at his father's house while he was in residence. It irritated him, having men and women underfoot. Especially when he had a prisoner.

Aisling reached up to a braid of dried onions he'd hung from the ceiling. She touched one of the vegetables and asked, "May I?"

He shrugged, and she reached up for the onion. After checking it for signs of rot, she peeled it with her fingers. "If I may borrow your knife, I'll cut this up for the stew."

"You already have a blade," he reminded her.

Her eyes narrowed. "That one is for later. It will be used to cut out the heart of any man who dares to touch me."

Self-assured, wasn't she? He moved into her space, keeping the knife gripped in his palm. With his other hand, he reached out to her waist. "I'll dare to touch you."

He wasn't about to let this outspoken slip of a girl defy him. The knife rested between them, a reminder that she could not win this battle. "Will you cut out my heart?" He drew so close his thigh moved between her legs, daring her.

"I can't," she whispered. "You don't have one."

The journey to Lutus's home was far more uncomfortable than he'd expected. With the slave seated in front of him on the horse, Tharand was forced to hold her while riding. His arm held steady against the curve of her breast, while her slim body rested within his legs. He had wrapped her in his cloak for warmth, and yet she leaned into him for protection against the cold.

High above them, storm clouds bided their time. He urged his horse Ymir to move faster. The stallion sensed the impending need to reach their destination, and Tharand held her tighter.

He still didn't know why he'd let her keep the knife. Somehow he sensed there would be no danger from her. At least, not yet.

The lush scent of her body invited him, tantalizing him with the motion of her hips rocking against his manhood. He grew hard, his length aching to sheathe itself inside her.

Odin's bones. He'd intended to deliver her to Magnus, an exchange for his sister's life. A beautiful slave, bound to pleasure her master. Instead, he found himself wanting to discover her secrets. He wanted to slide his hands beneath the soft linen underdress. Feel the round breasts, her nipples pebbling beneath his thumbs.

Her shoulders lowered, and he sensed a change. She knew of his arousal, tensing against him. A groan caught in his throat when she turned toward him. Her dark eyes hardened into ice. "I am not yours to take, *Lochlannach*."

The words challenged him, as surely as one sword striking against another. "I've already taken you, *kjæreste*." And with that, he reached forward, lifting the edge of her skirts until his palm touched her bare thigh. He let the woolen cloth fall back into place, though he kept his hand upon the softness of her skin.

She hissed, jerking her attention back to him. Though she tried to pull his hand away, he kept it in place. Lowering his mouth to her ear, he whispered, "When I bring you to Magnus, he will not be wanting a shy virgin." He slid his hand up to the slit of her womanhood. Cupping her, he let the rhythm of the horse move his hand. She fought him, trying to reach the dagger. But a moment later, he felt her begin to bloom.

Warm wetness coated his thumb, her honeyed arousal. Encouraged by it, he stroked her intimately until he was rewarded by the arch of her back. A low moan sounded in her throat.

"Have you ever sheathed a man?" he murmured, sliding his fingers into her silken entrance. "Did he give you pleasure?"

Her breathing quickened as he teased her folds, feeling for the hard center that would send her over the edge.

"I don't...want you," she managed, struggling not to let herself go. His fingers were bathed in her wetness, her body denying the words she spoke.

He slowed the horse, deliberately letting it trot so that she bounced against his hand. His own breathing had grown harsh, his length hard and hot against her buttocks. If he lifted the back of her gown, he could lift her up and impale her on his shaft.

He rubbed her faster, and her skin grew fevered with desire.

No, she didn't want him. And Odin's throne, he was a bastard for arousing her in this way. He'd never been able to resist a challenge. Especially not one as sweet as this.

He entered her with two long fingers, pressing hard against her sweet flesh until she cried out. He kept his strokes in a deliberate imitation of lovemaking, drawing out her frustration until at last she crumpled, shaking with the fierce aftershocks of pleasure.

And still he didn't stop. He rubbed her until she wept, her hands gripping his thighs as though begging him to join with her. When her muscles grew boneless, he stopped, withdrawing his fingers and pressing a soft kiss against her nape.

"We'll be stopping for the night soon."

She leaned forward, her shoulders slumped forward. "I hate you."

As the sun started to slip lower in the sky, he told himself he would not regret arousing her. She had to be ready for Magnus, to become his concubine.

And though he craved joining his body with hers, he would leave her untouched. Even if it killed him.

Aisling awoke in the middle of the night, her spirits bruised and battered. It wasn't far now, and within another day Tharand would hand her over to the Norse king.

The cold floor had made it nearly impossible to sleep. Tharand had offered her the chance to sleep beside him upon a humble pallet. The thought of feeling his warm body against her own made her shudder. Not from fear, but from her own forbidden desires.

He'd touched her in a way no man ever had. She'd despised the feeling of being so trapped, so helpless to his strength. Like a lover, arousing her until her body opened to his. It tormented her, the way he'd brought her to the edge of ecstasy and sent her drowning into an abyss of wild need.

She sat up, pulling her gown around her, as if to shut him out from her mind. Only a few feet away, she heard the steady rhythm of his breath. Beyond them, the other inhabitants slept, Ludin and his family. The presence of people should have made her feel better, but she knew that these were his allies, his friends.

The earthen floor was so very cold, the air so frigid her breath formed clouds within the longhouse. Tears began to fall once again. Not so he could hear; she wouldn't give him that satisfaction. But the burden of what had happened swept over her until she could no longer hold it in. She lowered her head and gave in to a good cry.

"I know you're awake." His deep voice slid into the silence. "And my offer still stands if you wish to sleep beside me."

"I would sooner sleep with a viper," Aisling retorted. Her teeth chattered, and she bit her lip, trying to keep warm. She had enough willpower to resist the temptation of his body heat. It was simply difficult convincing her freezing feet that they were better off without warmth.

Aisling glanced around, hoping that someone would awaken. But no one paid any heed to their conversation, their slumber unbroken.

"You enjoyed my hands upon you," he murmured. "You're afraid of what else you might feel." He sat up, his large frame silhouetted in the shadows. Though she could not see his face, her heart raced in fear.

And undeniable anticipation.

He could have forced himself upon her, time and again, but he had not. Her body broke out in a sweat, just thinking of his touch earlier. The rough wool of her *léine* abraded her skin, her body completely at war with her mind.

"I'm not afraid of you." The lie did nothing to allay her fear, and she hugged her knees, keeping her body covered.

"You're terrified I'll force myself upon you." His deep voice brushed over her like a wicked caress. "And worse, that you'll enjoy it."

Her pulse pounded so fast, she couldn't answer. But he sensed it, and in the dark, he closed the distance. His fingers threaded through her hair, loosening the strands. Though he did nothing more, she was shaking so hard, she couldn't face him.

"Don't touch me." The words were ripped from her mouth with a confidence she didn't feel.

He bent in so near, she could smell the spiciness of his skin. Like winter's breath, mingled with the exotic tang of foreign lands. A raider's scent.

When his mouth tasted the skin of her neck, a dark heat raced through her blood. She couldn't move, her body rising to his forbidden call.

"You've never been touched by a man, have you?" He drew back, and let her go.

A denial tangled in her mouth, for she had shared in the *Bealtaine* rituals, taking a lover as most women did. "I haven't been touched by a murderer," she corrected. "Or a thief."

"I've been called both." His hands moved to the sides of her breasts. Lazily, his thumbs traced circles over the fabric, so close to her nipples, the tips grew erect. "I'm not a good man, *kjæreste*."

Another brush of his lips grazed her mouth. A heated flame kindled between her legs, a rising fire to experience more of what he'd taught her that afternoon.

"I've changed my mind," he said, tossing her his own coverlet. "Stay where you are, Aisling Ó Brannon. For if you join me here, you'll find yourself on your back and I'll be inside you."

* * *

The nightmare strangled him, tearing out any hope of peaceful sleep. Tharand's hand clenched in a fist, as though it held a dagger. Stifling air clogged his lungs, while memories of his sister's screams tormented him.

His heartbeat pulsed within his chest, a slight dampening of sweat upon his skin despite the frigid air. He rolled over, but the space beside him remained empty. Aisling insisted on sleeping upon the floor beside the fire, huddled beneath the woolen coverlet.

The instinctive desire to take her into his bed had not dimmed. Though her skin would be freezing cold, he wanted to warm her. Hours ago, he'd succumbed to his curiosity, tasting the softness of her skin. It was everything he'd imagined it would be, with her hair falling over his hands. The way a breath caught in her throat, and the soft sigh when he'd kissed the tender space. She might loathe him, but she had been caught up in the moment as well. The very thought made him shift uncomfortably.

As the hours crept toward dawn, Tharand could feel the temperature dropping. He stared up at the ceiling for a long moment. The easiest way was simply to drag her to his bed. Why should he allow a captive to choose?

He sat up and saw that Aisling was seated, no longer sleeping. All senses went on alert, for he knew nothing of her intent.

When he dropped to one knee before her, she didn't raise her face to his. She'd been weeping. Her reddened eyes and quiet demeanor gave the evidence.

"Did you kill them?" she asked quietly.

"Who?"

"My brothers." She closed her eyes, refusing to look at him. "Kieran and Egan."

"Many tribesmen were taken," he answered. "Most were sold into slavery. Your brothers might have been among them."

"If they aren't dead," she finished. Her posture remained downtrodden, her voice dull. "I want to know what happened to them."

He reached out and tipped her chin to look at him. "No one is going to rescue you, Aisling. Your fate rests in the hands of King Magnus now."

"No," she whispered. "My fate rests in your hands." Her voice pleaded with him, while she covered his palms with her own.

"You want me to let you go."

"Yes." She laced her fingers with his. "I want to believe that you possess honor. That somewhere beneath your heritage lies a man who will do the right thing."

She didn't know. Couldn't know that he had no choice. He owed her no explanations, for she was nothing but a captive.

He jerked his hands from hers. "I'm not a man of honor. I kill when my king commands it. I seize whatever I can find upon the battlefield, for that is a warrior's right." He rose and tossed her a pair of battered shoes that had once belonged to Jóra. "Nothing you say will change your fate. Prepare yourself, Aisling. For today I will give you over to the king."

Aisling voiced silent prayers throughout each mile of the journey. As soon as they stopped to let the horses drink, she would have to make her escape.

But how? Every plan seemed foolish. Even if she did manage to get away from Tharand, she didn't know her surroundings. They were north of Dubh Linn, and she had never traveled this far before. The freezing weather made it even more impossible, for there was no shelter.

You have to stay with him, her mind reasoned. *You'll die if you don't.*

Was death worse than surrendering to a man's pleasure?

Embarrassment flooded her at the memory of Tharand's touch. She had wanted him to kiss her, wanted his touch. Even now, she could not forget the way he'd touched her upon horseback. He attracted her in a way she'd never anticipated. Her body had responded to him, bowing beneath his rigid strength and evoking unwanted yearnings.

She rubbed her hands together, struggling to get them warm. "What can I do to win my freedom?"

"There is nothing." Like ancient standing stones, he would not be moved.

"I don't believe you."

He didn't spare her a glance. "Believe what you will. You will be given to him." But the sharp tone in his voice suggested that there was another reason. He stopped the horse and dismounted, lifting her down.

"You're getting something in return," she predicted. When he still kept his eyes averted, another truth dawned. "*Someone* in return."

At that, his blue eyes pierced her with certainty. "As I've said. There is no other choice."

Her mind turned over the situation, searching for a way out. The tension in his muscles, the unyielding cast to his face, made her feel even more helpless.

"Is it a woman?" She took a hesitant step toward him, unsure of how to read his expression. Was he truly a man who intended to use her to his advantage? Or was he trapped, just as she was?

From the stoic lines in his eyes, the bitterness, she almost stopped short. Tharand's silence confirmed his answer. A strange heaviness weighed down upon her, to think of him riding this far for another woman.

Her face flushed, for he'd touched her intimately. The thought of him caressing another woman made her insides twist.

Why should you care? her mind demanded. *He is nothing but a thief and a murderer. A man who cares only for himself.*

But if that were true, why had he not forced her into his bed? She couldn't see past the cloak of his silence.

He moved toward her, watching her like a predator. Aisling almost fled backwards, but at the last moment managed to stand her ground. "What do you want?"

"I think you know."

A heartbeat later, his mouth crashed down upon hers. And Danu, his kiss eradicated every thought in her mind. His hands slid up to capture her nape, his lips plundering hers. No longer did she feel the winter's cold as the heat of his body burned against her own.

He kissed her as though he didn't want to give her up, as though she meant something to him, more than just a slave.

She let him take from her, and before she could realize what was happening, she was kissing him back. She ignored the panicked voices that warned her not to do this. Palming his shoulders, she trailed her fingertips over his muscles, down to the runes tattooed on his wrists.

His hard erection moved against the juncture of her hips, and she parted her legs slightly. The thick length rubbed her, tempting her to surrender to him.

Tharand never stopped kissing her, and when his tongue probed the entrance to her mouth, she let him inside. The wet heat mimicked the sensation of joining with a man.

"You were watching me," he murmured against her lips. "And I wondered what the taste of you would be like."

Aisling's legs stumbled beneath her, and she clung to him for support. Before she could ask what he meant, he lowered the shoulder of her *léine*. In the snowy chill, her skin puckered, her nipples tightening.

"You're cold," he said huskily. "And I haven't tasted all of you yet." He bared her breast, stroking the nipple with his thumb. Hot blood rushed to her face, and her palm closed over the dagger strapped to her thigh.

Without taking his gaze off her face, he trapped her hand in place, lowering his mouth to her breast. Warm heat enclosed the nipple, and the sensation made her wet.

She yearned to be filled with him, to know the weight of his body upon hers. As he suckled, her hands fisted in his hair, the dagger forgotten.

All of her willpower disappeared, like a snowflake upon warm skin. She wanted him. God help her, she sensed that it would not be like this with another man. Perhaps it was the forbidden nature of being a raider's captive. Or perhaps she was losing her sense of reason the longer she stayed with him. Whatever the cause, she yearned to feel him inside.

His hand moved beneath her skirts, and he unsheathed the dagger, dropping it into the snow. A rough palm cupped her center. Using his thumb, he stroked her until a rush of wetness coated his hand.

"Don't," she pleaded. She didn't want to desire him, and she loathed herself for even thinking of letting him do whatever he wanted.

Tharand parted her, sliding his finger inside her warmth. Then another finger, until he gently stretched her open. He penetrated her with his fingers, while he conquered her mouth once again.

The shallow strokes tortured her with the promise of a joining.

"Your body is awakening," he whispered, flicking his thumb against her swollen cleft. A jolt of fire permeated her, making her moan against his mouth. His wicked hands were making her ready for him, until she trembled.

"You are cruel." Shaking with need, she tried to block out the rising frustration.

"Yes." He withdrew his hand, letting her skirt fall back into place. Gruffly, he added, "But you will please the king. That is all that matters."

"My feelings don't matter." She threw the words back at him, wishing he had never touched her.

Tharand reached down and handed her the dagger, hilt first. "You might need this, as protection against Magnus's men."

Aisling hid her face as she replaced the weapon. Her mood only darkened as he lifted her upon the horse. Deeply aroused, Tharand had taught her a lesson she'd not soon forget. It was best to shield herself from this *Lochlannach*, to pretend that he did not even exist.

For she meant nothing to him.

Chapter 3

Tharand's own mood had soured. Over and over, he reminded himself that Aisling Ó Brannon was a slave, a woman no different from the others he'd captured. And though none could compare to her beauty, he could not lose sight of his purpose.

Time and again, she'd surprised him. The sweetness of her arousal, the driving need to watch her come apart, was slowly stealing away his mind.

And when he'd kissed her...

Odin's bones, she had a mouth that was made to be savored. When she'd kissed him back, he'd caught a sense of what it would be like to have her willing. And if he didn't keep his hands off her, he would break his own vow not to get involved. It would only make it harder to give her up.

Abruptly, he stopped the horse. He couldn't say why, but they would arrive at the king's estate by nightfall. Once he gave her into Magnus's custody, he could no longer protect her. The thought of other men bruising her fair skin made his fist tighten.

"Why did you stop?" she asked.

Without answering, he lifted her down and led her

toward a small grove of trees. "You don't know how to use a knife, do you?"

She eyed him with distrust. "Why would you think that?"

He held out his hand. "Give me the blade."

"Why?"

"Because I want to show you how to defend yourself with it."

"My brothers taught me," she argued, keeping her hand upon the outline of the weapon beneath her skirt.

Tharand kept his hand outstretched, waiting for her to acquiesce. He couldn't let her go to Magnus without a means of defense. Even if he stayed with her, he could not be with her at all times.

"Show me what you know," he asked. As she withdrew the blade, he fell into a defensive stance. "Try to stab me."

Aisling shook her head. "That isn't really what I—"

"Do it," he ordered, adjusting his stance so that his foot was anchored against one of the oak trees.

She reached beneath her skirt, giving him a quick view of a long bare leg. He tried to ignore the distraction, focusing on the weapon she held.

"Now aim for my heart."

"And as I said before. You don't have one."

Didn't she realize he was trying to help her? Damn it, didn't she know what kind of men served Magnus? They would dishonor her in an instant, unless she made it clear that she belonged only to the king.

Tharand waited for her to make a move. He needed to see her technique before he could correct her.

The last thing he expected was to be pinned against the tree, the dagger embedded in his tunic. Aisling crossed her arms and regarded him. "You know that I could have killed you. I suppose I should have."

He gaped at her, understanding that she was trained to throw the weapon, not to stab with it.

"Perhaps I should leave you here," she mused, taking a step backwards, toward his horse. "You'd be warm enough with your cloak. Someone would come along eventually and free you."

He reached over and wrenched the dagger from the wood, tearing the fabric. Holding the weapon, he stared at her. "Who taught you to throw a knife like that?"

"My brother Kieran."

"Show me again." He used the blade to peel off a small fraction of bark. Handing her the knife, he stepped back to watch. She couldn't possibly hit such a tiny target. None of his own men were trained to do so, and they practiced daily with their blades.

With the flick of her wrist, she embedded the knife exactly in the tiny space.

Odin's blood. He couldn't believe what he was seeing. "Once more."

And she did, without hesitation.

"Kieran wanted me to be able to protect myself." Aisling withdrew the knife from the wood, strapping it to her thigh once again.

"You're good," he acceded. That was when it struck him. He'd completely misjudged her. She wasn't a helpless maiden at all. Time and again, she could have used the blade against him. He could be dead right now. Why hadn't she tried to kill him?

The questions ate at him until finally he took her hand. He held it lightly, unsure of why he was touching her. "You had the chance, just now, to take my life. Why didn't you?"

She raised soft brown eyes to his. "I should have."

Tentatively, she touched his cheek, her fingertips moving down his jaw. The gentleness startled him. Snowflakes came down from the clouded sky, lighting upon his mouth.

Her hands moved down to his shoulders, as though she were healing each part of him she touched. He didn't move, his pulse beating beneath his skin.

"You're killing me now," he murmured, and was rewarded with a seductive smile.

"Good."

Her hands slipped beneath his tunic, and at the touch of her icy fingertips, he yelped. A throaty laugh wound around him, seductive and rich.

The snow fell thicker, and he ignored it as he leaned down to kiss her. This time, it wasn't meant to subdue her, only to give in to his own longing.

He tasted her victory and his own regret. He hadn't expected to admire her, nor to want her for his own. The kiss warmed him in a way nothing else had.

Her arms wrapped around his waist, her cool hands moving up his bare back. He winced as goose flesh rose up. "You're still cold."

"Am I?"

He nodded. "Let me warm you."

In answer, she pulled his mouth down to hers. He took from her, transforming the kiss into the desire he felt. He'd not expected her to reach out to him, and his sense of honor went on alert.

She didn't mean this. She didn't truly want him. It was about negotiating, trying to coerce him into letting her go. And though it was the hardest thing in the world to do, he broke away from her.

"We have to go." He lifted her into his arms, walking toward the horse. When he raised her onto the horse and then swung on behind her, he was careful not to get too close. It didn't matter. He breathed in the scent of her hair, like a cool May morning.

Innocent, she was. And he was about to give her over to the king. Magnus would not hesitate to accept the beautiful slave.

But afterwards…

If Aisling did not please him, Magnus would give her to his men. He suspected that she would not hesitate to kill any man who threatened her. She would lose her life, if she did.

Strands of her hair whipped against his face, and he pressed them gently away. A sense of unease came over him, at the thought of her coming to harm.

His arms curled around her while they rode, and the fit of her body to his felt right. Against the snowy whiteness, the black runes upon his forearms stood out. Would Aisling's life be marked by one of them? He tightened his hold upon her.

Though it went against his duty, he no longer wanted to surrender her to the king. And Odin help him, he didn't know what he could do about it. She was here only as an offering, a gift to secure his sister's safe return.

He had tried on numerous occasions to talk Magnus into letting Jóra go, even offering gold as a ransom. But the king wanted her with an unnatural longing. Already he might have defiled her.

Tharand quickened the pace of his stallion. They needed shelter before the snow grew too deep for travel. With each mile, his guilt intensified.

Hours later, just as the sun began to sink into the hills, the *rath* stood before them. It was one of many estates conquered by King Magnus, taken from the Irish who had dwelled there before him. The stronghold was meant to defend the eastern coast of Erin. Already there were murmurings of a war brewing north of Dubh Linn.

When they arrived, Tharand gave his horse over to a slave

and drew Aisling to his side. He kept his arm around her, in an unspoken message that she was not to be touched by any man.

Any man, save the king.

Jealousy snaked through his gut, strangling his good sense. But though he turned over different possibilities in his mind, none of them would save Aisling.

The slave led him to the visitor's quarters, and after a repast of wine and venison, they were given a small pallet for sleeping. The room had no privacy, with several couples sharing the space.

Aisling folded back the coverlet and slid beneath it. She propped her face up on one elbow, waiting for him to join her. He half expected her to keep the blade in her hand, as a warning. Instead, she met his gaze with a steadiness.

"You may sleep alone." He sat up against the wooden walls, his hand resting upon the handle of a bronze battle-ax. It was easier to guard her this way. For this night, he would keep her safe from harm.

And after that, he'd have to let her go.

Aisling tried to sleep, but her mind wouldn't allow it. She watched Tharand keeping guard, knowing that he had no intention of sleeping.

Such a paradox, it was. He'd brought her here as his prisoner. And yet he'd never treated her in that way.

She closed her eyes, remembering how he'd defended her from one of his own men. He'd given her the coverlet from his bed the night before, the wool still warm from his body. He'd held her close while riding, teaching her what it meant to feel desire.

When he'd kissed her, it shattered every image she held. It wasn't the kiss of a lover, but of a man starving for a woman's touch. This afternoon when she'd reached out to him, the ground beneath her had shifted. She wanted to kiss him, though it was wrong. He was her captor and a man she should despise.

Instead, he seemed ready to surrender his life for hers. He watched every man as though anticipating a threat. As though she were a treasure to be guarded instead of a slave.

The empty void stretching inside startled her. She wasn't supposed to feel anything for him, this stranger who had stolen her away. Especially not the unfamiliar sensitivity, the longing to kiss him again.

Aisling drew her legs together, crossing her ankles. The motion tightened the aching within her woman's flesh. Sinful, wanton thoughts poured through her as she imagined his strong body moving upon her. His hips driving against hers as he filled her.

Her breath caught and she fisted the coverlet. In the morning, he would leave. She'd not lay eyes upon him again.

But there was still tonight. A chance to quench this thirst, to understand him.

He possessed a deep sense of honor, despite his *Lochlan-nach* heritage. And even when he'd taken her body to an ecstasy she'd never known, despite her unwillingness, he'd wanted to please her.

That, perhaps, was why she hadn't used the knife against him.

Aisling sat up and drew her knees forward, resting her wrists upon them. *Look at me,* she bade him. For in his eyes, she would find her answer.

His gaze snapped toward her. The raw need was almost savage in its nature. He did not relinquish the sight of her, and she unbound her hair for him while he watched.

"What are you doing, Aisling?"

She stood and held out her hand. Like a stranger inside her

own body, she hardly knew herself. But right now, she wanted a night with no regrets.

Tharand rose and followed her outside, his large hand covering hers. The storm had ceased, but the frozen earth held a light dusting of snow.

"I want to be alone with you."

He cupped her nape, resting his forehead upon hers. "You don't belong to me."

The reluctance in his voice had nothing to do with lack of desire, she realized. It gave her a measure of hope. "I won't see you again, after this night."

"No," he answered.

She rested her arms around his shoulders, leaning in to touch him. "Who is she, Tharand? This woman you seek."

He hesitated, but when she kissed his mouth, he answered against her lips, "My sister."

"Is she the king's lover?"

"She is his hostage. And only fifteen." Tharand hissed when she pressed her body to his, cradling his length against her softness.

"You're trying to save her. By sending me in her place."

His shoulders lowered, and she had the answer she needed.

"You could save us both," she ventured. "Let me help you." She refused to believe that he would discard her so easily, that there was no hope.

He pulled her into a tight embrace, his breath warm against her cheek. "Would to the gods it were possible. But I am commander of the soldiers at Vedrarfjord. Magnus would not take kindly to a betrayal."

"Could you free your sister without his knowledge?"

"I have already tried." The dark, haunted look in his eyes returned.

"Tomorrow," she whispered, touching his upper arms. "We will free her tomorrow." She slid her hands down his muscles to the dark tattoos upon his forearms. From his stance, she sensed him starting to pull away. "Why haven't you given me to the king already?"

He ran his thumb over her mouth. "Because I am weak."

Aisling took his hand again, but this time, he gripped her wrist in return. "You should go back inside. Sleep."

"Is that what you want?"

His eyes raked over hers, leaving no doubt of his need. "If you don't go now—"

"You'll touch me in the way I want you to?" she whispered. At the disbelief in his blue eyes, she wound her arms around his neck. "One night, Tharand. Give me a memory to hold."

He cursed beneath his breath, lifting her into his arms. Aisling held tight, as though he were her shield in the midst of a battle.

Thank God. She needed him, if for only a few hours.

He picked up a torch and led her down to one of the underground cellars used for storing food. Though the temperature was freezing, Aisling felt none of the cold.

Tharand set the torch into an iron sconce and regarded her. In the flickering light, his dark-gold hair gleamed. His eyes pierced her with disbelief. "Why?" he demanded. "I am your enemy."

She touched her hand to his, not at all certain of what she felt for him. "I don't believe that anymore."

"Then you are a fool."

"As you say." Aisling took the lead, bringing his hands around her waist. Leaning in, she kissed him. Against his mouth, she felt his reluctance. Did he no longer want her? She shivered in the cool air, wondering if she'd made a mistake. "Shall I stop?"

He responded with words in the Norse tongue, endearments that made her blush. He kissed her temple, cradling her face in his hands. "I will try," he swore, "to get both of you out."

It was enough. Aisling released the edges of the cloak she was wearing. The cloth pooled to the ground in the moment that he took her mouth.

Like the invader he was, he commanded the kiss until she surrendered. She held fast to him for balance as each new layer of clothing joined the cloak upon the ground. When she stood naked before him, he knelt. With his mouth, he worshipped her, kneading her bare bottom as he kissed a path up her thighs. He disarmed her, tossing both daggers to the ground.

When he probed at the juncture of her legs, Aisling froze. "What are you—"

"Open for me." His mouth teased her, soft bites that made her legs tremble.

"I can't."

He would not allow a refusal, and used his hands to ease her apart. At once, she felt like a true captive, unable to free herself from his touch. He spread her apart and caught her gaze for a moment.

"You're a gift to me, Aisling Ó Brannon. One I intend to savor." With that, his hot mouth kissed her wetness, his tongue invading where she wanted him most.

His arms supported her against the wall while his tongue moved against her, driving her into such desperation she couldn't think, couldn't breathe, as the fist of pleasure broke through her, spiraling until she sank against him.

"We have hours yet," he promised, removing his own clothing until he stood naked before her. Lean and muscled, his body resembled a god's. The dark tattoos entranced her as he lifted her hips.

And then, she felt the tip of him at her entrance. Thick and hard, he eased himself into her tight well. While he filled her, she wrapped her legs around his waist. It took a moment for her body to adjust to his size.

In his eyes, his own awakening dawned. Deliberately, he moved against her, raising her up before letting her slide down his manhood.

"I dreamed of holding a woman like you in my arms," he said.

He didn't ravage her, nor treat her like the slave she was. Instead, he made love to her as though she were cherished. Like a woman he wanted to keep at his side.

The swelling need intensified with each stroke. She gripped his hair, fighting not to cry out as he withdrew and entered her body.

"Don't leave me here alone," she responded, pressing herself against him until he increased his rhythm. "Stay."

Be with me.

He groaned, taking her down to the floor. Though she winced at the freezing earth, the thought vanished when he thrust inside her once more. Aisling lifted her knees, and he drove himself within, marking her as his own.

This was not about conquering her body, but instead a gift of himself. With each joining, she pressed herself closer, wanting to merge her body with his.

He never ceased the rhythm, pushing her higher while his shaft hardened even more. Unexpectedly, she crossed over the edge, her body gripping him in a rush of fierce satisfaction.

When at last he released his own desire, covering her with his weight, she held fast to him while he broke apart. Power filled her, knowing that she had made him feel this way.

He whispered against her skin, and no longer was he her master. Lying in her arms, he caressed her. As an equal.

Stay. The thought reverberated in her head, gathering intensity. A foreigner, he might be. A *Lochlannach*, and a man who knew nothing of her people.

But he'd sworn not to abandon her. And she held fast to her faith, hoping he would keep the vow.

Tharand didn't move, resting his weight atop her. He still couldn't understand why Aisling had offered herself, and though he wanted to believe she desired him, his common sense denied it.

She was an Irish noblewoman, a chieftain's daughter. He hadn't expected her to be any different from the other female slaves. But like a warrior, she had fought to survive. And she possessed the skills to kill anyone who stood in her path.

He rolled to his side, withdrawing from her warmth. "If a man tries to touch you, use the blade. Do not hesitate to kill."

She traced a pattern over his chest. "You will be there to protect me."

"Not always." He could not be within the king's private chambers. As time crept forward, he had no idea what he would do to save both Aisling and Jóra.

Her mouth covered his in a light kiss. "I trust you."

Tharand closed his eyes at the words, knowing he was unworthy of her trust. And as he took her for the second time, it tormented him to imagine giving her up.

Chapter 4

Aisling stood beside Tharand, her wrists lightly bound. She didn't like it, but had not questioned him. He knew the king's men better than she. Afterwards, he'd run his fingers beneath the ropes to ensure that they weren't too tight.

She wore a new gown that he'd purchased, a saffron silk overdress and *léine*. Though slaves did not wear such expensive colors, she supposed it would help raise her status.

Tharand had also returned the two daggers. One knife was strapped to her thigh, the other near her ankle. Neither was easy to grasp beneath the weight of the skirts, and she prayed she would not need them.

"Don't let anyone see your weapons," he'd warned. "Slaves are not permitted to carry them."

As they moved through the crowd, Tharand's hand tightened upon her wrist. Aisling kept her gaze forward, but her skin prickled as the eyes of the Norse warriors watched her.

Among the men she also spied a few Irish chiefs, which startled her. Whether they were allies or enemies of the king, she couldn't be sure. She doubted if any of them would help her escape.

"Why have you come to the north, Tharand? Have there been problems in Vedrarfjord?" The king sat upon a dais, a man of strength and power. Perhaps eight and twenty years of age, he held a determined air.

"No, my king." Tharand knelt in deference, then stood when the king commanded it. "I have come for my sister, Jóra."

The king's expression turned displeased. "Jóra has received many marriage offers, thus far." He signaled to one of his men and added, "She will make a suitable bride to one of my loyal warriors. I have seen to it."

Aisling didn't miss the way Tharand's hand moved toward the handle of his battle-ax. Grim lines settled upon his mouth. "I am honored by your care for her, sire. But I have come to bring her home." He drew Aisling forward and added, "And in return for your generosity, I have brought you a gift. This Irish slave, who was once daughter to a chieftain."

Fear bolted in her stomach as Tharand released her into the king's custody. His eyes remained locked upon Magnus, as though she didn't exist, nor matter to anyone.

Her discomfort multiplied, for fear that he'd broken his promise. Perhaps he had lied, accepting her embrace without caring anything about her.

The memory of last night resonated within her. Dear God, what had she done?

A slight smile played upon the king's mouth. Aisling found it hard to look at him, but worst of all was Tharand. His stony expression was that of a mercenary.

Moments later, a young girl with fair, braided hair appeared within the hall. She wore a blue silk gown, with golden brooches clipping the overdress to her shoulders. It had to be Jóra, from the way Tharand's tension dissipated.

Aisling had no time to think upon it, for two soldiers

dragged her forward. One gripped her by the hair, while the other held fast to her arm.

Tharand didn't react, and his denial hurt worse than any physical pain.

You were wrong about him. He said only what you wanted to hear.

Aisling bit her lip so hard she tasted blood. As the soldiers dragged her forward, she stumbled upon the dais.

King Magnus studied her. He reached out to touch her arm, then cupped her face. Heat rose up in her cheeks, but she didn't move. The taste of betrayal soured her mouth.

The king shrugged. "I've seen more interesting slaves." With a nod of his head, he ordered his men to take her. Tharand didn't even glance in her direction.

Her lungs tightened, her eyes stinging with tears she could not cry. He'd used her. Taken her body without any intention of helping her. And now she would become the Norse king's prisoner.

"Jóra will remain here until I have seen to her marriage," the king added. Though Tharand bowed in reticence, the gesture was stiff.

Before she could respond, the men took her outside the hall, toward one of the longhouses. Lust gleamed in their expressions.

And still, Tharand did not come.

She closed her eyes, preparing herself for the fight to come. No man would violate her. She would die before letting it happen.

Inside the longhouse, the first man tore at her gown, his hand groping her breast. Aisling wrenched her hands free of the ropes and reached for her knife. With a sudden slash, she drew blood across the man's arm.

"Don't," she warned in the Norse language. "I am not yours."

A blur of motion caught her eye, and she threw the knife from sheer instinct. Without thinking, she unsheathed the second blade beside her ankle and poised to fight. The first soldier stared in disbelief at his dead companion.

"If you move, you'll join him," Aisling warned. She stepped backwards into the light, keeping the blade ready. Her heartbeat raced, while she searched the settlement for a way out.

There was no time. The first soldier sounded an alarm, and while she fled toward the gates, a row of warriors moved to block her exit. Aisling halted, the knife locked in her palm.

As they advanced upon her, she prepared to meet her death.

Tharand's fury had reached its limit. He hadn't expected King Magnus to refuse Aisling. It nearly snapped his control, watching the men take her, while he was helpless to do anything.

If he showed any sign that she held value to him, Magnus would exploit it. And Aisling, like Jóra, would be lost.

She can protect herself. She has weapons, he told himself. But his hand curved over his battle-ax while he waited for the chance to defend her.

The surge of possession drowned out all reasoning. He needed to keep her safe, needed to keep her at his side. He didn't even realize he'd taken a few steps backwards until the king addressed him again.

"You seem restless," Magnus commented. Jóra paled, and Tharand forced his attention back to the dais. It was as if the king had torn him in half, forcing him to choose between Jóra and Aisling.

And though his loyalty should have belonged to his sister, he couldn't let Aisling go. Not anymore.

Tharand's knuckles whitened, and he chose his words carefully. "The slave was meant for you alone. She was not intended to be treated thusly." *And if any man does, I will sever his head from his body.*

"Such is the fate of a captive." Magnus underscored his words by resting his hand upon Jóra. His sister's innocent eyes grew worried. He wanted to reassure her, but he no longer knew what he could do to save her.

A din of noise interrupted them, and Tharand spun around. Aisling tore into the hall, her eyes wild. In her hand, she held one of the blades he'd given her.

Behind her, he saw the soldiers. Somehow she'd broken free of her captors, and the ensuing chaos gave rise to fighting.

One of the *hird* strode forward, the warrior lifting his battle-ax to strike her down. Tharand blocked the blow before it could threaten Aisling. The crash of metal sent a reverberation through his arm, and he forced her behind him.

"Take my knife," he ordered, and she unsheathed the weapon from his belt. Back to back, he defended her.

"You left me with them." In her voice, he heard the anger and hurt.

"I was trying to negotiate for your release." His ax swung wide, and she moved with him.

"You said you would try to save both of us. Instead, you let them take me."

"What would you have me do? Betray my king and risk your death?" His ax cut into the flesh of an enemy. He defended another blow. "Already have I shed the blood of my own people. For you."

She fell silent, the warmth of her back pressing against him. "What will happen to us?"

"I don't know." He didn't tell her that their lives depended upon his ax now. Even if he emerged victorious, he doubted if Magnus would spare them.

Abruptly, Aisling left him. The distraction caused him to turn his attention away from the soldiers. Only instinct protected him from the sword slicing toward his gut.

The Irish chiefs had joined together against the *hird*, the hall becoming a battlefield. Tharand searched for Aisling and found her moving toward the dais.

In horror, he watched her pull back and aim the knife toward the king. He was too far away to stop her. The blade spun from her fingers, while a roar resounded from his own throat.

Aisling's blade lay embedded in the throat of an Irish chief. The dead man held a spear in his palm, his body sprawled upon the dais.

King Magnus's face was black with rage. He jerked the spear from the chief's hand. "Cease your fighting!" He punctuated the order by hurling the spear into the crowd.

The men halted, swords and battle-axes poised in mid-air. Tharand lowered his weapon, and moved to Aisling's side, pulling her to him.

No doubt Magnus would sentence her to death. She'd thrown a knife toward him; all had seen it. The thought of watching her die was like a blade tearing into his own throat. He couldn't let it happen.

"My king." He dropped to his knees, knowing that Magnus would never grant her mercy. "Let whatever judgment you pass upon her fall upon my shoulders instead."

Aisling paled, and knelt beside him. She buried her face in his tunic, and he threaded his hands through her dark hair.

"Why?" the king asked sharply. "She has committed treason, attempting to take my life. And she killed one of the *hird*, as well."

"I saved your life," Aisling asserted, lifting her face in defiance.

Tharand knew it, but the king had no knowledge of her skill. Magnus would believe only that she'd attempted to murder him.

"She speaks the truth, sire." Tharand lowered his head once more. "But regardless of your decision, I ask that you grant me her punishment."

"And if I sentence her to death?" Magnus asked.

Tharand expelled a hard breath. "So be it."

A knot closed up in Aisling's throat. No. She couldn't let him die. His hand gripped hers, as though he couldn't let go. She embraced him, holding fast. "You cannot do this."

His only answer was to rest his palm upon her cheek. The roughened skin was calloused from years of holding a sword. His blue eyes held no regrets.

The knowledge shattered every barrier, filling her up with the need to be with him. Whether in life or in death no longer mattered.

"If he dies, let it fall upon me as well."

Tharand tried to speak, but she touched her fingertips to his mouth. "You will not make such a journey alone."

When the king spoke at last, she barely heard his command to come forward, so intent was she upon remaining with Tharand.

"Rise, Aisling." Her warrior took her hand and led her up the dais.

King Magnus offered no leniency. To Tharand he demanded, "Give me your sword."

Icy fear filled her up inside, and she knew there was no escape. Tharand gripped her hand so tightly, he nearly crushed the bones.

"I am not afraid," she whispered.

Tharand offered the king his sword, hilt-first. As the blade left his hands, Aisling saw the smear of blood upon his palms. Then he knelt beside her once more.

"She means much to you, this slave." The king lifted the sword, testing its balance.

Tharand inclined his head. "She does."

The words held intensity, and when he looked upon her face, Aisling saw the feelings he did not name. And though she had spent naught but a few days at his side, she would willingly surrender her life to be with him.

King Magnus lowered the sword. "I accept this sword as payment for the soldier she killed." He regarded Aisling next, his expression softening. "In return for my own life, I grant you your freedom."

Nothing could have stunned her more. The relief upon Tharand's face mirrored her own, but behind the king, she spied Jóra. The young girl would remain the king's hostage, a failure that would haunt Tharand.

But there was something she could do.

"Sire, I would ask that you release Jóra Hardrata instead." Aisling bowed her head in deference. "Grant her the freedom to return home."

Hope filled up the young girl's face, and Aisling knew she had made the right decision. The king deliberated for a long moment, not at all willing to let her go.

"What of the marriage offers?" King Magnus asked, his reluctance clear.

"Please, my king," Jóra begged. "If you would but let me see my family again, I give you my vow to return."

Tharand did not look happy about such an offer. It seemed to appease the king, however. "One moon, then. You may visit your homeland and then return."

Though it was not what Tharand had wanted, it was a single step forward, Aisling knew. It would be enough for now.

The king gestured for Jóra to join them, and the girl flew into her brother's arms. "I will expect your loyalty, as commander of my troops at Vedrarfjord. And your sword, whenever there is need."

Tharand acknowledged the king's command. "You have it."

Aisling waited alone in Tharand's bed, inside his longhouse. She lay naked beneath the coverlet, although she kept two daggers nearby, in case anyone arrived before he did.

The door swung open, and she gripped the hilt.

"Don't throw it. Please." Tharand's mouth curved in a slight smile. "I know your skill and there is no need to demonstrate."

She set the weapons aside. "I wanted to be sure it was you."

He hung up his cloak. The garment slipped from his fingers when she sat up, revealing her bare skin. The hunger in his eyes raised her confidence.

"Were your parents glad to see Jóra?" she asked.

He nodded, removing his tunic. His muscled chest gleamed in the firelight, making her long to touch him. He prowled toward her, shedding clothes as he walked. "You could have come to meet them."

"I am only a slave."

He tore back the coverlet, revealing the rest of her body. "My slave." The mattress sank beneath his weight as he drew her body to his. Skin to skin, she welcomed the length of his shaft and parted her legs to cradle him.

The hot satin of him nestled against her secret place, and already she was slick with moisture. "I waited for you," she murmured.

He raised her body up until he slid an inch inside. *"Kjæreste."*

The endearment washed over her and she framed his face with her hands. "I want to stay with you. Even without my freedom."

He filled her up, his hardness caressing her in a way that warmed her blood. "I want you as my bride, Aisling Ó Brannon. No longer my slave."

His offer was completely unexpected. She couldn't find the words, and when his mouth covered her nipple, he added, "I suppose I'll have to convince you."

"You could try." The teasing words were cut off when he withdrew from inside her. She pulled at his hips, trying to bring him back. "Or you could tempt me."

He shackled her wrists with his hands, penetrating her heat once more. Helpless, Aisling could only accept him as he thrust deeply, ravaging her body and filling her with a desperate pleasure. Her skin grew damp with sweat, her womanhood welcoming him as he claimed her for his own.

"Tharand," she cried out as the first tremors shook her.

It wasn't enough for him, and he took her down, forcing her to accept the wild spasms of ecstasy. "Say yes."

She held out a little longer, weeping with the dark torment. At last he shuddered in his release, plunging within until she clenched him to her breast. She held him, her body and mind filled with such longing. For him and him alone.

"Yes," she whispered.

The charred remains of Duncarrick crowned the hilltop, and Aisling's heart ached to see it. Would Kieran and Egan be there? Had her brothers managed to break free of the slavers?

Tharand slowed his horse when they reached the entrance, his hands still resting around her waist. "Do you want me to come with you?"

"I'm afraid of what I'll find." She turned and kissed him, gathering strength from his arms.

Tharand captured her lips, kissing her until she lost sight of where they were. Her body melted against his, liquid with wanting him. But she forced herself to break free of his embrace. "I want to see my family again," she admitted. "I need to know what happened to Kieran and Egan."

"Go to them." He dismounted and lifted her down. "And when you return, I will be waiting."

Aisling shielded her eyes from the sun. Her warrior rested his hand upon the flanks of his stallion, and she knew with a certainty that he would never leave her. "Let us go together."

* * * * *

Discover what happens to
Kieran and Egan Ó Brannon in the novel
HER WARRIOR SLAVE,
available now from Harlequin Historical
in both ebook and print format
wherever books are sold.

DISROBED AND DISHONORED

Louise Allen

Author Note

"Disrobed and Dishonored" is the story of what happens when a respectable young lady with a problem meets a rakish highwayman whose solution to her dilemma is anything *but* respectable.

Jonathan's suggestion gets Miss Sarah Tatton out of one predicament and into his bed—which is no place for a virtuous young lady. Luckily for her she knows the new Lady Standon (wife of *The Shocking Lord Standon*) and through her meets more of the Ravenhurst clan (from my series THOSE SCANDALOUS RAVENHURSTS), who throw themselves with characteristically unconventional enthusiasm into rescuing the ill-matched pair of lovers.

I hope you enjoy glimpsing two of the heroines from the Ravenhurst books. To read this family miniseries, please visit eHarlequin.com.

To the brilliant team at Richmond with thanks
for all their support.

Look for Louise Allen's
The Lord and the Wayward Lady
in June 2010
This launches the Regency Silk & Scandal miniseries

Chapter 1

July 1816, Norfolk

The man in the mask ran one hand down the neck of the ugly gray hunter. 'Patience, Tolly. One more to go and then it's oats for you and two dozen of the finest old brandy for me.'

The horse snorted, his ear flicking back to listen to his rider's voice as Jonathan slouched into the familiar comfort of the saddle, eyes narrowed against the late-evening light. It was past eight now and no traffic had passed along the lane for half an hour. Up to then business had been brisk and last night's wager seemed easily won. He dug a hand in his pocket and drew out the tokens he had claimed, proofs of a kiss from each of the first five women who passed down the lane on their way back from market in St. Margaret's to the villages of Saint's Mead and Saint's Ford.

There was a downy feather from the empty egg bucket of the country lass who had giggled and returned his kiss with relish; a tiny corn dolly from the elderly dame driving her donkey cart back, her baskets of straw plait almost empty, a twinkle in her eyes as she pinched his chin; a paper of pins from the thin-faced spinster who had blushed like a peony when he had respectfully saluted her papery cheek; and a promissory note for one ginger kitten (guaranteed of good mousing stock) from the farmer's wife who had roared with laughter and tipped up her round red face with cheerful anticipation.

Jonathan pinned the corn dolly to his lapel, stuck the feather in his hat brim and wondered which of his housekeepers would most appreciate a kitten. His pleasure in the evening's sport began to wane. He had another hour before he was due to join his friends at The Golden Lion for supper to present evidence of his success and the chances of the required fifth female happening along seemed increasingly poor.

Tolly lifted his head and pricked his ears. 'Hoofbeats,' Jonathan concurred. 'One horse—likely to be a man.' He nudged the gray through a gap in the thick hedgerow, drew the empty pistol, laid it along his thigh and waited.

'Despicable, hypocritical swine,' Sarah Tatton repeated, reining in her mare to a walk and dashing the tears out of her eyes with an impatient hand. Careering around the countryside sidesaddle in evening dress was far from comfortable now that her initial fury had simmered down, to be replaced by something approaching panic.

How could she have been so meek, so trustingly innocent? Eighteen months sitting in the country, perfecting her wifely skills in domestic management, needlework and entertaining, while Papa boasted to all and sundry of the excellent match he had made for his daughter—and what had she to show for it? Her linen cupboard was immaculate, her stillroom a marvel, she could play a sonata and hold her own in the most trying dinner-party conversation and, *finally*, her betrothed had deigned to turn up to discuss the wedding.

Sir Jeremy Peters might be only moderately good-looking and not possess a sparkling wit, but he was, as everyone had told her during the course of her second Season, *a catch* for the daughter of a country baronet with moderate looks and a moderate dowry to match. Wealthy, well-connected—she could not hope to do better to oblige her papa.

'Respectable?' Sarah swore under her breath. Half an hour in his company, during which he had congratulated her on her modest gown and presented her with a hideous string of lumpy freshwater pearls, had made her heart sink; she had not remembered him as being so dull. But when she had gone upstairs to change for dinner Mary, her maid, had broken down in floods of tears as she fastened her gown.

'I've got to tell you, Miss Sarah. I cannot let you marry him, not even if it means my place,' she had wailed. What Sarah had heard took her breath away and left her sick and shaken. Sir Jeremy had assaulted Mary at the house party where he had proposed to Sarah and threatened that he would tell Sir Hugh Tatton that she had offered herself for money if she said one word of it.

So Sarah confronted her father with the fact that she had discovered her betrothed was the sort of man who would ravish defenseless young women—and Papa had dismissed the matter.

'Nonsense,' he blustered, slapping his newspaper down on his desk in irritation. 'Some young trollop looking to earn herself a few shillings, I've no doubt. Asking for it.'

'But no, Papa! This is a respectable girl.' She did not dare tell him who, not with the memory of the housemaid turned off without a character when Cousin William's visit had left her pregnant. Her father was of the old school when it came to domestic discipline. 'And even if it were the case that she was willing, you cannot expect me to marry a man of such loose morals.'

'A lady ignores such matters. It is her duty to remain faithful, above reproach, and to raise her children. Her husband may seek diversion elsewhere—'

'Diversion!'

He scowled. 'Diversion. It means nothing and no lady of refined mind should think of such things, let alone admit to knowing of them.'

'I cannot possibly marry Sir Jeremy,' she announced flatly.

'You most certainly will, my girl! I'm not letting a good match like that slip through my fingers because of some missish scruples. You marry him—or I will find out who has been filling your head with this scurrilous nonsense and see they suffer for it. Do you understand me?'

How could she find Mary a suitable new post, one where she would be safe from her father's wrath? If she had been in London she could have gone to a good agency, given her glowing references, but here, deep in the country, such a plan would have to be conducted by letter and Papa insisted on her chaperone reading all her correspondence.

And how she was going to be able to keep a civil tongue in her head over dinner she had no idea. She had stood outside the drawing room gathering her composure to enter when she heard the men talking inside.

'Modest virtue, that is the thing about Miss Tatton,' Sir Jeremy was saying. 'The assurance that one is marrying a virgin of impeccable upbringing and not one of those flighty girls who live for nothing but their beaux and their parties. How precious is a lady's purity! I searched long and hard before I was confident I had found such a prize.'

The hypocrite valued only her *virginity*? He debauched young women and yet he could say such things to her father who would smugly accept them?

Sarah turned on her heel. 'Tell Sir Hugh that I have a migraine and regret I will not be able to come down this evening,' she said to the footman. The moment his back was turned she was away to the stables.

Leaving the house for an hour or so at least gave her a chance to cool her temper, but what to do now? Fear was beginning to overcome the fury as her imagination took hold, presenting her with a vivid image of what life with Sir Jeremy would be like. Her instinct was to run, but that was pointless; how would she live?

The question became academic as she rounded a corner and found herself staring down the barrel of a large horse pistol. 'Stand and deliver.'

A highwayman? They really said that? Sarah discovered her mouth was open and shut it. The figure confronting her was straight off any broadsheet telling the shocking stories of Dick Turpin or "Hell" Hawley. A big, ugly gray horse, a tricorne hat, a cloak thrown back over his shoulders despite the heat and a black mask covering the upper half his face.

She dragged Sir Jeremy's string of pearls over her head and held it out. He was welcome to them.

'No, I don't want those, sweetheart.' His voice was amused, educated and deep; it seemed to resonate at the base of her spine. A gentleman gone to the bad?

From somewhere she found her voice. 'What do you want, then?'

'One kiss and a little token to show for it.' He urged the horse up alongside her mare and she realized it was not just the horse that was big. She made herself sit still and not flinch away.

And then she found she did not want to. 'A kiss?' He was clean-shaven, his teeth white as he smiled in the evening light. The breeze brought her not the rank smell of unwashed robber that she had been expecting, but the clean odors of leather and citrus. 'It is not gallant to jest! You may have the pearls and welcome.'

'No.' He took the pearls in an ungloved hand and dropped them back around her neck, holstered the pistol and leaned toward her, doffing his hat. 'I do not jest.'

His hair was dark brown, overlong, waving from the pressure of the hat. His eyes were green, shadowed by the mask, and yet when he smiled she could just see the laughter lines in the corners, the humor.

'Just one kiss?'

He nodded as she bit her lip in indecision, his mouth curving in a way that made her want to touch it. 'If you will grant it. I do not steal from women.'

What if she should kick her heels and send the mare plunging past him? He leaned down and took the reins as though he could read her mind. Sarah stared at him, wondering why she did not scream. He really was a very strange highwayman. And she was in a very strange mood. She was conscious of her heartbeat—that was trepidation, no doubt—but what to make of the warm feeling low in her belly or the fact that her lips were dry? Sarah licked them and saw his eyes follow the movement.

'Why have you a corn dolly in your buttonhole?'

'A token from the donor of my second kiss. It is a fertility symbol, I believe, but don't worry, kisses are harmless.'

An interesting definition of harmless! 'Very well. I have nothing better to be doing this evening, after all.' She tipped up her face, turning her cheek toward him and closing her eyes. And then she felt his breath warm on her skin and realized he really was only going to take what she offered and some madness seized her.

She opened her eyes and moved her head and met the hooded green gaze and his mouth found hers. 'Oh!' As she gasped his tongue slid between her lips and his free arm went around her shoulders and he lifted her against him so she was standing in the stirrup while the kiss went on…and on…and the warm evening world spun around her and his heat and the questing invasion of his tongue filled her senses and she gripped his lapels and touched her tongue to his and thought she would faint from the intensity of it.

And then she was back in the saddle and they were looking at each other as though the earth had just shifted beneath them. He seemed to be breathing rather heavily. She rather thought that if she did not loosen her stay laces, breathing would no longer be possible.

'Madam,' he said at last. 'I must thank you for giving me the most precious thing in your possession. May I ask for a token, also?'

Sarah took hold of three or four hairs that had come down from her topknot of curls, tugged them free and held them out to him. He bowed slightly and curled them with care around the corn dolly. He thought her kiss precious? A highwayman's opinion of her kiss was certainly more acceptable than Sir Jeremy's hypocritical valuation of her virginity.

'Sir, that is not the most precious thing I possess.' The words left her lips without conscious thought.

'It is not?' The green eyes rested on her face.

'No. I am a virgin.'

The gray tossed its head as though its rider had clenched his hand on the reins. 'Ma'am?' She saw him swallow.

'And that is something of a burden to me, just now,' she confessed.

'Indeed?' He looked not shocked, but interested.

Somehow the story tumbled out. How she came to be recounting such intimate details to a complete stranger, a man—a rogue—Sarah could not fathom. Why she was not sliding from Daisy's back in a pool of embarrassment, she had no idea, but she did not even seem to be blushing. It could only be her desperation and the utter seriousness with which he was listening to her.

'In short,' she concluded, 'my father plans to marry me to a lecherous, hypocritical excuse for a gentleman for whom my only virtue appears to be my—well, my *virtue*.'

'If you were not a virgin, he would not be interested,' the highwayman remarked.

'Well, I am, so there's nothing to be done about it.'

'You could have a frank discussion with a married lady, discover some, er…details and inform your chaperone that you have lost your virtue, describing the experience so she had no doubts,' he suggested in a matter-of-fact manner, as though they were puzzling over some trivial problem.

'There is no one I could talk to.' If only her good friend Jessica was home from her honeymoon by now! She would enter into this scheme with complete frankness, but it would be another two weeks and that was too late. 'I do not think that anything less than firsthand experience would do. I can hardly make it up. But thank you, it was a very good idea.' She sighed, feeling the tears beginning to well up in her eyes again. She bit down hard on her lip to stop them; weeping and moaning was not going to get her out of this fix.

The gray backed away and she glanced up at its rider's face.

Below the mask his mouth was set. He looked somewhat grim. 'I could help you.'

'Describe...*it*?' she faltered, finding she could blush, after all.

'No. I doubt I could, from a woman's point of view. No, more practically, we—'

'You want to take my virginity?' Her voice emerged as a squeak. Daisy tossed her head, catching her mistress's sudden panic.

'No, but I could *almost* take your virginity.'

'Almost.' The light was beginning to fade and she was not able to make out the nuances of his expression beneath the mask. His tone was pitched somewhere between appalled and amused.

'Almost. Just so you get the idea. Have you any knowledge of the theory, Miss, er...?'

'Sarah,' she said shortly. 'No, not much. I know it hurts and I know there is the danger of becoming pregnant and I have no desire for the former experience and certainly none for the latter.'

'I promise that neither would be the case.'

'Are you mad?' she inquired, more of herself than of him. He did not appear to be deranged and if he was an evil seducer, he was certainly going about it in a most original way. And she was beginning to find the preposterous, shocking suggestion positively...possible.

'I know you did not rob me just now, or ravish me,' she said, frowning at him in the twilight. 'And you could have done either, quite easily. I liked the way you kissed me, although I should not. You appear to be a man of principle, even if you do earn your living in an illegal manner.'

He shook his head, seeming to withdraw from the idea even as she became convinced. 'You are right, I was mad to suggest it. There must be some other way out of your predicament.'

Sarah contemplated her situation. She was not lacking, she

felt, in either determination or imagination, but she could see no other way out of this. 'No, you are quite right: it is the perfect solution. And if you will not then I must find someone who will help me.' There wasn't anyone, of course, but she put every ounce of conviction she could muster into the statement.

Jonathan could feel his will being sapped by the intensity in the gray eyes fixed on his face. He believed she was in trouble, else why would she be riding alone in evening dress? She appeared to be in her right mind—which was more than he had been a moment ago as he had articulated, without thinking, the idea that had come to him.

There was an edge of desperation in her tone that convinced him that what she said of her betrothed was true and it was not simply a matter of a lovers' quarrel. And now that he had put the idea into her mind he feared she really would seek out another man if he refused her. And then there was that kiss. The taste of her like honey and roses and a hint of spice and the heat and the response that he would swear was instinctive, innocent—and deadly.

She had no idea, of course, of what he would be letting himself in for. No concept of the willpower it would take to go so far and then stop, to pleasure her just so far and no further. 'Very well.' Her expression made him smile. Her eyes widened with surprise, relief and apprehension in almost equal measure. 'I know an inn not far from here.'

'The Golden Lion.' She nodded. Of course, she must live hereabouts and know it. And be known, if only by sight. This would take some care.

He led her back along the woodland path he had come by, stopping at the shepherd's hut he had noticed earlier. 'We'll leave your mare here. There is shelter and water.' She let him lift her down, silk and light boning and warm, slender waist under his hands making his imagination run riot while he saw to the mare, conscious of Sarah's eyes on his back as he worked.

'What is your name?'

'Jonathan. Here, take this.' He swung off his cloak and tied it around her neck, flipping up the hood to cover hair and face, then boosted her up onto Tolly's broad back and swung into the saddle behind her. Ah, more torture, the soft weight of her on his thighs, the little wriggle she gave to get her balance, the scent of her body pressed warm to his chest.

'You are a successful highwayman then, Jonathan, to be able to afford The Golden Lion and yet resist my pearls?'

'Shall we say it is more of a recreation than a business?' he suggested, guiding Tolly toward the stable yard, puzzling about the woman in his arms. Not just out, certainly. Twenty-two or -three, he would guess, with some authority about her. Well-bred, respectable and, presumably, an obedient daughter up to the point her father introduced this undesirable suitor. He had never seen her before, which meant she did not move in his circles, but even so, to avoid embarrassment he rather thought he would keep his mask on.

He helped her down in the shadows and led her up the side stairs and to his room without being seen. 'Wait here. I'll not be long.'

His six friends were in the private parlor, cards on the table, bottles open, food spread out on the sideboard. They got to their feet, grinning, as he came in, still masked. 'Well,' Griffin demanded, 'have I won back the money I lost on yesterday's prizefight or am I out a dozen of my best cognac?'

'You're out.' Jonathan tossed his hat on the table. 'Here— a feather from a maid who'd taken her eggs to market and came back with a kiss to spare for me, black hairs from a fancy young thing with her nose in the air, a corn dolly from an old duck in a donkey cart and a paper of pins from a severe dame who is doubtless still blushing. Oh yes, and the promise of a ginger kitten should I care to collect it.'

'Damn me, I never thought you'd do it.' Lord Gray splashed port into his glass and downed it in one gulp. 'I wagered against you. Get some food and come and help me win it back.' He gestured at the litter of vowels on the table.

'No, I'll leave you to it.' Jonathan walked over to the sideboard, rubbing his back. 'Pulled a muscle somehow. Damn sore. I'll take some food up and see if bed will put it to rights.'

He retreated, with a laden plate and a wine bottle in his pocket, amid gibes about what had caused the strain and ribald suggestions for curing it.

Sarah perched on the edge of the bed and wondered if she had gone mad. If she had misjudged her man, she was in serious trouble. Even if she had not, she was deliberately setting out to ruin herself. And then there was the undeniable fact that she was about to commit acts of shocking intimacy with a man. A stranger.

What was almost more disturbing, she found her heart was beating with wild anticipation at the thought of it. She wanted him in almost equal measure to the fear. Her highwayman. Jonathan. She had never wanted a man before; at least she had never wanted more than a mild flirtation, a daring kiss to set her a-flutter for an evening, to be forgotten in the morning along with the champagne and the foolish flirting.

Now… She jumped as the door opened and he came in, locking it behind him. He handed her the key before putting a plate on the table and taking knife, fork and bottle from his pocket.

'Food first?'

That voice seemed to curl round inside her, making her hot and flustered and strangely jumpy. 'No.' *Eat? Is he mad?*

'Wine, then?'

'Yes.' That would help. She studied him as he eased out the cork. Long legs, broad shoulders, enough muscle to be a fighter and a smile on him that turned the hot, flustered feeling into a deep, disturbing, low ache. He still wore the mask and she was glad of it; somehow it made him less real. 'Thank you.' She gulped the wine and handed him back the glass. 'I am a little nervous, I confess.'

'Understandably. Do you still want to go through with this?' Sarah thought of Sir Jeremy, thought of Mary's tears, and nodded. 'We will proceed to the matter at hand then? Would you like to undress first, or shall I?'

Chapter 2

'You will have to help me.' Sarah got to her feet and turned her back. That was easier, she did not have to look at him. She tried not to flinch as his fingers, busy on the buttons, brushed the bare skin of her neck, then her shoulders, then were kept from her naked skin by her chemise. The gown sagged and she caught it, stepping out and standing there, his warmth at her back as he began to untie her stay laces.

'You are very adept at this,' she said, attempting to sound cool and sophisticated and aware she was achieving neither. The release of pressure on her ribs was not, oddly, helping her breathing at all. *I can still stop, I can still say no…*

'I have had a little practice,' Jonathan conceded. She could hear he was smiling. 'You can turn round now.'

He was standing there shrugging out of coat and waistcoat. Despite the mask she could see his eyes on her, a dark heat smoldering there. 'Will you untie my neck cloth?'

That brought her close, as he no doubt intended, her fingers clumsy on the simple folds. His clothes were respectable, but plain; she tried to concentrate on that while she unwound the warm muslin from his throat and pulled it free. He was waiting, it seemed, for her to unbutton his shirt, so she did that too, feeling a little light-headed as so much chest became visible right in front of her face. It was a very impressive chest, with flat, sculpted muscle and lightly tanned skin as though, perhaps, he had swum that summer or worked with his shirt off. He must undertake other, more honest, labor from time to time.

And then there was the hair, crisp and startling as it brushed her knuckles, growing thicker and more focused as she worked down, until it vanished into his breeches. Sarah undid the last button and tugged so the shirt came free. And then there he was, clad in nothing but buckskins and boots and there she was, feeling as though she was wearing nothing but a blush.

'It isn't compulsory to proceed, you know,' Jonathan said, watching her face. 'We can just have some supper and I'll escort you home.'

'Oh, yes, it is,' she retorted, suddenly sure, despite feeling more nervous than she could ever remember. 'It is this or marriage to the swine who raped my maid and then threatened her. Papa considers him such a good match in material terms that I cannot think of any other way than this to get free from him.' He still seemed to hesitate. Sarah swallowed down the lump in her throat. 'Are you going to take your boots off?'

That provoked a snort of laughter. 'But of course. It is *de rigeur* to remove one's boots before making love to a lady.' He sat and began to pull them off.

'You are a very strange highwayman.' She supposed she should remove her petticoats. Was there an etiquette to this lovemaking? Sarah stood there in chemise and stockings watching the play of muscle on Jonathan's back as he tugged. It was important to be able to describe the intimate appearance of her lover if she was to convince Mrs. Catchpole, her chaperone, of her ruin, she thought, finding strength in the reminder of why she was doing this.

'I have had a sad life,' Jonathan explained, glancing up and catching her staring.

'No doubt.' He was, thank goodness, retaining his breeches. The amount of bare man on display was already rather more overpowering than she had bargained on. For some reason she had thought this would all take place in the dark.

'Now, I have been wanting, for the past hour, to kiss you again.'

It was interesting, Sarah thought, striving for rational thought, how different a kiss was when there were so few clothes in the way. His arms around her seemed to caress her skin, she could smell his warmth and the intriguing male scent of sweat and plain soap and something citrusy and horse and leather, and he tasted of wine and man. And his mouth on hers was not smiling any longer.

Rationality slid away to be replaced by a need Sarah did not know she had. She was shocked by the intimacy of his tongue in her mouth, inciting hers to touch and invade in its turn and surprised to discover that without having any idea what she should be doing, she was twining into his embrace and pressing herself against the outrageously hard ridge that lay against her stomach.

She gave a gasp, startled and embarrassed and not a little fearful until Jonathan's hands came down to cup her buttocks, lifting her against himself, rocking her into the hardness until she moaned, the fear subtly becoming another kind of trembling altogether. 'Oh, yes, sweetheart,' he murmured against her neck. 'Oh, yes.'

She was on the bed, Sarah realized, as her chemise was lifted over her head, and then there they were, her against the pillows wearing nothing but her stockings and Jonathan leaning against the bedpost breathing hard and looking as though he was counting.

'Oh!' One arm across her breasts and one hand flat at the junction of her thighs were not a great deal of covering, not when he was still in his breeches. He was watching her and she should be dying of shame—and part of her was and part of her was trembling with the need for him to hold her again. 'Aren't you going to take those off?' she blurted, suddenly anxious to have this over and done with.

He did, dropping them to the floor and making no attempt to cover himself. 'Oh,' Sarah said again. Her gaze skidded away, up his body, and met the masked green eyes. Now, his body naked, the mask seemed sinister and she swallowed, hard.

Something must have shown on her face, for he raised one hand to the black silk, hesitated, and pulled it off. 'Better?' She nodded, studying his face intently, fearful of finding something there that the mask had hidden, but the green eyes were clear and frank and his expression serious. Removing the mask made him look younger.

'Good,' he said, his mouth curving up into a slow smile. 'Are you all right?'

She managed another nod as he came and lay down next to her, pulling her against him. 'Stockings?'

'I like the stockings.' His voice, coming as it did from the valley between her breasts, was somewhat muffled.

'Oh.' She stroked his hair, then found the curl of his ear and played with that with one hand while the other pressed him to her breast and she became aware that she was whimpering softly and his lips and teeth had found a nipple and were tormenting it until she thought she would scream.

Then he released her and propped himself up on one elbow, smiling down. 'Is this what you had in mind?'

'Mind?' Sarah blinked at him. 'I don't think I have one.'

'Oh, well, I'll just have to carry on then.' He moved down the bed and began to untie her garters while Sarah lay back, panting. She knew what happened with animals: the male pounced and it was all very hurried and rather violent. Not like this at all.

This seemed a little safer; he showed no intention of pouncing… 'Oh!' Jonathan was licking up her leg from her ankle, up to the back of her knee. Her legs, with no conscious thought from her, fell apart shamelessly, and with a chuckle he lowered his head between them as she tried to close them, feeling that she would die of shame. What had come over her? 'No!'

'Yes.' And his mouth was *there*, flicking and teasing a tiny point of intense sensation that seemed to dominate every other feeling. It was outrageous, inflammatory, something was going to break, shatter—she had to resist, to hold on, to… She shattered.

'Jonathan?'

'Welcome back.' He sounded pleased with her. 'More wine?'

'What was that?' Sarah blinked in the candlelight. Jonathan was off the bed, pouring wine, still shamelessly naked. Still very aroused.

'An orgasm.' He handed her the glass.

'But we didn't…'

'No. We don't have to,' he explained, comfortably matter-of-fact as he sat beside her and took his turn with the wine.

'But if we had been doing…doing everything?'

'Same result, some extra preliminaries.' He dipped a finger in the wine and dripped the red drops onto her left nipple, then bent his head and began to lick.

Sarah surrendered to the sensation, her hands clutching his

shoulders as his hand slid down, touched where his mouth had been, his thumb circling the sensitised nub. Jonathan lifted his head. 'Relax.'

'I am!'

'More.' And he slid a finger into the wet heat, into the aching tightness and she arched, panting. Then another, and still his thumb wove its wicked pattern of arousal and her body clenched around the intrusion and her groping fingers found him and closed on mobile satin skin and bone hardness and heat and he moaned and thrust into her grasp as she lifted against his hand and there was darkness and stars and his mouth hard over hers as she screamed and he surged against her. And then a slow slide into oblivion.

Jonathan was asleep when she awoke. She lay there for perhaps ten minutes, just looking at him while her mind and her body returned to something like normality and the impact of what she had done came to her.

She was naked, in bed with a naked man with whom she had been utterly shameless, with whom she had experienced pleasure she had no idea existed. And now she was ruined. Sarah had no idea whether she wanted to laugh or cry, but she knew she had to go before he awoke, slip away, get to the hut and saddle up Daisy, ride home—all without him following her, discovering who she was.

She sat up and Jonathan stirred. No, she had to delay him. He would be alert in a second if she tried to creep out. One silk stocking curled across the rumpled bedspread. She eyed the man beside her, sprawled in utter relaxation on his back, arms thrown above his head.

So, she wanted to play games? Amused and aroused, Jonathan kept his eyes closed as silk trailed up his arm, caressed his wrists. How very sophisticated for such an innocent! He let her imprison his wrists, felt her fumble at the bed head. Then the knots tightened, something rattled and he was wide awake, straining to be free against bonds that did not yield one inch.

'What the hell!' Sarah was dressing, her hair scraped back into a tail and tied with one stocking. The other, presumably, was what was imprisoning him.

'I'm sorry, but I cannot risk you finding out who I am,' she explained, her face rather pale in the candlelight. 'I am very grateful.'

'Grateful!' he exploded, bucking futilely against the knots.

'It was wonderful and so…helpful. And I really appreciate that you did not take advantage of me.' She picked up his cloak and edged toward the door. 'I will leave the cloak in the hut.'

'Helpful?' Jonathan demanded of the door as it closed softly behind her. '*Helpful?*'

The storm that shook Saint's Ford Manor had subsided to merely hurricane velocity by ten the next night. Mrs. Catchpole eventually recovered from the hysterics brought on by her charge's careful description of exactly how a man's member felt when held in the hand and had braced herself sufficiently to assure Sir Hugh that, indeed, it would appear his virginal daughter had been deflowered. And what was worse, that the young woman was so far abandoned to propriety that she was threatening to tell Sir Jeremy about it, in detail, if she was compelled to persist with the betrothal.

Sir Hugh had subsided from puce to mottled crimson and stopped shouting long enough to agree that, to prevent scandal, he would inform Sir Jeremy that Sarah had changed her mind and there was nothing to be done about it. The spurned suitor had driven off in high dudgeon.

That had all taken until midafternoon. The rest of the day had been filled with recriminations, more hysterics, demands to know who the man was—and firm refusals by Sarah to say—and dire warnings of what would become of her should she prove to be with child.

She nearly blurted out that there was no danger of that and bit her tongue, concentrating on looking determined—which she was—and ashamed of herself, which she most assuredly was not. What she was also feeling was an alarming awareness of her own body and an utterly immodest desire to do it all over again. And again.

Finally Sir Hugh had retired, muttering, to his study with a full set of decanters, Mrs. Catchpole had succumbed to a migraine and Sarah deemed it tactful to retire to her bedchamber for the night.

Mary, beaming with delight that somehow her mistress had routed the feared Sir Jeremy, was agog to know how she had done it, but all Sarah would say was that she had stood up to her papa and that finally he had accepted, with very bad grace, that she could not be forced into the match.

The maid left Sarah in nightgown and robe, a book of poetry in her hand, and went off to raid the cooking sherry in celebration.

Quite how Sarah realized she was not alone, she was uncertain. There was no sound, no stirring of the air—just a tingling down her spine. She put down the unopened book with care and turned, her fingers closing around the candlestick. A tall, masked figure materialized from the shadows in the corner by the window.

'Jonathan! How long have you been there?'

'An hour.' His voice sounded cold as he put up his hands to untie the mask, tossing it aside, his eyes not leaving hers.

'While I was undressing?' she demanded, then realized how foolish it was, after yesterday, to be indignant about that. 'How did you find me?'

'I followed the hoofprints of your horse, made some inquiries in the village. It was not hard.'

'No.' Her heartbeat was all over the place. 'You must have heard me talking to Mary; you know my plan succeeded, thanks to you.' He must have done more than listen; he had been there in her most private, feminine space, a space she had expected only a husband to enter. 'Why have you come?'

'To return these.' He tossed the long rope of pearls on to the bed and this time she could hear the anger in his voice.

'I'm sorry I tied you up.' Sarah found she was stammering more than she had when she confronted her father. 'I did not want you to find out who I was.'

'It certainly gave my friends considerable entertainment to find me tied naked to the bed by one silk stocking and a string of pearls,' he said, his lips thin.

'Oh, no!' Sarah stared back, aghast. 'I thought it would be easy to get free.'

'Silk tightens under stress and those pearls are an expensive string, the thread is strong. No, Sarah, I was trussed like a gamecock in a basket and had to wait to be rescued.'

'I am so sorry. I can understand why you are angry,' she murmured.

'I am hardly angry about that. My friends dismissed it as a drunken, amorous romp—they just want to meet the lady involved, whom they think must be a most inventive playmate. No, what angers me is the fact that you saw fit to pay me for my *services* last night.' He gestured abruptly toward the pearls.

'I didn't! At least, they seemed like something useful to help tie you and then I thought, you have a living to make…' Her voice trailed away.

'Not as a male whore,' he said harshly.

'Oh, no, never that,' she whispered. 'You did me a favor. I had not thought of payment, just a gift.' He was right, it had been insensitive, insulting. She straightened her spine. 'I apologize. I have no idea how I can make amends. I just wish I could.'

She saw his eyes close and the harsh line of his mouth relax into a rueful smile. 'I am a stiff-rumped idiot to take offense. It was a miracle you were thinking straight at all, and as you say, you thought I had a living to earn.'

'You haven't?'

Jonathan smiled, silent.

'Who are you?' He shook his head.

'That is unfair,' Sarah protested. 'You know my name now.'

He grinned. 'All part of your punishment for the offense to my pride.' The smile was positively wicked now. Something inside her tightened in fearful excitement.

'Part?'

He withdrew his hand from his pocket and there was the silk stocking, dangling from one long finger.

She edged toward the bed. 'You…you want to tie *me* up?' Her voice rose to a squeak as the excitement turned hot and lodged low, sending shocks of anticipation into the secret places that were becoming damp even as he watched her so intently. 'And make love to me? Here?'

'Mmm. If you would like me to.' Jonathan seemed so cool, but she could see the pulse hammering in his throat where his shirt lay open and his lips were parted, so very temptingly.

It was madness. They would have to be so quiet—*could*

she be quiet if he touched her as he had before? Could she trust him to untie her again? But the excitement was building, coiling, making her feel different—dangerous, reckless. Jonathan had awakened something inside her that she could hardly recognize.

'Only if you promise to untie me before you leave,' she said, trying to match his teasing tone.

'I promise.' And the look in his eyes was no longer teasing, no longer hot. For a moment she saw tenderness and melted. He locked the door, then moved suddenly, like a cat, to spin her into his arms. The robe was off her shoulders, the night-gown sliding toward the floor, even as his mouth crushed down on hers and his arms lifted her, tossing her onto the bed, gasping with laughter and a delicious, fearful anticipation. 'I need another stocking.'

'Top drawer of the dresser.' She watched him tear his own clothes off as he walked across the room, his very urgency arousing her. He was so beautiful, she thought, feasting her eyes on taut buttocks and the elegant dip of his spine at the waist, the length of his legs and the definition of the muscles. Last night she had been too apprehensive to really look at him. Even his feet, with their long tendons and the flexible toes curling into the Chinese rug, were beautiful.

He came back, stocking in hand, and stood contemplating the bed head. He was already aroused, she saw with gathering excitement, as he tied one stocking to each of the top corner posts, then looped the free ends around her wrists so that she was lying back against the pillows, her arms outstretched. 'Comfortable?'

'Yes,' she admitted, wary.

'I will not take any notice of demands to stop or cries of *No!* If you want me to free you, say *Release me,* and I will, at once.'

'Promise?'

'Promise.' Jonathan strolled round to the foot of the bed and took her right foot in his hand, lifting it to his mouth. 'Are you ticklish?'

'No,' Sarah said, lying, as he began to suck her toes. *Toes? Toes were not sexual, toes were... Oh!* By the time both feet had been nibbled, sucked and licked she was in a state of bemused desperation. Was he punishing her? Was he never going to kiss her, touch her breasts, do any of those things he had done last night, or would he drive her insane just by sucking her toes and never move above her ankles?

Chapter 3

'Jonathan!'

'Yes?' He looked up, face serious, an unholy twinkle in his eyes.

'Please?' Sarah was not sure what she wanted, she just knew she needed it *now*. He grinned and began to lick upward. *Oh, yes.* At last he was going to stop tormenting her and tip her over into that blissful state… He just kept going, up her thigh, lingering on her hipbone, across her belly to her naval. 'Oh.' It was nice, it was more than nice, but it wasn't *that*. The skin across her belly tightened as though to control the heat that was swirling inside her and she tilted her hips up, hoping he would take the hint. If she only had her hands free!

Then he reached her breasts and settled down, comfortably propped on one elbow, to continue tormenting her, nibbling and licking like a man with a bowl of strawberries who wanted to savor the scent and the taste for as long as possible. He reached out for something with his free hand, drew it toward her and she felt the snaking slither of the pearls, cool against her skin as they trailed over her hipbone and slid between her thighs.

Jonathan began to tweak the string and they grazed over

the sensitized soft skin, touching, just, the aching nub that she so wanted him to caress, a teasing, frustrating counterpoint to the shocks of sensation his lips and teeth were sending direct from her nipples to her groin.

She was moaning, her head restless on the pillows as she felt him sit back on his heels, one hand still trailing the pearls through the moist, swollen ache between her thighs. He was watching her, she knew it, but fear and shame had dissolved in the cauldron of sensation he was stirring up within her.

Sarah opened her eyes and looked at him, his erection straining up against his flat stomach, and realized, through her own haze of desire, just how rigidly he was controlling himself to pleasure her and how much she wanted to touch him. As he bent to flick his tongue across the track of the pearls, she felt, with an intensity that shocked her, that she wanted to caress him like that.

'Release me,' she said, wriggling back so she was half sitting against the pillows. 'Please, release me.'

As she hoped, he straddled her body, moving up the bed so he was astride her rib cage as he reached for her right wrist. His erection was right in front of her face, so close she could see a pearl of liquid at the tip. As he stretched across she raised her head and took him into her mouth and they both froze, he with a gasp of shock, she with the rush of sensation.

'Sarah!' He tried to pull away, but she closed her teeth in delicate warning and he was still again while she moved her lips, her tongue, fascinated by the taste and the texture and the effect she was having. Jonathan began to work at the knots and suddenly her hand was free and she could flatten it against the taut buttocks, holding him to her while he freed the other wrist, and then his weight shifted and she realized he was gripping the rail above her head.

He was so still, his breath rasping as she sucked, drawing her tongue up and down, loving the intimacy and the power. She could sense, as her hands held him, the effort it was taking him not to thrust into her mouth, realized the strain she was putting him under and somehow summoned up the will to release him. He moved with the speed of a lunging swordsman, sliding down her body, crushing her under his weight, his pelvis pressing against hers, and she reacted instinctively, opening to him even as her fingers bit into his shoulders.

Jonathan found himself stretched over Sarah's body, her legs cradling him, his hips tensed to thrust. He caught himself, the effort wrenching a groan from deep in his chest. 'God!' He rolled off her, forearm flung across his eyes, fighting for control. She had trusted him and he had damn nearly...then her hand took him, sure and generous, and he turned back to caress her, shaking in her embrace as they fell into ecstasy and darkness together.

Sarah was curled against him, sleeping, he realized, as he came to himself. That had never happened to him before. His mistresses had never shown any inclination to snuggle confidingly against him, and that avoidance of feigned sentiment suited him perfectly. Caroline, his current *maîtresse*, most certainly never clung. The thought of appearing anything less than perfect sent her from the bed the moment he left it to retreat behind a screen and emerge ten or so minutes later, cool and immaculate. And by then he would be in his robe pouring champagne, ready for an uninvolved exchange of civilized pleasantries. All so very sophisticated, all so very...cold.

This was not cold. Sarah's body hugged his with the trusting, innocently sensual abandon of a sleeping kitten, her breath tickling the hairs around his left nipple, her right arm flung over his rib cage, her right leg across his thighs. They were both hot and damp, sticky and tousled, and he found that strangely pleasurable.

Jonathan wondered how long he had slept, then stopped caring and rubbed his cheek against the tangle of brown curls that was all he could reach. After a moment he dropped a kiss on the crown of Sarah's head and smiled as she stirred, muttering, and caught his nipple between her lips, playing with it in her sleep. It hardened and other parts of his body began to react. Jonathan shifted a little, so she let go with a soft sound of protest and lay still again.

He had not reckoned on feeling like this when he had let his temper and his pride ride him that morning. He had spent the day tracking her down and the evening finding his way into the house. An unlocked storeroom window had given him access, then he had slipped upstairs to check each bedroom until he had found hers.

The alcove with its swathe of drapery had been perfect— perfect to wait unobserved as the maid closed the curtains across the windows, and perfect, as he had rapidly discovered, to torment him with first the scent and then the sight of Sarah.

He had closed his eyes as the maid undressed her: he had not lost all control. But his eyes might just as well have been wide open as he followed every whisper of silk, every rustle of petticoats, the sound of her sigh of relief as her stays were unlaced, the maid's comments on the pretty clocking at the ankle of her stockings.

Then there had been the soft sound of a loose nightgown falling over her head to toes that, his imagination was telling him, were bare, and the murmur of their conversation. All so intimate, so feminine, as the two young women shared their joy that the unwelcome suitor had been routed.

Sarah had not confided how she had achieved that to her maid, he noticed, realizing he would have been well served for his intrusion if he had had to spend long minutes listening to a dissection of his performance.

But that realization did nothing to dampen the heat of the anger that the discovery of the pearls had ignited. His friends' teasing had been bearable, rooted more in admiration of his prowess at finding a bedmate so inventive rather than scorn at the predicament he had found himself in. No, it was the fact that she had carelessly left him jewelry worth a considerable sum laced mockingly into his bonds.

It was not until he had seen the remorse in her wide, gray eyes and understood that she genuinely had not counted their value, had thought only of delaying him long enough to escape, that the hurt pride vanished like smoke in the wind.

Idiot, he thought now, stroking the warm, soft skin of her shoulder with his palm. Sarah was not some pouting Society beauty buying what she wanted, careless of the feelings of those she used. She was different, and he was beginning to find that very difference disturbingly appealing.

The clock struck one as he pulled the light coverlet up over their bodies and let himself drift off to sleep, his mind full of new and disconcerting possibilities, his arms full of curves and fragrance.

'Sarah.' She came up out of a dream of Jonathan to find him there, bending over her, fully dressed.

'You are real,' she observed, half-fuddled with sleep and pleasure, then smiled as his eyes crinkled with amusement at her folly. 'Of course you are. What time is it?'

'Four. I must go before the household stirs.'

She sat up, careless of the way the sheet fell to her waist, and surprised at how quickly she had become so shameless in his presence. 'You are leaving Saint's Ford, aren't you? You will not be coming back.' Of course he would not; this was merely an unusual incident for him. For her, she realized, watching his face in the candlelight, it was everything. She had solved the problem of Sir Jeremy and paid with her heart for it.

Jonathan stroked the back of his hand down her cheek. 'Your highwayman will never come back, Sarah. Would you be glad to think that perhaps you have reformed me?'

'I do not think you were ever a very dangerous highwayman,' she observed, fighting to keep her tone light. 'So I doubt I can claim much merit for any reformation that has occurred. But yes, it is not a safe occupation for a man such as yourself: I would not like to think you might have ended on a gallows.'

'A man such as myself?' he asked, his mouth twisting into a smile that seemed to mock himself, not her.

'Honorable, kind, brave and clever,' Sarah said, wondering at Jonathan's sudden stillness.

'Thank you,' he said softly, lifting her hand and pressing his lips to her knuckles. 'You give me something to live up to, my sweet.' He was on his feet and unlocking the door before she could say anything else. Then he paused in the open doorway before slipping like a ghost into the dark corridor and away.

'I suppose you expect me to allow you to go to that house party your school friend invited you to, despite your behavior,' Sir Hugh Tatton snapped as Sarah sat nibbling listlessly at her bread and butter ten days later.

'Jessica Gifford?' She had forgotten all about that invitation. Jessica, a firm friend despite a two-year difference in their ages, had left school to earn her own living as a governess, and then, by some miracle, had met and married Lord Standon.

'She is the Countess of Standon now, Papa. And it is Lady Dereham whose invitation it was. She is a cousin of Lord Standon's.'

'Lords, ladies—hah! Aye, and there was something smoky about that match, from what one hears,' Sir High grumbled. 'Henrietta wrote to me from London to say Standon was kicking up no end of a to-do, flaunting his new mistress all over Town, and the next thing we know he's off on the Continent marrying some governess he finds there, if you please.'

'She has obviously reformed him, Sir Hugh,' Mrs. Catchpole ventured nervously, still obviously expecting retribution for not exercising sufficient control over Sarah. 'And she must be a superior young woman if she went to Miss Fletching's Academy, as Sarah did.'

'Hah!'

'And it might be as well if dear Sarah does attend the party. There will be numerous eligible gentlemen present. Gentlemen who would be interested in making a speedy match if the dowry is right…' She let her voice trail away as Sarah felt her blushes mounting. Somehow she kept her mouth closed on the vehement rejection of any suggestion that she might try to palm off her love child on an unsuspecting husband.

'Indeed,' Sir Hugh said slowly. 'A point well made, ma'am. One trusts that there is no need for haste, but still, one cannot be too careful.'

As if I would, Sarah thought, laying her hand protectively over her belly, then realizing the hollowness of the gesture. There was no chance she was pregnant, thanks to Jonathan's care of her, but if she were, under no circumstances would she let his child grow up as any other man's. Not the child of the man she loved.

'Sarah?' Mrs. Catchpole was on her feet.

'I…I'm sorry, a crumb…' Sarah said, wildly catching at any excuse for leaping to her feet, her hands pressed to her mouth. 'Water, I'll just go and get…' She fled. *Love? I am in love? Of course I am. I am in love with an utterly unsuitable man whose full name I do not know, who is never coming back and who, obviously, does not love me.*

'Mary,' she said firmly, startling the maid, who was standing in the middle of her bedroom frowning at the black silk mask in her hands, 'we have to think about what to pack for Lady Standon's party. It seems I must catch myself a husband.'

'Yes, Miss Sarah. What is this? I found it at the bottom of your stocking drawer.' The maid held out the band of silk.

'A souvenir of an adventure,' Sarah said, blinking back a tear. 'One that is about to become just the memory of a dream.'

Chapter 4

'Jessica!' Careless of waiting servants or other houseguests, Sarah threw herself into her friend's arms. 'Oh, Jessica, I am so happy to see you!'

Reeling slightly from the impact, Lady Standon hugged her tight, then held her at arm's length, the better to look at her. Jessica looked radiant, Sarah thought.

'What's wrong?' She tucked Sarah's hand under her arm and drew her into the house. 'Come and meet Bel—Lady Dereham—and the others and then I'll show you your room and you can tell me all about it. Whatever it is.'

Coppergate, the Derehams' country house, was deep in the Hertfordshire countryside and had the warm feel of a home. Lady Dereham greeted her with a smile, introducing her to the other guests, who were all relaxing, comfortably informal, in the big salon. Sarah did her best to commit the names of the host of assorted Ravenhurst relatives to memory before letting Jessica whisk her away.

'So, tell me what is wrong. There are dark circles under your eyes and I would swear you have lost weight. Is it Sir Jeremy?'

Jessica curled up in the window seat and listened as Sarah

paced the room recounting the tale of Sir Jeremy's infamy, her impetuous ride and her meeting with Jonathan. When Sarah got to the part where he made his outrageous suggestion to rescue her from her fiancé, Jessica clapped her hands over her mouth and stared in horrified amazement.

'Sarah! You let him deflower you?'

'No! I told you—he *almost* did.' Jessica closed her eyes for a moment. 'Jessica, I am in love with him.'

'My dear! It is impossibly romantic. Does he have a nickname for the broadsheets and ride a black stallion?'

'He has a very ugly horse and no nickname I am aware of.' Sarah sighed. 'It is mad of me even to dream. He's a gentleman gone to the bad, I think.'

'It won't do,' Jessica said with a shake of her head. 'You know that. This isn't a Minerva Press novel and he won't appear in the nick of time transformed into a duke.'

'I know.' She was resigned to it, after so many days of sighing for him.

'Well, the last thing you'll want is to be flirting with the young men at the party, that's for sure. You can always take refuge with Elinor Ravenhurst, who is very rational and regards all men as unnecessary frivolity, and Lady Maude Templeton, who declares she knows who she wants to marry but hasn't organized it yet. The poor man has no idea he is about to be organized, of course, and he is quite hopelessly ineligible.

'Falling in love is painful, but will get better in time,' Jessica murmured. 'I just hope you do not truly *love* him, because if you do, that will take a long time to heal.'

There was a difference, Sarah thought, as she went down to dinner attempting to ignore Mrs. Catchpole's prattling.

Being in love or loving. Which was it? Loving implied knowing a person deeply and truly. What did she know about Jonathan?

He was intelligent and honorable, he had a sense of humor, he was forgiving, he made love like… 'A devil or an angel?' she murmured, causing her chaperone to glance sharply at her.

'Sarah, this is no time for wool gathering. This is a significant opportunity for you to meet not just eligible young men, but influential hostesses. Now smile!'

'Yes, Priscilla,' Sarah said meekly to Mrs. Catchpole, pulling herself together. She owed it to her hostess to be an amiable guest, and that would not be aided by her thinking about the caress of Jonathan's mouth at her breast or paying attention to the low, demanding pulse that made her fidget and ache.

Informal Lady Dereham might be, but she arranged her dining table in accordance with precedence, and Sarah was partnered by the vicar and had, on her left side, Lieutenant Harris, a cheerful military man with a bluff sense of humor.

Her mood, when the ladies rose to leave the men to their port and politics, was therefore rather more tranquil. It would be interesting to seek out the two young ladies Jessica had mentioned. Miss Elinor Ravenhurst was easy enough to locate, a tall redhead sitting in a corner with her nose in a book and dressed in a gown of a depressing beige.

'Miss Ravenhurst? I am Sarah Tatton. I hope I do not interrupt, but Lady Standon mentioned you as someone with a very rational turn of mind and I thought I would like to speak with you.'

'Rational?' Miss Ravenhurst smiled and closed her book. 'She means that she despairs of interesting me in a young man or finding any young man prepared to take an interest in me. Are you a scholar, too, Miss Tatton?'

'No, I am not in the mood for masculine company,' Sarah confessed, sitting down.

Intelligent hazel eyes studied her. 'Either you are in retreat from an unwelcome suitor or you are in love with someone unsuitable.'

'Both,' Sarah confessed, startled.

'Then you must meet Maude.' Elinor waved her fan, a battered affair that seemed to have been sat upon, and received an answering wave from a handsome young woman chatting with three army officers.

'She will not wish to be interrupted,' Sarah began, but Lady Maude abandoned her swains with a flirtatious smile and came across.

'Maude, this is Sarah Tatton, who is unsuitably in love,' Miss Ravenhurst announced with the air of a scholar identifying an interesting specimen.

'Really?' Lady Maude sat down in a flurry of expensive silk skirts and held out her hand. 'Is it mutual?'

'No, Lady Maude. He has no idea of my feelings and I have no idea of his name, his whereabouts or anything, other than that he is entirely ineligible.'

'Call me Maude, please.' Her ladyship, dark, vivacious and enviably pretty, perched on the sofa next to Miss Ravenhurst, a contrast in styles. 'And I see you've already met Elinor, who is a lost cause as far as men are concerned, but who will talk common sense and try to persuade us from rash action. Mind you, I cannot help but believe that somewhere is exactly the right man for her, just as there is for you and for me.'

'Not rash, merely irrational, Maude,' Elinor corrected. 'A female should not be dependent upon a mere male for her every happiness.'

'I quite agree, insofar as most things are concerned. But

there are areas of happiness for which one must depend upon mere males, are there not, Sarah?' Maude's wicked twinkle left no doubt which areas she was referring to and Sarah felt herself color. 'Oh, my! You blush. Is he such a great lover, this unsuitable man of yours?'

'Wonderful,' Sarah admitted, amazed that she could confide so easily. But she sensed that these two young women, so very different, would be both kind and discreet. 'I will tell you what occurred, if you promise not to say anything to anyone else.'

'We are both,' Elinor announced, leaning forward, 'agog.'

Sarah awoke the next morning feeling somewhat better. True, Jonathan was still lost to her, but she had made two new friends and had found that her old friendship with Jessica was as strong as ever. Confiding in all three of them had stilled her uncomfortably active conscience. They had reassured her that of course she should not have obliged her father and married Sir Jeremy, having discovered his unpleasant character.

When she went down to breakfast she found it an exclusively female company, for the men, Bel informed her, had all gone out to inspect the stables.

'We are having a dance this evening,' Bel announced. 'A nice, formal, *refined* dance. Everyone will have arrived by then and the men may wash off the smell of the stables and behave like civilized human beings. Discussion of politics, horses and hunting will be forbidden and no one under the age of sixty-five may play cards.'

The last thing that Sarah felt like doing was participating in a ball, but she knew what was expected of a good guest. 'Lovely! I am so glad I brought a new ball gown,' she declared brightly.

* * *

It had not occurred to Sarah, until she was standing in the doorway and watching the houseguests and the neighboring gentry mingling and laughing in the long room, that being hopelessly in love did not just entail the pain of losing the man of her dreams. It also meant that either she must remain a spinster, and childless, all her days or marry a man she did not love.

'Sarah?'

'Elinor, I am sorry, I am blocking the door. What a delightful scene, is it not?'

'Very animated,' Elinor agreed, as they entered side by side. She was dressed in gray silk with a cream lace trim, both of which colors effectively killed any glow in her cheeks. 'And noisy. However, I have a book hidden behind the sofa cushions in the retiring room, so once I have been observed treading on at least one pair of male toes, I can probably escape.'

Maude, who was, of course, surrounded by young men, waved and Sarah heard her companion sigh as they crossed to her. Feeling she had to compensate for Elinor's lack of enthusiasm, she assumed her best social smile and soon found her dance card much in demand.

When she had first come out such popularity would have thrilled her; now she felt like someone who had an antipathy to cats but who was proving irresistible to the creatures.

'No,' she said firmly to one of Lord Dereham's friends, 'Thank you, Major Piper, but I do not waltz.' Never having achieved the exalted status of holding a voucher for Almack's, Sarah had not been approved by a Patroness and knew that to waltz without such blessing would label her as fast.

So she danced the first set of country dances, then the

quadrille, and wondered that she could still keep smiling and pretending to flirt when what she wanted was to be alone with a big man with smiling green eyes and a deep voice and a mouth made for sin.

The third set was a waltz, so she could make her excuses and go to where Elinor was sitting out in an alcove sipping lemonade and reading a small book behind her fan.

She had almost reached her when Bel spoke behind her. 'Miss Tatton! I believe you have no partner for the next set.'

'No, ma'am,' Sarah said, turning. 'I have not been approved to—'

The man beside Lady Dereham was tall, powerfully built, and in formal evening attire. His dark brown hair was cropped fashionably, his expression one of polite expectation. But the look in his green eyes was one of shock that matched her own and the lips of his sensual mouth were slightly parted as though on a sharp intake of breath.

'Oh, that is of no matter in a family party.' Bel dismissed the rules with a flick of her exquisite French fan. 'May I introduce the Earl of Redcliffe? He is hoping you will stand up for him for this set. Lord Redcliffe, Miss Tatton is a dear friend of Lady Standon's.'

'Miss Tatton.' His bow was immaculate, his voice deep and achingly familiar. It could not be. It was impossible that her highwayman—*her love*—was standing there in front of her, a respectable member of the aristocracy.

'Redcliffe!' It was Gareth, Lord Standon. He slapped the big man on the shoulder, then took his hand. 'You are so late I thought you weren't coming.'

'I apologize.' Jonathan shook hands with his friend. 'I had to go into Town unexpectedly. Things to arrange. But nothing would make me miss your party.' He glanced at Sarah. 'Almost nothing.'

And then the paralysis that had come over her when she had seen him began to ebb away, and she realized the hot sensation that coursed through her was anger.

Chapter 5

'Thank you, *my lord.*' A fine line appeared between Bel's brows at the emphasis. 'I do not waltz.' Her voice rose, heads turned.

'Sarah—'

'I do not want to dance.' She could hear her tone becoming shrill and modulated it, forcing something close to a smile. 'Thank you.'

'Miss Tatton,' Jonathan said. 'I would not *constrain* you to anything against your will.' She felt the color rise in her cheeks. It was as though the scene in the ballroom was shifting in and out of focus and the man in front of her was alternately formally attired and standing against a background of chattering couples, and stark naked in her bedchamber, a wicked smile on his lips and her stocking dangling from his fingers.

'Let us try, shall we?' he suggested. 'You can always tell me to *release* you, should you find the experience disturbing.'

Disturbing? The heat was gathering low in her belly, she felt light-headed and breathless and *wanting*, and the anger pulsed through the arousal and the ache and she just needed to hit him and kiss him and…

Her hand was in his and she could not, without making a scene, escape. Jonathan drew her onto the floor and took her in a firm hold. 'You are doubtless as surprised as I am, to meet like this.'

'I am most certainly surprised, my lord,' she said. *Oh, God, he smells the same. Leather and citrus and man.*

'My lord?' He quirked an eyebrow at her as the music began. 'What has happened to *Jonathan*?'

'I do not know. Tell me, what *has* happened to Jonathan?'

The fact that she was angry and upset and not merely shocked seemed finally to penetrate his consciousness. 'What is the matter?'

'Matter?' Somehow she managed to keep her voice down as he swept her the length of the room and round into a complicated turn at the end. She had never danced the waltz except with a dancing master; now, she realized, she was so preoccupied that she simply followed Jonathan's lead through the most difficult steps.

'You lied to me, you deceived me, you took advantage of me and you wonder why I am angry?'

'Yes,' he said bluntly, the arched dark brows lowering in answering anger. 'I never took advantage of you, I never deceived you, I never lied to you—'

'You lied by omission.' He forced her into a tight, swooping turn, her skirts swinging out, the room shifting dizzyingly about her. Sarah glimpsed Maude's face, staring. 'I thought you were a highwayman, or if not that, at least an ordinary man, a gentleman who had fallen on hard times. How could you not tell me who you were?'

Then the reason he had not, and the real reason she was so upset, hit her like a blow and she stopped dead in the middle of the floor as couples swerved to avoid them.

'But of course you could not tell me,' she whispered. 'Because if you had, you thought I would say that you had compromised me, that as a gentleman you must marry me and you would have been trapped. That is it, is it not?'

'No!' Jonathan somehow managed to keep his voice down from a bellow.

'And I suppose you laughed about it with your friends,' Sarah added. 'It was all for a bet, I presume? The highwayman act.'

'Of course it was a damn bet!' A couple gliding past stared at him. Sarah was glaring at him as if he was some kind of libertine bent on ravishment. 'And of course I said nothing about you to them. For God's sake, let's get out of this confounded dance.'

'Certainly, if only to take myself out of range of your blaspheming and bad language.' She turned on her heel and stalked off the floor, leaving him standing there, the focus of all eyes.

'I trod on her feet,' he explained to those couples within hearing and followed her, attempting to look ruefully amused when all he wanted to do was snarl.

By the time he reached the edge Sarah had vanished. Jonathan, despite his height, could see no topknot of glossy brown curls, no slender figure in almond silk. A dark-haired beauty with a heart-shaped face and an expression of exasperation appeared in front of him. He dredged into his memories of last Season. Lady Maude Templeton. 'She's gone out onto the terrace. That way.' She pointed, then walked off. Jonathan thought he heard her add, 'Men!' as she went.

Jaw set, Jonathan stalked off in the direction indicated. Idiot woman, of course he hadn't told her who he was! Couldn't she see why? And why wasn't she pleased to see him? He was pleased to see her. More than pleased. It upset his plans, but to hell with that; Sarah was here and he wanted her. After he'd boxed her ears.

The torch-lit terrace held a scattering of couples strolling and flirting. There was no sign of Sarah, but he had not expected her to stop here, in full view. He took the sweeping steps down onto the lawns and glimpsed the flutter of pale skirts in the darkness.

When he reached the same spot, treading quietly, his dancing pumps making no sound on the close-scythed turf, he could not see her. Then he realized that the shrubs that had been planted along this wing of the house had a narrow gap in them. Slipping through, he found a graveled walk between them and the house walls. Sarah had her back to one of the sloping buttresses of the old wall, her gaze fixed on a group of tumbling cherubs set amongst the greenery.

Her head came round as he stepped onto the gravel and he felt his body tighten at the sight of her wide eyes, the rise and fall of her breasts in the low-cut silk.

'Go away.' She stood her ground, chin up.

Jonathan kept walking. 'No. Why are you so angry with me?'

'I told you!'

'Did you really expect me, when we first met and we made our extraordinary decision, to whip off my mask and introduce myself as the Earl of Redcliffe? My concern was for your protection.'

'Poppycock!' Sarah snapped. 'Have you any idea how humiliated I feel? Had you not thought that this might happen if we met again? Or was it impossible to believe that humble Miss Tatton might move in the same circles as yourself?'

'Well, you hadn't up to then,' he retorted.

'No, and I imagine you are none too pleased to find I am now!' The color was flying in her cheeks, he could see angry tears sparkling, and the effort not to seize hold of her and shake her and kiss her and take her was almost overwhelming.

'It was certainly not what I planned. I intended—' He never got the words out. Sarah thumped him on the chest with her clenched fist. 'Damn it, that hurt!'

'*Good.*' She did it again. 'That's how I feel, as if someone has punched me in the chest. I *trusted* you and all the time you were just amusing yourself with some silly little gentry virgin who had got herself into a pickle.'

'Amusing myself? If I had been amusing myself, Miss Tatton, you wouldn't still be a virgin, believe me.' Jonathan grabbed her wrists before she could land another blow and yanked her hard against himself. 'If I had been *amusing myself* things might have gone rather differently.'

She glared up at him, lips parted, face flushed, the scent of hot, angry woman filling his senses and bringing with it the prickle of awareness that she was not afraid of him, not just angry with him, but that she desired him and that he wanted her. Here and now.

Sarah gasped as he pushed her back against the buttress, its slight slope bringing his weight down on her, crushing his loins against her pelvis as he spread his legs to trap her. Her wriggling thrust her against him, and he thrust back, gasping as the heat of her met the aching length of his erection, their naked flesh separated only by thin, silk breeches and the flimsy defenses of her gown.

He trapped her hands above her head, his big hand enveloping both wrists easily, and smiled down into her face, lit by the spill of light from the window above. 'Now *this* is amusing myself. Be honest, sweeting: do you want me to let you go?'

Sarah went still beneath him, her eyes searching his

face, her heart beating against his shirtfront. Then her eyelids closed as though they were too heavy and she whispered, 'No.'

Shaken by her reaction, he schooled himself to be gentle, lowering his mouth over hers, determined to coax her, but she nipped at his lower lip with sharp teeth, took his mouth with a raw need that was fueled still by anger, and his own frustration rose to meet hers and the kiss became fierce and rough and she matched him, grazing teeth, thrusting, tongues dueling, pressure and demand, with no yielding, no softness.

Beneath his weight her body bucked, not to throw him off but seeking the friction of his hardness against her soft core. His hand left her breast to pull at her skirts until his fingers touched her thigh and he could push between their straining bodies, find the hot, wet folds and part them.

Sarah went still, hanging, waiting for the touch he had taught her to expect, but he slipped one finger past the tight, desperate knot of flesh and slid it into her, gasping against her mouth at the sensation, muffling her own cry of shock and arousal as he added another finger, feeling her tighten around him instinctively.

Her reaction was so arousing he thought he would come just from that alone, and forced himself to stillness, only his mouth ravishing hers, as though to release her would be to cease to breathe. Then she whimpered against his lips and he began to thrust and she arched under him, clenching, matching his strokes until he felt the quivering desperation building, building, and took pity on her, brushing his thumb against her, one touch sending her over into shuddering collapse.

Sarah sagged, her head thrown back against the warm stone, only the weight of Jonathan's body and his grip on her wrists keeping her upright. The anger had burned away. All she knew was that the man she loved had driven her into a mindless inferno of sensation and need and the impossibly wonderful satisfaction of that need.

'Sarah,' he murmured against her neck. 'Sweetheart. Are you all right?' He released her wrists and her hands fell to his shoulders and he stood upright, bringing her with him.

'Mmm,' she managed to murmur, every inch of her aware of him, his strength and the scent of aroused man and the hardness pressed against her.

'I didn't hurt you?' She shook her head, the world gradually stopping spinning. 'You were angry. I was, too, because you were. I didn't know you would be here, any more than you knew I would. Listen, sweet—' he cradled her against himself, rocking her gently '—this can't go on, we have to talk…to resolve this.'

'No, I don't want…' she began, trying to explain, terrified what his sense of honor might compel him to say. One moment she thought herself in love with a man who knew he could never offer for her, even should he wish to, the next she found he was a man who would feel obliged to do so. Which, her spinning brain tried to fathom, was better? Or were they both too bad to bear?

'You don't want me?' he asked softly, holding her tenderly now as though that turmoil of exciting, angry passion had never been. 'I might have something to say to that.'

'You cannot force me,' Sarah began and felt him stiffen as though she had hit him again. 'I—'

'Was that a bat?' an alarmed feminine voice demanded just the other side of the bushes. 'Because if it is, I am going right back inside, Elinor Ravenhurst. I don't care how interesting the stars are.'

Maude? Elinor?

'Don't be foolish.' That was Elinor. 'It is an old wives' tale that they get into your hair.'

'Lady Maude, Miss Ravenhurst! Have you seen Miss Tatton?' Mrs. Catchpole sounded breathless. 'I do not know where she can have got to. I am most alarmed. Lady Dereham must organize a search party.'

Jonathan appeared to be shaking, then she realized he was laughing. Sarah elbowed him sharply in the ribs.

'Oh, she's here, Mrs. Catchpole,' Elinor said blithely. 'In those bushes. It was the bats, you see. We came out to look at the stars, the three of us, and then the bats swooped down and Sarah screamed and dived into the bush.'

Jonathan reacted faster than she did, brushing down her skirts, pushing a loose curl behind her ear. 'We will speak tomorrow,' he whispered, giving her a little push.

Sarah stumbled out onto the lawn looking, she was certain, as though she had been pulled through the hedge backward, rather than having merely taken refuge in it.

'Sarah! Look at you,' Mrs. Catchpole fussed.

'We'll go to my room and tidy up.' Maude tucked her hand into Sarah's arm and whisked her away down the path toward the house, leaving the chaperone trapped by Elinor's careful explanation of how one could identify the constellation Leo.

'What is going on?' Sarah demanded as Maude shut the door and stood there beaming at her.

'It's him, isn't it? Your highwayman, only he's really Jonathan Kirkland, Lord Redcliffe. I've known him for years, so I could see he'd had a shock, and then I saw your face and the two of you were having that really splendid tiff, so we thought, Elinor and I, that we had better leave you to it, but keep an eye on you. And then Mrs. Catchpole started flapping about so we came to rescue you.' She sat down on the bed. 'But what was he doing pretending to be a highwayman?'

'It was a bet,' Sarah said as Elinor came in.

'Well, you've found each other now,' she said prosaically. 'I wonder why lovers so often have such huge rows? It seems most strange.'

'I know why *I'm* angry,' Sarah said, sitting down before her knees gave way. 'But I don't know what he has to be cross about. He didn't tell me who he was because he thinks I'd have expected him to offer for me.'

'Did he say so?' Maude began to brush the back of Sarah's dress. 'Tsk! Lichen everywhere.'

'No, but what other reason could there be for not saying, once he knew my name?'

'Have you asked him?' Elinor inquired, looking up from her notebook.

'Not exactly.' Sarah bit her lip. 'I hit him. On the chest with my fists and I shouted at him. He was quite angry.'

Maude began to giggle. 'I'm not surprised. Wait until the morning. I am sure you will both be in a better frame of mind by then.'

The morning, after a night of restless sleep disturbed by quite shocking dreams, hardly seemed more promising. The breakfast parlor was populated by heavy-eyed guests sipping coffee, while many seemed to have decided to stay in their rooms.

Jonathan was seated at the far end of the table when Sarah entered with Mrs. Catchpole. He rose with the other men, then resumed his seat with a fleeting glance in her direction.

She was still pushing her omelette listlessly around her

plate half an hour later when Lady Dereham appeared at her side. 'Lord Redcliffe has asked if he might speak with you in my sitting room at your convenience.'

Sarah stared. Her chaperone sat bolt upright, looking for all the world like a pointer that had sighted game. 'Sarah, dear! We must—'

'Do not disturb yourself, ma'am. I will escort Sarah.' Bel had her out of the room before Mrs. Catchpole could react. 'You look very well, my dear. There is no need to go and primp. Here we are.' Bel opened the door, gave her a little push and closed it, leaving her alone with the Earl of Redcliffe.

'Oh.' It was not the most intelligent thing she could have found to say. Sarah bit her lip and regarded his unsmiling face.

'Sarah. I have, this morning, written to your father. I thought I should show it to you before I send it.' He held out a sheet of paper.

'Written?' She took it. The words were out of focus.

'Yes. I realize that to call would be more conventional. It was my intention to return to Saint's Ford Manor and do the thing in style, but now... Sarah, there is no way I can wait.'

'You intended to come back to me?' She stared at the firm black letters, willing them to make sense.

'Of course. I had to lose the highwayman, speak to my bankers about the settlement, have a haircut—all the things a hopeful suitor needs to do.'

'Suitor? Why?' She thrust the letter back at him. 'I cannot seem to focus.'

'Sit down then, and I will read to you.' He guided her to the sofa, then stood before the hearth and cleared his throat.

'"Sir Hugh, I write to inform you of my intention to pay my addresses to your daughter, Miss Sarah Tatton. I cannot pretend that my attachment to her was not sudden. In fact I believe it was, if not love at first sight, then most certainly love from the first moment she allowed me to press a respectful salutation upon her lips.'

'You spoke?'

Sarah shook her head, dumb with delight. *Respectful salutation?* That must be the first kiss that he took when they met. He was making it sound as if he had met her for the first time here, when in fact…

'"My standing and circumstances you may ascertain from an inspection of the *Peerage*. In regard to my intentions as to settlements, I trust the enclosed papers from my lawyer will prove satisfactory…" etc., etc.' Jonathan folded the paper.

'Well, Miss Tatton? You are, I believe, of age, which means that I need not await a response from your father but may do this now.' He went down on one knee beside her. 'Sarah.' His voice was husky and she found she could not breathe, just stare into his eyes, trapped by the intensity in them. 'I love you. I think I loved you from that first kiss. I *knew* I loved you when I felt the pain of thinking you had offered me payment for lying with you. My fault, I confess, was to go and leave you without explanation, but I did it intending to return as an entirely respectable suitor. Like an idiot I wanted to surprise you, to have everything in place, perfect. Do you forgive me?'

'Oh, yes. I love you, too, you see. I don't need everything to be perfect, I just need you.' She had found her tongue, and her eyes focused clearly on his face and she reached out and cupped his cheek with a hand that was steady.

'And you will marry me?'

And instead of answering, she simply leaned forward and kissed him and never noticed until afterward that her cheeks were wet.

* * *

'Lady Redcliffe, you are blushing.' Her new husband set Sarah on her feet beside the wide bed and bent to kiss her. 'Now what, after all the things we have enjoyed together, can be making you shy now?'

'This is different,' she confessed, reaching up to undo his neckcloth.

'Yes,' Jonathan agreed, leaving her fully clothed while she undressed him and then slowly, gently, unveiling her body until they stood facing each other in the twilit room, naked. 'I love you and now you are mine.'

'I know. And you are my husband and we no longer have to be careful. Will you show me how to love you?'

And without answering with words he lifted her onto the bed and began to woo her with lips and tongue and gentle, wicked fingers until the familiar, insistent throb took over and her head began to turn, restless on the pillow, and her own hands stopped caressing and could only hold him and he shifted his weight and lay between her thighs.

'Don't be frightened.' He moved slowly, nudging, and she smiled, heady with pleasure, tingling with anticipation.

'I'm not frightened. I just want you so much. Want you inside me, to be around you, to hold you in every way I can.' It felt strange and powerful, the inexorable, heavy pressure, but her body seemed to know what to do and was accepting him. She shifted, searching for the best position, and then he smiled and surged against her and she gasped, pain flickering past to be replaced by an overwhelming sense of completion.

Jonathan stilled above her, his eyes intense on her face. They were so closely joined that she could feel the pressure of his hipbones, the tantalizing brush and weight of his testicles, the friction of his body hair. And then, as she dared to breathe again, to relax, she could feel him inside her and realized that she could tighten around him and that when she did he groaned and closed his eyes and thrust.

She could match the surging, deep rhythm, tightening, caressing, and his eyes opened again and the look in them took her breath and she held on and let herself fly until he thrust deeper than ever with a hoarse cry and she felt him convulse inside her, spilling life and heat into her, and she let go and joined him in the velvet darkness.

Sarah came to herself to find they were wrapped together, her head on his breast, their legs twined. 'In August,' Jonathan said, his hand stroking possessively down her body, 'I asked you for the most precious thing you possessed. Thank you for giving it to me.'

'My virginity?' Sarah queried, raising herself on her elbow to smile at him.

'No.' The deep green eyes smiled back. 'Your heart, my darling.'

'How could I help it?' She bent and kissed him. 'A highwayman stole it quite away.'

* * * * *

A NIGHT FOR HER PLEASURE

Terri Brisbin

Author Note

Welcome to the beginning of my new series of stories about the knights of Brittany! Four sexy, brave warriors—three illegitimate and one noble—were fostered and raised together and became a fighting force in Brittany during the rise of William of Normandy. Three followed him to England in the hopes of wealth and lands and power—oh, and wives, of course!

This short story, "A Night for Her Pleasure," is loosely based on the theme of the O. Henry story, *The Gift of the Magi,* and is about two people in love who only want to do or be what the other person wants or needs. Trying to ignore their own desires and dreams, Simon and Elise spend their wedding day learning about each other and pledging that they will be exactly what the other wants in a spouse. The results are not quite what either expects, but when the heart is involved, nothing goes as expected.

I hope you enjoy this sensual story about the path of love, which is linked to *The Conqueror's Lady.* Please visit my Web site at www.terribrisbin.com for more information about me and my current and upcoming releases.

Enjoy!

Look for the second in Terri Brisbin's
Knights of Brittany trilogy
The Mercenary's Bride
Coming July 2010

Chapter 1

Rennes, Brittany
Spring, 1066

"Look at her," Simon ordered, nodding in the direction of his—wife. It still felt strange and new to him to call her that—not difficult to understand, because they had only married that morning. "Just look at her." His blood heated just glancing at her.

Giles, Brice and Soren all turned to look across the crowded hall to where the women sat in various groups during the wedding feast. Elise had made her way over to her mother and her cousins and sat chatting with them, all the while enticing him with her innocent demeanor and simple beauty.

"She seems to be in good spirits, Simon," Brice offered. "Though I am surprised she is here."

Simon turned and realized that his friends were looking at the wrong woman. Before he could correct them, Giles interrupted.

"As am I. Alianor looks unseemly happy for a woman who is losing her lover and protector to the clutches of a wife." Giles held up his cup in a salute to Simon and then to Soren.

"Mayhap she will be looking for a new one, Soren. What think you of her beauty and manners?"

Soren opened his mouth to speak, but laughed instead. "I will wait to see how smoothly things go between Simon and his wife. He may be back in Alianor's bed sooner rather than later and my efforts would all be for naught."

Simon's graphic curse stopped further discussion of his mistress and startled some who stood close by their group. Turning his back to them, he lowered his voice.

"I was speaking about Elise, you fools, not Alianor." Simon drank the rest of his wine in one swallow. "Bastards," he cursed under his breath.

"Without a doubt, my lord," Giles said, nodding to Simon. Stepping closer, he smacked Simon on the back and laughed. "We but sought to ease the moment."

"Am I that obvious then?" Simon could feel the tension growing within him over the coming night…and taking Elise to his bed. He'd wanted her from the moment he watched her dismount in front of his keep, and now that she was his in the eyes of the law, he only wanted her more.

"Just as much as any other groom, Simon," Brice offered.

Glancing across the room again, he watched as she smiled and nodded at something one of her women said. His body reacted strongly to her beauty and femininity. And the thought of holding her in his arms, touching her skin, tasting her essence and initiating her into the pleasures of the marriage bed this night made him harden yet again.

Then, as he watched his friends appraise her, the heat of jealousy pierced him. The three drew women to them like flies to the sweet, and he had no doubt that with their experience in the ways of wooing women, if any of them turned their real attentions to her, they could show him up for the rough, brutish man he truly was. It was only the hope that he could be different for her, different *to* her, that allowed him to believe he could make her happy in this marriage.

As though his thoughts had called her name, Elise raised her pale blue eyes and met his gaze. Tossing the hip-length waves of auburn hair over her shoulder, she tilted her head to the side. His throat tightened and his mouth grew dry, but his blood pulsed and his heart raced as the corners of her mouth lifted into the gentle smile he was coming to crave. Soon, she would truly be his. The sound of his friends' whispers drew him from his lost moment and back to the problem facing him of the coming night.

"She is yours, Simon. Surely you know that even as everyone in this gathering does," Soren assured him. "What is it that has your ball—trews twisted in a knot?"

The others laughed at their friend's witticism, but Simon did not. Taking in a breath and letting it out, he turned to face them. In a lowered voice, he finally admitted his deepest fear.

"She is a virgin."

The others looked one to the other and then back at him.

"Of course she is, Simon. Her virtue has been well guarded by her family. Even her dimwitted father knew enough to keep her from his plans," Giles answered.

Elise's father had backed the wrong noble in the dispute between the imprisoned Duke Conan and his usurping uncle Count Eudes who tried to wrest control of the region from him. Simon's family, connected to both sides of the embattled family by blood, had remained out of the fray, but he suspected that Eudes and his progeny would still come back into power in the duchy. With their cousin William making noises of war in their direction and pressing ahead with his plans to claim England as his own, Simon could believe any number of machinations would move those out of favor back into favor and change the balance of power between Breton, Normandy and the other duchies and kingdoms.

"Ladies such as she deserve poetry to woo her and to gain her love. Contracts and marriage will not do it," Simon began. He might be known as a lover of women, but he'd never wooed one in his life—certainly not one so fair and so feminine. "She is so delicate, and I," he said, "I am so…so…"

"Worldly?" Soren asked, finishing Simon's sentence but not with the word of his choosing. "Most women appreciate those years of experience in a man." Soren laughed loudly and smacked Simon on his back. "Lady Alianor was heard to say just that on many occasions."

Simon wheeled around and walked away from his friends. Even knowing that too much wine and the festive, somewhat bawdy mood had loosened their tongues, Simon would probably punch one or all of them soon—and *that* would bring an end he did not want to their marriage feast. It would show Elise the very side of him he anguished over even now. So he grabbed a pitcher of wine from one of the servants and stalked off up the stairs to the top floor, where he could be alone and watch the hall from the balcony.

By the time he reached the alcove above, a lovely widow had already approached Soren, clearly with hopes of a liaison for the coming night. Shaking his head over how easily the fairer sex fell over themselves at the feet of the "Beautiful Bastard," Simon took a deep drink of the wine in his cup and swallowed it.

"The lady is in love with you already, Simon. You have nothing to fear with her." Giles reached his side and looked down over those gathered below them. "Take her gently, and all will be well between you."

He held out his empty cup and Simon filled it before his. "I have always favored my father's family," he offered. "We are not known for our grace or small statures."

"Ah, but to have watched you fight with your sword in battle is to know the lie of those words. And small or large, it will all work out if you have but a care for the lady's pleasure first."

Simon again drank down most of the wine in his cup before Giles pulled it from his grasp.

"If you continue to drink at this rate, the only thing the fair Elise has to worry about is you falling asleep on top of her." Giles eyed him once more. "Have you never taken a virgin before?"

He said nothing, but that was answer enough for his knowing friend.

"See to her pleasure first and then to your own. Once she has found hers, she will be more accepting of allowing you yours." Giles drank the rest of his wine.

It seemed like a sound plan, but the strength of Simon's desire for Elise was there in his body already for his manhood rose hard against his breeches. Would he be able to maintain control of his passionate urges when presented with Elise, naked in his embrace, finally his alone to claim?

Then, as though he had the ability to read another's thoughts, Giles added, "You might want to seek relief before you approach your lady's bed this evening." Giles did not meet his gaze, but looked instead at those below.

In spite of having not visited the fair Alianor's bed since Elise's arrival two months ago, somehow the thought of seeking another did not sit right on him, so Simon shrugged in reply.

Giles reached out and smacked him heartily on his back. "Begin mayhap by settling her to your nearness and your touch? Surely you have kissed her? Touched her, even? Pray tell me that you have managed at least that, in spite of her mother's constant presence and ever-watchful eye."

Simon laughed aloud at that. "Her lady mother would do well as a jailer in Duke Conan's prison tower. Nothing, I fear, gets past her steely gaze or biting tongue."

Giles laughed too and shook his head. "Now that she is yours, you must begin to claim her. Step-by-step, my lord, much as you train your horses."

Simon barely controlled his laugh at that one. Giles and the others, with their illegitimate status, had little need to use finesse and little opportunity to approach virginal ladies. Most wellborn ladies did not welcome their interest.

"My friend, I would advise you never to let any woman, especially a lady, hear you compare her to a horse. You will find yourself without the warm welcome you so crave before you can blink your eyes." Simon turned to the stairs and nodded. "Come. I think it is time to begin gentling my wife to my touch."

"Fear not, Simon. All will be well by morning. The lady truly wedded-and-bedded and you will be at ease." Giles's expression grew serious. "But just in case your way is not successful, I will place a book of poetry by your bed so that you can use it if needed. 'Twould seem that ladies do like the soft words and pledges of love."

Simon did smile then at his friend's attempt to take his fears seriously. Agreeing with a nod, he made his way down the stone steps to seek out his wife. He had hours of feasting before nightfall and he was eager to begin wooing his wife.

Chapter 2

Lady Elise of Nantes watched as her husband and his friend left the rim of the balcony above and walked towards the stairway that led back to the main floor. The castle was appointed with several floors, bright and beautiful tapestries lining the walls around them, and a hall that could seat hundreds without crowding. All Simon's possessions were grand, as befitted the very wealthy and powerful count of Rennes.

All except her.

Elise smoothed some imagined wrinkle from her gown and considered her good fortune yet again. Even without her mother's urgings, it was difficult not to do so when faced with Simon's beneficence. In simple words, she owed him everything.

Her cousin leaned over and handed her a cup of wine and Elise took a small sip. Her mother's mouth formed a tight line; Elise knew immediately that she disapproved. After seeing Simon's warm gaze on her, she pulled some remnants of pride and bravery together and emptied the last of the wine into her mouth. If it burned a bit and hit her stomach with a thump, she would never say.

"You will disgrace us, Elise, if you fall asleep or lose your composure in your marriage bed," her mother whispered in a furious tone. "Cease drinking this instant."

Elise nearly dropped the cup at her mother's order, but she did not. She was married now, married to Simon, Count of Rennes, and answered to no one else. Not her mother and certainly not her foolish father who'd endangered them all. Simon alone ruled her now. A shudder passed through her at the thought of what lay ahead of her this night and of the power one man now held over her.

"My lady, surely a small cup of wine will but soothe her maidenly nerves," her cousin Petronilla offered. Her mother's frozen gaze made Petronilla cease her attempt to intercede.

"There is no reason for nerves or hesitation, you silly girl. My daughter knows her place and her duty to the count, in his bed or out of it." Lady Bertrade then lowered her voice so that only Elise could hear her words. "When you lie beneath him, fight naught that he does and acquiesce in all things. Let him have his way."

"Come, cousin," Elise said as she stood. If she had to listen to one more of her mother's audacious commands about the approaching night in her marriage bed, she was sure she would scream. "I need some cool air to refresh me."

Elise turned to leave, a brazen move on her part, but her mother grabbed her arm and pulled her close.

"Remember, you will give him leave to do whatever he wishes with you. Refuse him nothing," she whispered furiously.

"I have heard your words, Mother. I understand," she whispered back as she tugged her arm free. As bold as she may have sounded, the truth was that she knew not what to expect from her new husband.

Her mother had issued those words of warning for months; as soon as the marriage contracts had been signed, she had begun her instructions to prepare Elise for marriage. All were the same and excluded details of what she should lie still through or what he would do that she must allow. Elise understood the basic process of marital relations with a man, but her mother's words clearly hinted at things more dangerous or repulsive.

Standing back, she took Petronilla's hand, pulling her cousin to escape with her. She nearly ran as she sidestepped couples who were dancing and those just lounging around the hall, drinking and eating and celebrating her marriage to Lord Simon. Finally, they made their way out of the hall, through the corridors to the door that led to the courtyard. The air, fresh and cool as befitted a spring morning, greeted her as she stepped out of the door.

"She means well," Elise began to explain to her cousin, but the frown on Petronilla's face stopped her from apologizing for her mother's behavior again.

"Lord Simon will not allow her to command you so, now that you are married," Petronilla declared forthrightly.

Elise nodded, not fully convinced that a simple marriage ceremony would bring her mother's controlling ways to an end. But, if being Simon's wife meant she would make her own decisions, she welcomed whatever must happen between them as a small price to pay.

Petronilla took her hand and patted it. "Lord Simon will be a kind husband to you, Elise. Alianor said..." Her cousin paused, realizing her error and looked across the courtyard waiting for the awkward moment to end. "I cannot believe I said that to you, and on your wedding day. Pray thee, forgive me?"

At first mortified that her cousin mentioned her husband's leman, Elise then realized that she, Lady Alianor, was the one person who could answer her questions about what to expect in her marriage bed. Certainly she could not speak to the woman who, in spite of being the noble-born widow of one of Simon's vassals, saw to her husband's private needs. She needed someone else…someone like Petronilla.

"There is no reason to apologize, Petronilla. My lord husband's attentions to the lady are not a secret here."

"Still, Elise, 'twas thoughtless of me to bring her to your attention."

Elise turned and took her cousin's hand, tugging her closer. Looking around first, to make certain that no one could overhear her words, she said, "To gain my pardon, I seek a small service from you."

"What service, Elise?" Petronilla asked, her hesitancy obvious.

"I wish you to speak of what Lady Alianor has told you about my husband."

Petronilla's otherwise pale face blushed deep red as she sputtered and gasped at the request. So, Lady Alianor had shared many details with her sister-by-marriage about Lord Simon. Good. Mayhap Elise would learn much before being faced with the reality of her husband in their bed?

"Nay, Elise! Alianor has told me nothing, truly, nothing."

"Petronilla, you are my friend. Would you send me forth to my husband's bed knowing only what my mother has told me? That I should lie quietly and accept anything he does. That I must refuse him nothing. Not knowing what he will do to me is worse than any suffering I have faced."

"Still, Elise. You are a maiden. He expects you to know little of bedplay. He is a kind man…"

Elise dropped her cousin's hand and walked away. Failure to please Simon was not an option for her this night. She must be ready to be his wife, to keep him happy, so that he would never regret, or question for a moment, his decision to stand by their betrothal and marriage. How could she do that without knowing?

And more than for those reasons, Elise had begun to fall in love with the kind man she met on her arrival. Every preparation for her comfort had been seen to and every request was fulfilled. He greeted her brother and assigned him to duties and training, taking over the responsibilities her father should have accepted. But mostly, although he appeared to be a large, gruff man, he was ever kind to her and solicitous of her feelings when they ate together or conversed. He tried to make her feel as though she was already the lady of his lands and, when he could circumvent her mother's oversight, he'd even quietly offered his affections to her.

She stopped by a stone wall that separated the main yard from the chapel, and took a breath. Petronilla joined her there and put a hand on her shoulder.

"You are the only one who can help me, Petra," she said. "I know he cares for Alianor and that he is happy when he is with her. If I know what he likes, what pleases him, I can make certain to keep him happy." She met her cousin's gaze. "I must give him no reason to turn from our marriage. Too much and too many are at risk."

Although the Church sought to gain control over marriages and thereby control more of the wealth and power of the nobles and royalty of the lands, many nobles married as they pleased, some taking concubine wives in addition to the wives the Church recognized. If she was unsuccessful in pleasing Simon or providing him with sons and heirs and if he then sought relief from his vows, her family would not only be in disgrace, but would be destitute and destroyed.

She thought Petra was not going to answer her, then her

cousin began to speak. The words poured out quickly, but never did the two women look at each other.

"Alianor said Lord Simon likes lusty, passionate women who…who…who are neither sheepish nor quiet during their bouts of bedplay."

Elise lost her breath at such a description. Even trying to sort out the possible meanings made her heart pound and heat rise in her cheeks.

Petra's words seemed to confirm the things she'd overheard some of the female servants shamelessly discussing after Lady Alianor had walked by them a few days ago. But Elise could not believe such things actually happened between a man and his wife. Yet Petra was not done.

"He likes women who…who…who use their hands…and their…their mouths on him and his…privy parts." Petra still did not meet her eyes.

"Oh!" Elise whispered as she put her hands on her fiery cheeks to cool them. Did women do such things? She was more confused now than before she'd gained the information about her husband's preferences from Petronilla. *Hands? Mouth? Privy parts?* Just as the servants had gossiped? Surely not!

Even though such thoughts shocked Elise, a frisson of some unrecognized heat pierced through her. Such scandalous things spoke of passion and lust, something forbidden and yet somehow alluring to her, even in her innocence. An ache began deep within her.

"Do you remember catching your brother with the laundry maid in the stables, Elise?" Petra reached for her hands and tried to tug them free. "Elise? Do you remember what we heard them saying? What he asked her to do? It must be that!"

"Nay!"

She was not completely ignorant in the way in which a man

and a woman joined, for many times coupling occurred in places more public than private within this keep and even at her family's. But coupling and this…shocking revelation…were simply too different to be considered. Why would a man want such a thing? Did Lord Simon truly expect it of her? Shaking her head at the images that now crept into her thoughts, she dropped her hands away from her face.

Unable to even believe such a thing between a man and his wife, she waved Petra away and walked towards the door. Now, more than at any time since her betrothal had been announced, she needed some wine to calm her nerves. She only hoped she could find some without having to face her mother first.

Or Lord Simon.

Elise heard Petra's steps close behind her and she continued down the corridor towards the noisy festivities where she could forget what awaited her in the night. Turning the corner, she must have taken a wrong step, for she walked into a wall. Or what felt like a wall. Just as Petra ran into the back of her, Elise looked up into Lord Simon's smiling face.

Chapter 3

Simon took Elise by the shoulders to steady her after she collided with him. Gazing past her petite figure, he recognized her cousin behind her, who offered a quick curtsy before walking on to the hall. Though tempted to let her go once she steadied on her feet, he remembered his plan and kept her in his grasp, gently drawing her into a nearby alcove.

"Are you well, lady? Your face is flushed and you seem out of breath."

Her cheeks, usually a lovely cream color, were splotched with red circles and her chest—he dared another quick glance, trying not to notice the voluptuous curves so close to his hands—was heaving as though she'd run a far distance. Simon reached up, touched her cheek with the back of his finger and found it heated. He could not resist sliding his hand along her shoulders and lifting the length of her dark hair away from her face, sending some of the flowers woven into it drifting to the floor.

"I am well, my lord," she said, without ever meeting his gaze. "'Twas colder outside than I thought and I carried no cloak with me."

He took her words as a sign to try his gentler method. Stepping closer, he slid his arms the rest of the way around her and held her against his chest.

"Warmer now, my lady?" he asked.

Elise stood still in his embrace, not moving her head or body as he rubbed her back, trying to infuse his heat into her, to warm her from the cold. Simon felt her shiver, so he continued rubbing gently until she stopped. The enticing scent of the flowers, early spring blossoms, woven through her hair wafted up, and he inhaled deeply. He loosened his grasp enough to bring one hand up to her face, tilting it higher so he could see her. Then, he leaned towards her and pressed his lips to hers.

Elise accepted his mouth on hers, standing in perfect acquiescence within his arms—not moving, not seeming to breathe, and neither resisting nor furthering his kiss. Simon moved his mouth over hers, sliding back and forth across her softness, trying to ease her under his touch. But when he lifted his head and met her wide-open eyes, the expression he found there was one not unlike that of a wild animal when caught in the sights of an experienced hunter's nocked arrow. Fear, for certain, and a full measure of what appeared to be shock filled her gaze.

Simon knew that he was overwhelming her. His body stood nearly a full foot taller than hers, and his bulk matched his height. Wrapping her in his large arms as he had must have scared the breath out of her, indeed, for she still had not taken one in. Releasing her, he tried to come up with soothing words of explanation, but was forestalled by her mother's call.

"Elise!" Lady Bertrade called down the very corridor where he stood next to his very bemused wife. "Oh, Lord Simon, here you are! I could not find Elise and worried at her whereabouts when she should be seeing to your guests."

The lady's briefly bowed head and lowering of tone did nothing to soften her shrill demand, and Simon felt Elise tense next to him.

"I called Elise to my side, Lady Bertrade," he said, taking Elise's trembling hand in his. "I sought but a few moments of privacy with her. Surely my guests would forgive a groom's eagerness to better acquaint himself with his newly wed wife?" For good measure, Simon lifted Elise's hand to his mouth and kissed along her knuckles.

With a look of extreme satisfaction, Lady Bertrade nodded. "I will leave you to her, then, my lord."

It was not until her mother was out of hearing distance that Elise spoke, for her mother's temper might be controlled when Lord Simon was present, but would be unleashed once they were alone. "Pray thee accept my thanks for that, my lord."

Instead of dropping her hand now that the ruse was not necessary, he held it still and kissed it, this time lingering as he pressed his lips on her knuckles and then on the sensitive skin of her wrist. "You are lady here now, Elise, and you answer to no one save me. Remember that."

His voice, though always deep, dropped in tone to something more as he spoke—a sound that vibrated through her— and his mouth seemed to grow hotter against her skin. She'd taken precious moments reacting to his embrace and kiss when he'd surprised her in the hall—forgetting everything her mother had warned about—but now realized she must be ready for his nearness and his touch. Still not certain of whether her mother's instructions or the shocking things she'd heard from Petra were the correct way to go in this situation, Elise watched as he turned back to face her without letting go of her hand.

"Come, ladywife. Let us see to our guests together."

She risked peeking up at him a time or two as they walked back into the hall and were greeted by various guests, mostly those known or vassals to him. He introduced her to many she did not know, and always he held her hand in his. With her father in disgrace, most of her relatives did not risk traveling here to Lord Simon's lands or facing those who triumphed over them. Soon, she noticed his hand on her back, guiding her around the hall, then remaining there in a reassuring touch.

Elise had just decided she would use the information that Petra shared rather than her mother's remonstrations, when Lord Simon began a more personal approach, his attentions growing more blatant and more intimate. When they sat at the high table to eat, his leg pressed against hers under the linen cloth that covered the table's surface. At first, she thought he had just shifted in his chair, so she moved a bit to give him space. But his leg followed hers, his foot slid between hers, and she felt him rub against her.

On purpose! A flittering began in her belly, and suddenly a nervous anticipation filled her.

Certain now that he meant such a contact between them, Elise allowed him to do so, feeling the strong muscles in his thigh against hers. Any doubt of his intentions was answered by the look in his eyes when he turned to feed her a morsel of roasted beef dripping with juices from their shared plate. Lord Simon slid his right hand down from her shoulders, where it had rested, to her waist, tangling it in her hair. Then he lifted the piece of meat to her mouth, rubbing it first against her lips.

Elise fought a battle within herself while she accepted the food offered by her husband, indeed even as others at the table engaged them in conversation. When Petra caught her eye from one of the lower tables and nodded at her, she knew she must seize her chance to be more like the woman she knew her husband wanted. Sliding her hand down onto her lap, Elise held her breath, then moved it slowly over onto Lord Simon's thigh.

If he lived to reach one hundred years, Simon would never have expected such an action from Elise than the one she'd just taken. So light that he nearly missed it at first, her hand slid onto his leg and rested there—only inches from that part of him that reacted immediately. She moved it slightly along his thigh towards his knee and then back upwards again.

His blood pounded through his body, and blistering heat followed from her gentle caress. Torn between the temptation to throw her to the floor and claim her as his own in the way his body now demanded and the need to protect her and to be gentle with so delicate a lady, he tried to swallow the small bite of meat he'd taken just as she'd touched him. It remained stuck there in his throat, and he fought the urge to choke on it, for surely that would force Elise's hand from his leg and end the sweet torture and all the urges that her touch caused him. Finally, Simon was able to wash the food down with a mouthful of ale. Turning the cup so that her mouth would rest on the same spot his had, he offered Elise a drink.

He would have sworn that she'd placed her lips on him; the reaction to seeing her pink lips touch the same spot where his had been surged through him and he pulled together every iota of self-control he could find within himself to keep from placing her hand on the other part of him that surged as well. Simon attempted to look casual in his posture, trying not to let anyone see that her hand rested on him, trying not to let his raging desire loose on his innocent wife. A glance from Giles told him that his struggles were witnessed—and with a certain amount of sympathy, from the nod his friend made in his direction.

How was he to last until nightfall? How could he sit at her side, touch her, even hold her close, and not simply drag her off to their chambers and make her his? A man only had so much control and his was sorely tested even now, now with her soft hand lying on his hard leg near his harder cock. How? Mayhap if he focused his thoughts on her innocence? Mayhap if he made himself think on the fact that she came to him a sheltered virgin, regardless that the temptress would discover his true nature if she slipped her hand only an inch or two farther? As her hand did move—ever so slightly, but move indeed—he held his breath and tried to remember all of his good resolve. But the wide-eyed expression she gifted him with when he did look at her—a mix of siren and innocent at once—undid him and nearly unmanned him in an instant.

Elise felt Lord Simon's surprise when she boldly placed her hand on his leg and she thought he would object to so forward a gesture, but he did not. Now, meeting his gaze as he lifted the cup to her mouth, she saw a hunger there that any woman would recognize. The centers of his green eyes darkened, making the lighter ring on the edges of the color appear brighter and revealing that his reaction was much stronger than a simple touch should cause. His breathing sounded shallow and irregular as he gazed into her eyes, and she discovered she had trouble breathing too. As he tilted the cup, she felt his hand move from her waist to the back of her head, steadying her as she drank deeply of the hearty wedding ale.

A tiny drop escaped as she swallowed, and when she would have dabbed at it with her napkin to keep it from dripping, his mouth was there, open and hot, licking up the ale and then kissing her lips as though to share its taste. His hand, still behind her head, entwined itself in the loosened locks of her hair, something he seemed to like for he'd done it before. Then he pulled her closer and plundered her mouth.

Elise's body grew warm, her breasts swelled as they rubbed against her gown. First she did as her mother had ordered—opening her mouth wider to let him have his way. Then thinking on Petra's words, she let out a soft moan, meant only for his ears and then, even more boldly, she moved her hand, the one still hidden by the table's cloth, along the hard muscles of his leg once more. Not certain what his reaction would be, Elise felt only a moment's hesitation before he thrust his tongue farther into her mouth and tasted her more deeply.

Heat pierced her body, sending waves of pleasure from the places he touched to every place within her. Even between her legs began to pulse with that heat and she grew damp there and she shifted at the feeling of it. Whether it was moments or minutes, she knew not, but finally the sound of loud, raucous laughter conquered the haze of passion that surrounded them.

Oh, holy saints, they'd kissed so in front of all the wedding guests! She tried to draw back, but his hand held her mouth firmly against his, and Lord Simon showed no sign of allowing the cheering and bawdy calls to interrupt his pleasure. Elise lifted her hand from his leg and withdrew it, laying it against his chest then and trying to break the kiss. Finally, he opened his eyes and released her from both the kiss and his grasp, but not before gazing at her with an inscrutable expression. She could not tell if he was pleased or angered by her reactions to him.

Her heart pounded within her chest; she felt as though she could not draw a breath in deeply enough. Her lips swelled from his attentions, as did her breasts in a similar but different way, and she fought the urge to touch both her mouth and the tight buds that her nipples had become. Looking about for something to wet her now-dry mouth, she reached for the goblet he'd used before.

"Here, ladywife," he whispered, as he held the goblet out for a servant to fill and then handed it to her.

When he did not bring it to her mouth and when the fire left his green eyes, she worried that he was not pleased at all with her. Drinking some and then handing it back to him, she glanced around the room at their guests—the ones who had witnessed their public display. Other than her mother, with a grim expression on her face, most of their guests seemed to approve of their public kiss. Her mother, already rising from her chair, clearly did not.

Chapter 4

Simon knew he must gentle his touch and his kisses, but each time Elise moved closer or touched him—and that moment when a throaty moan escaped her during their kiss—he was goaded on. And his wayward arousal urged him forward as well, towards the rewards of this night. She seemed accepting of his kiss, so Giles's plan to accustom her step by step must be working. Now, as he watched her mother approach their table, he knew he must not allow the woman to interfere in his methods. Standing, he nodded to the musicians in the alcove to begin.

"Dance with me, my lady?"

Without waiting for her consent, Simon reached for Elise's hand and guided her to her feet. He kept her hand in his as they walked around the table to the place cleared for dancing, passing by her mother with only a nod. She might gainsay her daughter, but she would never think to do so to him. Many other guests rushed to join them, and soon they were moving through the steps of a lively dance.

Simon shamelessly held Elise closer than the dance dictated, taking advantage of his position as lord and husband to allow his hands to remain at her waist as they moved through the steps. During the portion of the dance that called for him to lift his partner and swing her around to his other side, he purposely let his hands slide up until he could feel the fullness of her breasts resting on them.

Though he heard the rushed intake of her breath at such an intimate touch, she did nothing to dissuade him from his actions. Indeed, after that first momentary hitch in her breath, he thought she may have leaned in closer and even placed herself more fully in his grasp. In spite of his own body's continuing arousal at her nearness, Simon held her aloft for the last maneuver and then let her body slide down his at a slower pace than the dance called for, enjoying the feel of her breasts against his chest and her hips and legs rubbing down his.

Unable and unwilling to resist such an opportunity, he met her mouth as he lowered her, and kissed her relentlessly until her feet finally touched the floor. Even then, he did not release her from his embrace, turning his head and kissing her once more. Simon could not help noticing that she looked both breathless and dazed as the music came to an end. It was how *he* felt, so he was glad she was as affected as he.

When she murmured a request for a few moments of privacy, he let go of her and watched as she walked away, towards the solar. Her cousin Petronilla followed behind, so Simon turned back to the table and sought his chair…and a reviving drink. It did not surprise him when his friends, ignoring all protocol and outraged glances, sat down around him, separating him from the others at table.

"'Twould seem Giles had the right of it, then?" asked Brice.

"Is she settling under your touch, Simon?" Soren asked. "Like your horse?"

Though Soren and Brice laughed then, raised their cups to him and drank deeply at the jest, Giles simply shook, then hung his head.

"I did not mean to tell them, Simon."

"It matters not now," he answered, waving their concerns off. He did not wish to discuss this personal matter with anyone right now, for he needed a few minutes to let his body and his lust cool.

"Did not the dance and her ease in your embrace erase your worries? You did not tumble over her and step on her feet. She seemed accepting of your affections. Surely good signs for the rest of it?" Soren asked.

"Truly, Simon, I do not understand why you worry so," Brice said as he glared at an approaching servant, warning him away. "Does not your marriage save her family and give her brother expectations lost by their father? Do you not honor her by making arrangements for her mother and for her own dower property?"

Giles had been silently watching the exchange, but had not offered a comment of his own since the first. Simon looked at him, eyebrows raised, waiting, for he knew one would come.

"The only problem I see for you is that night's fall is still three hours or so away. I suspect if you continue to 'settle her to your touch', you will end up between her legs against a wall in some darkened alcove or corner."

"Giles…" Simon warned with a growl. It was too damned close to the truth of it to speak of. "Enough."

"Ah! Here comes the lady now," Soren said, loud enough to interrupt any further discussion of her. He stood, as did Brice and Giles, stepping away from the table and allowing Elise to sit next to her husband.

"Are you well?" Simon asked, sliding his hand once more

to her back, and then resting it lower. Other than a lovely blush, she appeared just so, for he was trying to notice her comfort this day.

"I am, my lord," Elise said, feeling the light pressure of his hand on her back. As he slipped his fingers beneath her hair, they tickled her neck and sent tiny ripples down her spine. Just as in the dance, her body became a thing of its own, reacting and responding when her mind and her thoughts did not do so quickly enough.

Everything he did now seemed to involve touching her, she realized as he let his hand remain on her back, though he slid it down to rest beneath the jeweled belt she wore. Having anyone touch her, let alone having a man do so, was not something she was familiar with, and his touch aroused some stirring with her. From the gleam in his gaze when she met it, she thought it might be done apurpose.

She would like to ask him about it, but the presence of his men, his Bastard Knights, deterred her. Elise knew of them—Petra has spoken of little else on their arrival here—but these three men were of illegitimate birth and fostered against custom by the old lord, then befriended by the new one. Such men as these were not men she would ever deign to speak to in public, or even out of view, but it was clear to her and everyone in attendance that they held some special place here in Lord Simon's household and presence. As though knowing the subject of her thoughts, Lord Simon spoke of them.

"Lady, though 'tis not the usual manner of things, I wish to make these three known to you. Giles Fitzhenry—" Lord Simon pointed to the farthest man who bowed to her "—Brice Fitzwilliam there and Soren Fitzrobert here—" he slapped the nearest one "—are all sworn in my service and now in yours."

Surprised at how polite they were, Elise looked from one to the next as they bowed to her. Truly, from the rumors and stories she'd heard, she half expected them to leer openly at her or behave somewhat rudely. Instead, she could not miss their open affection and loyalty towards her husband and their apparent acceptance of her. Noticing their appearances now, their blatant manly appeal, she wondered how many women living or visiting this keep had not shared their beds at one time or another. These four were the kind of men that women whispered about and dreamed about and prayed for in their most secret conversations and moments.

They could, and probably did, have nearly any woman they chose in their beds for pleasures of the flesh and...

And she was now married to one of them!

Clearing her throat, she looked from one man to the next, taking note that the four were as different as any could be in appearance, but warriors one and all, with tall, muscular bodies, well able to do battle with any number of fierce opponents and well practiced from the look of them. Their coloring, with Simon's dark brown hair and green eyes, Giles's paler hair and blue eyes, Brice's blond hair and brown ones, and the giant called Soren had black hair and silver-gray eyes, this in spite of his name that usually spoke of reddish coloring, proclaimed their differences. But had she not known them, the three of them, to be by-blows and not of noble birth, she would have assumed by their height and bearing and manners to be so.

Elise heard a familiar cough and glanced over to where her mother sat. Her disapproving stare told her what was expected of a noble-born woman, and that was to shun such men as these. The expression in Lord Simon's eyes said otherwise. These men were important to him; he called them friends as well as vassals sworn to him. Though not certain of what their future dealings would be, Elise decided she must honor her husband's desires in this, for clearly if this was not important to him, he would never have introduced them so.

"Sirs," she said with a smile, "I am honored by your service and friendship to my lord husband and that you extend that to me now. Pray—" she held out her hand and motioned to the empty seats near them "—sit and be welcome at Lord Simon's table."

It was bold, something far bolder than even her intimate touch earlier, for this was something public, something witnessed by one and all at the feast, something that would set forth a practice for their lives together. Welcoming those who should, by birth, be seated at far lower tables than the lord's opened her to gossip and possible scorn, unless her husband supported such a gesture. If she'd thought for a moment that he would not, she was proven wrong quickly.

His friends, clearly uncertain whether to accept her invitation or to leave the dais as they should, waited for Lord Simon's sign. Simon rose, releasing her from his loose embrace, and smiled at the men.

"You heard my ladywife's words, join us at table," he said, raising his voice loud enough so that everyone in the hall heard.

Lord Simon took his seat once more, this time not resting his hand on her back. Though disappointed somehow at this lack, she did not have more than a moment or two to feel that, for Lord Simon made up for it quickly by placing his arm around her shoulders and drawing her close. Before she could react, he again brought his mouth to hers and kissed her...and then once more. Though quick kisses, they promised much more, later in private. And when she thought he would release her, instead he turned and whispered in her ear so that none would hear.

"You have pleased me in this, Elise."

His hot breath tickled her ear and made the skin on her neck tingle. She shivered and he held her closer still.

"For making them welcome, I will grant you anything you wish."

Already unable to breathe at the intimate gesture and the heat of his mouth so close, she gasped when he touched his tongue to the edge of her ear and then again when he kissed the place just below there. Her body pulsed once more with the excitement that such caresses and touches caused within her. For something so new to her, her body seemed to be recognizing and enjoying every moment of it.

"I but serve your needs, my lord, as any good wife would see to her husband's," she whispered back, noticing that Lord Simon's body shuddered then too, at her words.

She thought that he might steal another kiss, but he loosened his grasp and allowed her to sit back in her chair. If she thought this meant not touching her, she found she was mistaken, for he took her hand in his and rested them on her leg. Elise tried hard to concentrate now on the words flying around her, but as her husband released her hand and continued to caress her leg under the table, doing anything but feeling his touch became impossible for her.

Even through the layers of clothing—the chemise, the gown, the tunic and the stockings she wore—she felt as though he touched her bare skin with his fingers. He slid his hand along the top of her thigh, from knee to mid-thigh and then just a little higher, closer and closer to that private place between her legs.

Sensation warred with sense within her then and, though

she thought she should demur and not allow such things outside their bedchamber, the heat and the tiny shivers that pulsed through her were pleasant. It was invigorating, even as she felt so much for the first time. Trying to look at each of her husband's friends as they spoke to each other and to him, she felt she was quickly losing the battle, concentrating only on what her husband was making her feel.

Did he know? Did he know how her body ached for something more? Was this what consummation would be like? Would something that intimate make her feel this way? Could there be more to this than simply joining and allowing her husband to release his seed deep inside her? Losing the battle completely, she leaned against him, aching for more and mortified that he could cause such recklessness in her.

He stilled then, whether because her behavior was so wanton that he was shocked or for some other reason, she knew not. He began to lift his hand from her leg, but when she clutched it, instead he grazed the top of her leg and her belly, sending shudders through her whole body. Elise gritted her teeth then against such pleasure.

Suddenly those at table were silent; she dreaded meeting their gazes, for surely, those more experienced in such matters knew what was happening there. Keeping her eyes lowered, she took in and released a deep breath, hoping that she would gain some measure of control over the wayward and lustful urges in her.

When her husband's friends began to whisper amongst themselves, she did look up. They exchanged a few more words, but a look and a glance and a shrug were all she could see before her husband stood. If she thought what she had done in publicly accepting her husband's friends was scandalous, it did not come close to what her husband did next.

"My lords, ladies, good sirs and madams," he called out. "I find that my ladywife and I have need of some privacy." She blushed at some of the bawdy suggestions called out to them, but he continued, "Pray all of you remain and enjoy my hospitality. We will rejoin you…anon."

A mixture of fear and anticipation and excitement of the physical kind filled her then, making her want to laugh and cry at the same time. Before she could do either, Lord Simon pulled her to her feet and then lifted her in his arms. Throwing her arm around his neck to keep from falling, she leaned her head against his chest.

"I can wait no longer, Elise. I would make you mine now," he growled as he carried her down from the dais and towards the tower where his bedchamber was. "My back!" he called out to his friends who laughed aloud at his actions.

Chapter 5

Elise dared to peek over his shoulder then and found that many of the guests raced behind them, most likely intending to make merry on the way to the bedding and to witness what they could. Lord Simon's Bastards put a stop to that quickly, forming a wall behind them in the stairway that led to their chamber. As Lord Simon climbed the steps, carrying her towards her first true test of her ability to please him and protect her family, she could hear the shouted protests of those stymied by his friends.

"I wish no witnesses to our bedding, Elise. What happens between us is not for anyone else to see," he said as he swiftly reached the top floor and pushed open the door to their bedchamber with his foot. Once inside, he leaned against the door and waited for the latch to catch.

Elise worried then, for witnesses could prove the validity of a claim of consummation if questions were raised. If no one examined them for defects and saw them put to bed, there would be no one to speak on her behalf. He did not give her time to ask such questions; instead he carried her to the center of the room and put her on her feet. Shaking out her tunic and gown, she pushed her hair back from her face as she looked around his—*their*—chambers for the first time.

Larger than even the ones she shared with her mother, this boasted of two smaller rooms connected to the sleeping chamber. Although she knew he used his steward's room on the lower floor of the keep for his records and the official business of managing his lands here in Brittany as well as those in Normandy, the table—covered by various rolls of parchments and quill jars for ink—informed her that her husband also worked here in his chambers.

Turning around, she realized that the other smaller room contained trunks—hers was now placed next to his larger ones—as well as a table with a pitcher and bowl, and a chamber pot beneath it. The sight of her favorite bed robe there pleased her. Lord Simon had walked across the chamber and now returned with a goblet of wine for her. Trying to shake off any fear of what was to come, she thought on Petra's advice, scandalous as it was, and waited to see what he would do first.

Simon watched as a myriad of emotions crossed Elise's fair face—first, blatant curiosity, followed by recognition, and then fear. He hated seeing it and he pulled himself back under control, wanting to see her eyes darken with passion instead. Now that they were alone, Simon swore to take his time with her, for this one night would influence the course of their married life. He'd hastened this moment because he feared that his escalating lust would overwhelm him. Pushing his hair out of his face, he thought on how to ease the tension between them.

Giles's words came to mind once more.

After they each drank some of the wine, Simon lifted the cup from her hands and put it back on the table. Turning back to face her, he realized that all his steps taken so far were in danger of being lost. So, he grasped her by her shoulders and drew her near, pausing when she was close enough to kiss. His blood raged through his veins when she tilted her head back and offered herself to him. Touching his lips to hers, he tilted his own head and pressed more fully against her mouth, sliding his tongue inside when she allowed him.

Pleased by such trust, Simon moved on in his relentless campaign to woo his wife. Soon, kisses were not enough and he could feel her body trembling next to his. More than anything, he wanted to rid her of her clothing, to touch and taste her skin and feel her naked next to him. Lifting his head, he smiled at the dazed expression on her beautiful face and in those pale blue eyes.

"May I play maid for you, my lady?" he asked softly, knowing that someone must loosen the laces of Elise's gown and tunic for him to touch her skin. Either loosen them or cut them, though he was certain that she wanted to keep this gown in one piece, since it was a gift from the duke on their marriage.

With a nod of her head in agreement, she turned around, presenting her back to him. Simon took his time, examining her shapely form before he took a step closer and slid an arm around her. Held so close, he could feel her firm bottom against him. He could smell the flowers in her hair and he could, if he chose to, slide his hand down to explore the curves of her breasts, the flatness of her stomach or the place between her legs. Unable to control his wayward cock, he surged against her in that moment and felt the pleasure of being against her body.

Elise stood still, her mother's instructions running continuously through her mind: *lie still, allow him his way, acquiesce in all things, do not refuse him anything, a husband's right, be still, be quiet…acquiesce.*

When she felt his manhood hard against her bottom and felt his breath against her neck, it was difficult to remain quiet and still. Her body screamed for more…more of something that seemed to tease her even as his arm rested across her chest, holding her there. Her legs shook and the place between them wept with moisture. How could any woman remain still while such feelings rioted through her?

Lord Simon released her then and she nearly fell, saved only when he encircled her with both arms to unbuckle the jeweled belt that laid low on her hips. He tossed it on the bed and then he gathered her hair up in his hands and gently placed it all over one shoulder. He seemed fascinated by the length of it and by its scent. Thankfully, she'd used the rose-scented soap on it, for he appeared to like that. Then he began to unlace her dress, something no man had ever done, and it felt both scandalous and exciting to allow it. Her breasts swelled against the movements of the gown and her nipples tightened and grew very sensitive.

Allow him anything…acquiesce.

Elise let her head fall forward as his strong fingers tugged and pulled the laces on the back of the gown she wore. Soon, it was loosened enough to remove and she lifted her arms as he pulled the gown up and over her head. Her hair tumbled over both of them and his body shuddered behind hers. Standing before him in only her linen undergown, Elise felt exposed and naked, for the fine material hid nothing from view.

When she thought he would unlace the undergown, he did not. Instead, he pulled her against him once more and touched her. Not only with his hands, but also his mouth. He kissed the back of her neck, and his manhood pressed against her bottom. Every place on her body seemed his target—his hands sliding down over her breasts, cupping them and squeezing them before moving over her stomach and touching—finally, touching—the place between her legs where it ached so. Even through her gown, she felt the wondrous pleasure as he rubbed over her mons and tickled the hair that guarded the entrance to her core.

She tried, by the names of the holy saints she tried, but the sound escaped her before she could stop it. When he moved both hands back to her breasts, cupping them and rubbing his thumbs across the sensitive tips, she moaned at the exquisite sensations he caused. Remaining still while he plundered her body was simply not possible; Elise moved against him even as he teased the skin on her neck with his lips and tongue and teeth.

Simon stilled, not believing the passionate response in Elise's body to his kisses and caresses. She'd stood quietly, allowing him to touch her, until he used his hands over her breasts and even dared to stroke between her legs. Then she'd gifted him with such a moan that he nearly gained release in that moment. Realizing this was proceeding dangerously fast, he held her unmoving in his embrace until he could control his body's urges. He took a deep breath in and then released it, letting his hands drop from her body.

"Would you like to wear this to bed?" he asked, hoping that it was the thoughtful thing to do for his virgin bride.

"I confess that I do not know what is expected, my lord," she said in a husky voice. Dare he hope that passion caused such a response? "What is your pleasure?" she asked.

His pleasure? His pleasure would be to tear the thing off her, throw her on the bed, kiss and lick his way up and down her fair body, stopping in all the interesting curves and crevasses until she screamed out her release over and over again, and then swive her until neither of them could move. His manhood too thought that was a good idea, from its reaction to such wayward thoughts.

"Why do you not keep it on for now and climb into bed?" he asked, knowing he must cool down for at least a few moments or "his pleasure" would become the reality and surely scare her mindless of him.

She did as he asked, and he enjoyed watching the soft sway of her hips as she walked across the room, especially the view of her bottom as she climbed onto the bed. But the sight of those puckered, rose-colored nipples through the thin linen gown, her blue eyes wide in anticipation and arousal, and her auburn hair tumbling madly around her when she turned and sat nearly forced his control from him. Simon walked over and helped her get under the covers.

Turning away, he unbuckled his gold belt and lifted the jeweled chains from around his neck and placed them in the box on the table. Simon loosened the laces at his neck and tugged first the tunic and then the shirt over his head. Leaning against the side of the rope-strung bed, he slipped off his shoes and untied the crossed bands that held his hose in place. With only his braies remaining in place, he turned back to face his wife.

Her open curiosity pleased him. She had not turned away while he undressed or faced her bare-chested. Her own chest moved quickly, her breathing shallow and light, and her eyes growing wider with each step he took closer. What would her expression say when he revealed the extent of his arousal to her and her virgin gaze saw that part of him that would join his body to hers? Glancing around, he realized there was no way to darken the chamber, for the afternoon sun flooded through the three windows built into this side of the keep. He did not favor bed curtains, so there were none to mute the brightness around them.

Simon decided that it was best to continue while her body was still aroused. He turned away, untied the laces at his waist and dropped his hose and braies to the floor. He reached back and lifted the covers before climbing in next to Elise.

His skin was golden.

When Simon had removed his tunic and shirt, Elise had noticed the brown curls on his wide chest and that the golden color continued down all the way to his waist where his braies kept her from seeing more. Was he colored so by the sun all over? Heat crept into her cheeks as she considered him being naked outside where the sun's rays would darken his skin thus. Lord Simon turned, but she could not look away as he loosened his braies and dropped them.

The muscles of his back tightened as he shifted, and he moved quickly for she nearly missed the sight of his powerfully built buttocks and thighs before he sat down. Were they as hard and strong as they appeared to be? Remembering the feel of his thigh beneath her hand at table, she swallowed deeply.

Aye.

They were.

Nothing about him was not muscular or strongly built. And from the very quick look she got of his manhood as he slid in next to her, it matched the rest of his physique. Elise knew where it would go, but could not imagine how it could, especially now that she'd seen it and felt it against her.

Lie still…allow him his way…refuse him nothing.

The words repeated in her thoughts over and over until she could think of nothing else. Even when Lord Simon reached over and slid his arm behind her, guiding her closer to him. Or when he turned and his aroused manhood lay against her hip. Or even when he took her mouth and tasted her deeply with his tongue.

Acquiesce.

Elise closed her eyes as he rolled her onto her back. His mouth never left hers. Her breasts swelled more and ached as he touched them through the linen shift. He took the tips of them between his fingers and thumbs and rolled them until they tightened into hardened nubs and she nearly screamed out.

Fearing that she would lose control and disgrace herself or her honor, she tried to allow him to do as he pleased without struggling against his touch…or his mouth…or the wondrous heat that pulsed through her as he began to kiss his way down from her mouth to her neck to her shoulders and then on to her breasts. Proud that she could remain almost still through it all, she had no idea of what the feeling of his mouth sucking and licking those tightened nipples would do to her.

When her entire body shuddered and wetness wept between her legs, Elise understood that she could not do as her mother ordered. Worse, when Lord Simon moved his hand over her belly, gathering up the length of her shift so he could rub over the hair at the juncture of her legs and slide his finger into her cleft, she shook and shivered and moaned aloud at the aching pleasure it caused.

"Easy now," he whispered to her, and he yet continued to torment her breasts with his mouth. She felt the sound of his words against the wet linen and arched against his lips and teeth for more of it.

"Lord Simon," she whispered.

"Simon," he said thickly. "My name is Simon to you."

With the immense heat that poured through her and the throbbing ache building between her legs and deep inside her core, Elise knew that something was going to happen. Pleasure curled deep in her belly and she waited.

"Open for me, wife," he whispered even as he spread her legs with his knee.

Elise let her legs fall open and he knelt between them, spreading her wider and even rubbing that place that poured forth moisture and throbbed for more of his touch. His finger slid deep inside, then another joined the first and Simon used them to spread the wetness on the folds of skin there. The sensation shocked her so much that she finally realized her mistake.

Petra had told her how to please him and yet she'd ignored her advice, falling back on the words of her mother instead. Looking at the intense expression and the beads of sweat that covered his face as he continued to urge her body towards something—without, it seemed to her, much success—she knew what she must do.

Elise mustered all her courage and, reaching down between them, took his manhood in her hands. It pulsed like something alive in her grasp, but she did not let it go. Rubbing it up and down, she drew him closer to her cleft and moaned the words she'd heard the laundry maid say to her brother that day months ago.

"Take me, my lord," she whimpered, trying to imitate the girl's tone of voice. "Fill me now, my lord. Take—" she rubbed his member again "—me now."

And he did.

Chapter 6

⁓⁓⁓⁓⁓

The touch of her hands on his hard length was pure torture. Stunned by such a caress, he thrust twice into her grasp before he could stop himself. But when she begged him in that throaty moan to take her and fill her, he lost all semblance of control and drove into her as deeply as he could go. He took her and he filled her so full of himself that no fitted glove could have been so tight, skin against skin.

Lost in the haze of lust he'd given himself over to, Simon drew nearly out and plunged inside her again, feeling the heat of her core and letting his seed build to release. He'd wanted her so much for so long that it took but one more thrust, all the way to her womb, and his release was upon him. With a groan, he felt his cock pulse against her inner walls until he was empty.

Only then did he open his eyes and realize his mistake.

Elise lay beneath him, not moving, with an expression of pure horror and confusion on her face, and her hands pushed against his chest in an ineffective attempt to make him stop. He'd loosened his hold on his lust and let the ruffian inside him free to ravage his innocent wife. God forgive him, for he was certain Elise never would.

Simon eased out of her and climbed off her, sitting for a moment at her side. Her linen shift was pulled up to her waist and now marked with his sweat and seed and her blood. He went to the smaller chamber and brought the bowl and pitcher to the bedside.

His servants had thought of everything; he found a pot of heated water in the hearth, and the smell told him that someone had added herbs to it, hopefully those needed to soothe the hurt he had caused Elise with his fumbled claiming. Pouring the hot water in the basin first and tempering it with cool water from the pitcher, Simon brought it to the bed and offered his wife a cloth soaked in the steamy water.

"This should soothe the pain I caused," he said quietly. He thought he should say more, but what words could ever excuse his rough treatment of his virgin bride?

At first, she didn't move or say a word, but then she pushed herself up to sit and accepted the cloth from him. Without speaking, they passed the cloth back and forth, wetting it over and over, until Elise cleaned herself of the remnants of their joining. Only when her gaze focused on his groin did he realize that he was marked as well by her blood. Standing, he wiped himself clean and put the basin away. Pulling on his braies, he knew he must say something to her to explain, but what and how?

"May I get a clean gown, my lord?" she asked in a soft voice from her place in the bed.

"Please do not call me that, especially after all that has happened here. I would have you call me Simon." He walked over to her trunk, searched for a clean linen gown and brought it to her. "Here now, let me help you."

He reached over and took her hand, assisting her to the edge of the bed, where he could take the soiled shift off and let her put the clean one on. Once she was covered, as it was, she looked confused once more. Simon took her hand again and led her to an alcove near the windows that had two large, carved wooden chairs, each one cushioned and covered in velvet. He allowed her to sit and then, after tugging his own shirt back on, he stood at the window, staring out and trying to come up with the correct words to explain his terrible mistake in their marriage bed. Turning back to face her disappointment and fear, he nearly fell over her.

"Elise, what are you doing on the floor?" he asked, trying to pull her to her feet from the place where she knelt at his.

"I humbly beg for your forgiveness, my lord. I swear I will do whatever pleases you. If you do not forswear our marriage, I promise to allow you anything you ask," she cried out, grasping the edge of his shirt and touching it to her mouth. "I did not know," she said, shaking her head. "I did not know."

Shocked at such behavior, Simon realized that she thought herself to blame for things going badly between them and she was terrified by the thought he would repudiate her as his wife. Taking her by the shoulders and lifting her to her feet, he pulled her onto his lap where he could speak softly and calm her.

"I am the one who needs to beg your forgiveness, Elise. I was trying to be gentle with you, but when you touched me like that, I lost control of myself. I did not want you to see the barbarian I am and fear me. I wanted to be something different for you."

Though shaken to her very core by what had happened between them, his words now shocked her even more. Lord Simon, Simon, worried about her reaction to him? It was too much to accept, for it was her shortcomings and fears that caused things to go awry when he bedded her.

"I thought it would please you," she said, sitting up and meeting his gaze then. The dark green of his eyes softened and she found compassion and caring gleaming forth from them. "I only wanted to please you."

"Did your mother say such things to you? Did she tell you to…" His words drifted off. Would Lady Bertrade say such things to her innocent daughter?

"Oh, nay," Elise said, shaking her head. "Lady Alianor told—" Realizing her error by the way his gaze changed, she shook her head. "Not Lady Alianor, my lord. I meant to say—"

He lifted his hand and touched a finger to her lips to stop her. She watched as his brow furrowed and he shook his head now. Tilting his face, he scrutinized hers for a moment before speaking. When he leaned so, his hair drifted over his brow and she clenched her hands to keep from reaching up and pushing it aside for him.

"What did Lady Alianor say to you, Elise? Tell me the truth." Though his words were calm, she just wondered if he was as well.

Taking a breath and releasing it, she began. "Lord…Simon, I sought advice on how to please you in all things, but mostly in our marriage bed. Everyone knows that Lady Alianor pleases you—"

"*Pleased* me," he interrupted.

"*Pleased* you?" she asked back.

"I have not shared Lady Alianor's bed since our betrothal three months past, Elise."

"You have not?" Then she remembered her place, and she could not meet his gaze. "Forgive me. 'Twas not my place to ask such a thing of you."

He shifted beneath her then, turning them so that they faced one another. Taking her hand in his, he lifted it to his mouth and kissed it. "I have not taken any woman to my bed since our betrothal, Elise. I have only wanted you."

Her heart skipped a beat then, for his words were completely unexpected and his actions even more so. Before she could say anything, he repeated his question.

"What did Lady Alianor tell you?"

"I confess that I had neither the time nor the courage to ask her directly, my...Simon. But Petronilla is her sister-by-marriage and she related some of the things that Lady Alianor told her...to me." She stopped then, aware of what she would have to tell him if she continued.

"And Petronilla told you...what?" By the stern expression growing in his eyes, she knew she must tell him, and hopefully make him understand about her own shortcomings.

"That you liked women who were lusty and noisy and who...who..." She hesitated just as Petra had, finding it impossible to utter such words. Then, she just let them burst out. "You like lovers who use their hands and their mouths on your privy parts."

From the movement she detected beneath her, Elise knew his body had reacted to her words. From the guilty look there in his eyes and from the way they shifted to a deeper green, she also knew that he did, in truth, like such things.

"And so you used your hands on my...privy parts to try to please me?"

"I know that this was my first time in such an endeavor, Simon, but you did not look pleased by it. Indeed, you looked as though you were struggling to get through the ordeal."

He choked then and she jumped from his lap to get him some wine. Bringing it to him and thumping his back to help him clear himself of the coughing fit, his laughter surprised Elise.

"I was struggling, my innocent wife, to keep from ravaging

you during our first *endeavor* as you called it." Simon pulled her back onto his lap then. "I was almost able to move slowly when you grasped my privy parts and caressed them. It destroyed any remnants of control I had and I just plunged in to take you. 'Twas never my intention for it to end with such haste and without you receiving a full measure of satisfaction."

His words touched her then, and even her body, so recently used, began to respond to talk of privy parts, caressing, plunging and satisfying. She had been enjoying his affections until that moment when he broke through her maidenhead and brought pleasuring to a halt. Even the act of joining did not cause the pain she had been warned about, only a tightness and slight burning when he entered her so quickly.

"So, you were trying to please me by being bold and I was trying to please you by being gentle?" He laughed and the sound of it delighted her. "Mayhap the next time, you can simply ask me and not your friend or my last mistress for advice?"

"Your *last* mistress, Simon? What do you mean?"

"With a wife so willing to please me in my bed, what need have I of another woman?" Her husband leaned over and kissed her then. Between his words and his touching affection, she did not know which surprised or pleased her more.

"Mayhap you should wait to see if I am truly able to please you before you make such a vow? The first time did not proceed very well."

Simon stood then, holding her in his arms and carrying her towards the bed. Sitting on the edge, he lifted her to the center and then stood, looking down on her as she lay in only her linen gown. Instead of fear, waves of anticipation raced through her, heating the blood in her veins and making her heart pound.

"I think that instead of trying to be other than we are to

please each other, let us try to simply enjoy the things that please us together."

He tugged his shirt off in one move and his braies fell with another tug. This time he did not hide his body or his erect manhood from her sight. Simon simply stood there at the side of the bed and let her look her fill—as he did just moments later after easing her gown from her. Her body warmed, and that place between her legs grew moist and ready to accept him. Climbing to her knees on the bed in front of him, Elise reached out and ran her hands down from his shoulders over his broad, muscled chest, through the curls there and down as they made a path below his waist to his cock.

She knew he waited for her to grasp it, but she skimmed over it, much as he had when touching the hair on her mons, and slid her hands down his thighs and then back up again. Such strength, such power, she felt it ripple beneath her hands and wondered when his control would break again. Elise moved closer to him, bringing them in contact from chest to hips, enjoying the searing heat of his skin and the pulsing of his manhood between them.

Then it was his turn. Simon pulled her into his embrace, kissing her, plundering her mouth with his tongue, slipping it in and tasting hers, teasing it until she finally followed his lead and did the same, thrusting her tongue into his mouth. He suckled it gently and noticed that she moved even closer to him when he did that.

Lifting her off the bed, he wrapped her legs around his waist, allowing her to slide along his prick without entering her. Oh, no, he would make this time about her pleasure before releasing himself inside her. Elise gasped at the contact and then gasped again as he sat on the bed. He knew that having her like this opened her to his touch and he saw that she was beginning to realize it herself. Once he was leaning against the headboard of the bed, his hands were free to touch her.

"Does this please you, wife?" he asked as he stroked her breasts with his hands, cupping them and rubbing his thumbs over the nipples until they tightened.

"Aye, husband." She sighed, arching into his grasp.

Simon leaned forward then, taking one nipple into his mouth, sucking on it, teasing it with his tongue and lips and then tugging it gently with his teeth. She gasped at each touch of his tongue, each nip of his teeth, and probably did not even realize that she slid herself up and back on his hard length as he aroused her.

"And this," he said, sliding his hand down between them and stroking those sensitive folds between her legs. "Does this please you, wife?"

Not waiting for a response, he licked and tasted the other breast while still teasing the slick, tight passage of her with his fingers. Her body opened to him and swelled beneath his hand and beneath his mouth, giving him all the answers he needed. She pulled his head against her breasts, tangled her hands in his hair to hold him close and moaned.

"Aye, husband," echoed through their chambers and she gasped as the pleasure overwhelmed her.

Her body convulsed and shuddered on his hand and against his mouth, but this time he waited for her to gain its full measure before offering himself to her.

"Take me, lady. Take me now," he begged as he lifted her higher and showed her how to take control of him.

And she did.

It took her but moments to learn the way of it, and soon she was riding his cock, moving her hips and moaning with each slide up or settling down. Or mayhap it was him moaning as he guided her along his hardened member, losing himself in her tightness and in the pleasure he saw on her face this time. Or mayhap it was both of them, for just as he tightened and his seed began to spill, she leaned her head back and cried out another release. Simon held her still, as deep inside of her as he could be, and touched the small bud within her folds that made her entire body shudder another time.

It took moments or hours before their bodies calmed, neither one wanting to break the connection between them. Elise slumped forward against his chest, panting and sweating until both of their hearts had slowed, and he held her there. When they were no longer joined, she raised her head and gazed at him.

And her gaze filled with wonderment and something that looked like love to him. But could such a feminine, demure lady such as she ever love a brutish ruffian such as he?

"Did I please you, Simon?"

He captured her face between his hands and brought her close for a kiss. This time it was a tender one, filled with the hope that she could return his love someday.

"Aye, Elise. I am well-pleased."

She smiled at him, and he was filled with warmth and possibilities. "As am I, Simon," she said.

Simon slid them down onto the bed and pulled the coverings over them. The birds of night began singing their tunes, heralding the coming darkness. He gathered her hair in his hand and smoothed it away from her face. They still had the whole of the night ahead of them to explore their newly found passion and that thought made him smile.

Much later they grew tired of their exertions and Simon could feel himself drifting off to sleep, content to hold Elise in his arms for now. And he would have slept if not for her words.

"You said you would give me anything I wanted because I welcomed your friends to your table. Did you mean to promise such a thing?" He stroked her hair over her shoulder and down her back, enjoying the silky softness of her skin beneath his fingers. Even more, he took great pleasure that she seemed content to allow him such caresses.

"Aye, I did. And if it is in my power to grant your wish, I will do so, wife."

She leaned up on her elbows, exposing her exquisite breasts to his sight. "May I ask for three things?"

Startled by that, he tucked his hands behind his head, watching her and waiting to hear her requests. "You may ask."

"First, will you tell me how those men became your friends? I would know more about the three who hold such importance to you."

He did not expect her to ask such a thing. And it pleased him deeply, even as much as her initial welcome of Giles, Brice and Soren. He nodded. "I will tell you the whole and sordid story, if you so wish. But let us speak of them in the morning."

"Good!" she exclaimed. "My next request is something more personal." Elise explained, "Now that I have felt this passion that can exist between a man and a woman, the thought that the husband I love would enjoy such pleasures with another woman grieves me deeply." She paused and took a breath. "Would you share only my bed?"

Shocked more by her profession of love than her request that he be faithful only unto her, Simon responded, "About this second request…I told you I have not had any other woman since our betrothal. Now, having you in my bed and in my heart, I want no other."

Elise raised her eyes then and met his gaze, and his heart melted in that moment. If he thought her shy and unable to accept a man such as he—with his rough manners and bulky size—into her heart, the love shining there told him the truth of her feelings. Could it be true? He looked up then, watching her face as she explained more.

"I swear to try to please you, Simon, if you will give me the chance. I will even try—try—" she stuttered, then pushed herself up to sit at his side. She did not seem to notice that the sheets slipped, allowing him to gaze at her nakedness, and he enjoyed every moment of it. She stammered out the rest of her words, and luckily he was still lying down or he would have fallen over.

"I would like to try using my mouth on your privy parts."

Those privy parts leapt to life in spite of their recent exertions and stood waiting for her to try.

"Is that your third request, wife?" he forced out through gritted teeth. Simon was trying to gather his wits, which had escaped when she mentioned loving him, asking him to give up his mistress and offering to please him with her lips all in one conversation.

She nodded, not saying a word. Innocent as she was, Elise had no idea of the extreme pleasure that such attentions could bring. And she obviously had not considered that he could do the same to her.

"I am willing to show you how, Elise. So long, that is, as you let me do the same to you." Her faced colored with the deepest blush he'd ever seen, but he was not finished. "I want to lick and kiss you too, as I did your breasts and your nipples."

The effect on her, and him, was devastating. Now that she'd experience some of it, her body arched without even a touch from him. Much as his cock did at even the thought of her mouth sucking and tasting him like that.

"So, this is something we can both enjoy?" she asked, sliding down next to him and rubbing against his body with hers.

Her words alone nearly unmanned him, but he took several deep breaths before he could answer. "Aye, wife. We could indeed."

And they did.

Epilogue

They remained in their chambers the rest of that night and through most of the next day before Simon ventured out to see how his guests fared. Elise, more embarrassed because their guests would know what had happened between them, remained in their rooms, seeing only her friend Petronilla. Simon went in search of his friends and found them in the training yard.

"From the easy gait and the smile on your face, 'twould seem that all is well between you and your lady?" Giles asked first as they gathered in one corner near the fence.

Simon could not contain his joy and laughed aloud at the question. "Aye, friends," he said with a nod at them. "All is well between my lady and me."

"Did you finally pledge your love to her and accept hers to you?" Soren asked.

"Why would you ask such a thing? Ours is a modern marriage, we have no need to speak of such things," he said, even knowing the truth.

"Come now, Simon. 'Twas clear to any fool with eyes that you two have been falling in love since the day you met her,"

Soren confided. Smacking Simon on the back, he continued, "Why else do you think her fears mattered to you?"

"Why else did you set aside the fair Lady Alianor and ignore all the favors she had to offer?" asked Brice.

"I was so obvious then?" Simon asked.

"Hell, yes," they responded together, joining him in a hearty laugh.

"What are your plans now?" Giles asked.

Turning back to the keep, he spied Elise standing at the windows in their chambers and he waved to her. His body and his heart ached to return to her side, even now when he thought himself sated. "I am going to take her to see my lands in Normandy."

"Will the lady's mother accompany you?" Soren asked, with a sour expression on his face.

"Nay, we thought to leave her here while we traveled," he explained. The three nodded in agreement. "But Elise thought you might come with us."

He'd surprised them; he knew by the silence that it was something they'd not expected. Elise's suggestion, after hearing the story of how they'd become friends in his father's keep, had surprised him as well with her insight and understanding.

Simon turned back to face them. "William is gathering his forces to invade England and claim kingship there. I must stay here, to keep watch on Duke Conan's plans while William is gone. And to tend my lands and my wife." He could not help the smile that he knew covered his face, nor the warmth pulsing through him at just the thought of being with Elise. "But you three could find yourselves with opportunities not available to you now."

"Follow Duke William into war?" asked Giles.

"War can be the great leveler of men, Giles. On a battle-field, blood does not matter. Only skill and determination do."

"But we are sworn to your service, Simon," Brice said.

"Ah, but I will owe the duke scutage for my holdings there. I must either pay or provide men to fight for him."

"We must think on this and discuss it more before we reach Normandy," Giles suggested.

"Then you will come with us?" Simon asked.

Looking to the others first before replying, Brice nodded and said, "Aye, my lord. We will accompany you and your lady to your lands in Normandy."

Simon shook their hands and turned to leave.

"Would you not like to train with us, Simon?" Soren called out to him. "We should begin now if we are planning to go to war."

Simon did not stop, for he had better things to do that day than bash them into the ground. Without missing a step, he called out his response to them as he watched Elise step back from the windows to prepare for his return.

"I fear that my wife needs additional wooing and I must see to it anon."

Silence reigned for a few moments and then his friends broke out in a raucous laughter. He could only imagine the bawdy comments they were making between themselves.

But Simon could only think of the woman in his bed and in his heart—and how much wooing he could accomplish before they left for Normandy.

* * * * *

THE UNLACING OF
MISS LEIGH

Diane Gaston

Author Note

There is something about a hero who feels too damaged to be loved that always tugs at my heart. Such a hero needs a heroine who sees below the surface to the man underneath. Is that not what we all want? To be loved for the person we are at our very core?

I hope you enjoy "The Unlacing of Miss Leigh," my unabashed homage to *The Phantom of the Opera* and all Beauty and the Beast stories. This tale is linked to my story "Justine and the Noble Viscount" in the anthology *The Diamonds of Welbourne Manor.*

To Patty Suchy, who always told me I'd love
the movie *The Phantom of the Opera.*
She was s-o-o-o-o-o right!

Chapter 1

London, June, 1812

A thousand lamps blazed in the elms. Colonnades, fountains, cascades and porticos, while throngs of people of all sorts made up this night of masquerade in Vauxhall Gardens.

Amid this wonder, Margaret Leigh's heart raced. She was here to meet a gentleman, a man who would pay for her company.

"Are you certain you wish to do this, Maggie?" Her cousin's brow furrowed. "It is not at all proper."

She slanted him an amused look. "You are one to speak of propriety."

Henry had long been the scourge of the family. A schoolmaster's son and a vicar's nephew, Henry ran off to join a theater company when he'd barely begun to shave. Now, there was little family left to condemn him, only Margaret and her younger brother.

Henry nodded and waved a hand. "To the devil with propriety, anyway. Life is too short not to seek enjoyment where we can."

Margaret released a nervous breath. "Well, I cannot afford either enjoyment or propriety at the moment."

Henry pursed his lips in sympathy. Wearing horns on his head and tight-fitting green trousers and coat, his expression looked nothing more than comical.

Margaret stifled a laugh.

Henry was dressed as Puck in a costume from Covent Garden Theatre where he performed small parts. For Margaret, he had borrowed a fairy costume—a gown of palest blush, its skirts fashioned from so many layers of silk net that she seemed to float as she walked. It was quite the most beautiful gown she'd ever worn.

"Here we are." Henry stopped at the supper boxes along the South Walk.

Margaret, an impoverished vicar's daughter, and her cousin Henry, an actor of no renown, were to be guests of the Duke of Manning. For the festivities, the duke had engaged several boxes joined together, decorated with flowers and swags of colorful silks. Already, the boxes seemed filled with people. Most of the gentlemen wore black dominoes, but the women wore a variety of costumes, from rustic milkmaids' frocks to elaborate Egyptian princesses' gowns. The gentleman had arranged his rendezvous with Margaret to take place among the friends of the duke.

Margaret gave Henry a rueful smile. "If our parents could see us now."

Her cousin laughed. "I envision them collectively rolling over in their graves. I can almost hear your father." He made a dramatic gesture as if preaching from a pulpit. *"...I have written unto you not to keep company, if any man that is called a brother be a fornicator..."*

Tears pricked at Margaret's eyes. "You sound just like him."

Henry sobered. "My talent for mimicry."

Margaret's father had passed away of a sudden apoplexy not two months earlier and grief still overcame her at unforeseen moments. He'd been the last of that generation. They were orphans now, Margaret thought.

Henry's sympathetic look returned, but he quickly smiled and punched her on the arm. "I daresay your father would consider the Duke of Manning improper company for you."

"And his friend." The gentleman she was to meet.

The notorious Duke of Manning had run off with the Earl of Linwall's wife, set up housekeeping with her, and sired several children by her—the Fitzmanning Miscellany, the society gossips called them. In the supper box, the duke and his lady were easy to recognize, greeting their guests, both dressed in white wigs and colorful brocades that were fashionable decades ago.

Margaret turned back to Henry. "For a man and woman living in sin, they look very happy."

"They do indeed." Henry clasped her arm and stepped forward. "The rewards of impropriety."

They showed their invitation to the footman positioned at the entry to the boxes. As he admitted them, Margaret scanned the gentlemen in black dominoes. *His* would be lined in red, he'd written to her.

She glimpsed no red.

The words in his advertisement in *The Times* came back to her.

Seeking an educated lady of genteel birth for companionship. Gentleman of good fortune offers generous compensation.

Margaret had answered the advertisement. She answered every advertisement for companions or governesses, the most common professions for a woman of her station. None yielded any results. When the gentleman mentioned in the ad sent a footman with a written response, Margaret's hopes surged.

And were immediately dashed.

The companionship the gentleman sought was of a different nature entirely. He sought a mistress.

Behind his rather witty response to her had been a sense of aching loneliness. Margaret wrote back to him, even though it was highly improper to do so. She sent a polite refusal.

He wrote back.

He wrote to her again and again, charming letters of persistent persuasiveness, witty words and despairing loneliness. Each time, she sent back a refusal, but soon the greatest pleasure of her day was seeing his footman arrive at the door with the now-daily letter, then reading its contents.

Eventually, the gentleman proposed a meeting for which he would pay her twenty pounds. He suggested this masked ball at Vauxhall as the location. Twenty pounds was almost as much as she could earn in a year as a lady's companion or governess.

She needed that money quite desperately.

Her cousin led her to a table of refreshments. She picked up a glass of claret in hopes it would settle her nerves.

"It will be an adventure," Henry said.

"An adventure," she repeated under her breath, downing the claret and taking another.

"Good God," cried her cousin. "There is Daphne Blane."

Daphne Blane was the darling of the London stage, a most sought-after leading lady and one who often was seen on the arm of a peer.

"How can you tell?" Margaret saw only a woman in a Grecian costume, with a gold mask covering most of her face.

"There is no mistaking her." Henry put down his glass. "I must greet her. She will be impressed that I am one of the duke's guests."

Without Henry at her side, Margaret's courage flagged. She ought to flee, run down the Grand Walk to where the wherries waited to ferry guests across the river, hop into a hackney coach and return to Henrietta Street.

Instead, she took another fortifying sip of claret and looked for a corner in which to stand.

A young woman dressed as a shepherdess walked up to her. "Do I know you?"

God forbid anyone know her here, else she never would have come.

The masked young woman grimaced. "Oh, dear, that sounded rude, did it not? It is just you are near my age, I think, and if you should be one of my friends, I should be quite ashamed not to know it."

Margaret smiled. "I am certain you do not know me. I am Miss Leigh."

The woman offered her hand. "I am Justine Savard, the duke's daughter."

Savard was not the duke's surname, nor Lady Linwall's. Was Miss Savard the duke's daughter by another woman? Her father *would* roll over in his grave.

Miss Savard returned her smile. "Are you here with someone?"

"I am with my cousin." Margaret inclined her head in Henry's direction. "He is Puck."

"He is your cousin? I wondered who was speaking with Miss Blane." Apparently Henry was not the only one to recognize the famous actress.

Miss Savard glanced around again, then caught herself

and turned back to Margaret. "I fear my manners have quite gone begging." She looked apologetic. "I am expecting someone." Her color rose. "My sweetheart."

Margaret did not know what to say to this obvious confidence. "I hope he arrives soon."

"Oh, so do I." Miss Savard glanced around one more time. "More guests are arriving. Papa's friends. He and Lady Caroline invited everyone, I think. It is a shame his best friend could not attend. Papa and Baron Veall were schoolmates ages ago—"

"Baron Veall." The blood drained from Margaret's face.

"Do you know him?"

"No, I do not," Margaret said too sharply.

Her father's vicarage had been on land owned by Baron Veall, and one year the baron and his family summered in the great house there. Margaret had only encountered the younger son. One time.

She'd never forgotten him.

Miss Savard chattered on, "Well, the baron declined the invitation, but—it is the oddest thing—his son did not."

"His son?" Margaret squeezed the stem of her glass.

"His younger son, the captain."

Margaret's legs trembled.

"I pine to know why he accepted. My father would not tell me, but I had the distinct impression there was some negotiation—something clandestine—and I do love a mystery, as long as I can solve it." She looked thoughtful. "Perhaps it has something to do with Captain Veall's injuries. He was hurt terribly in the Battle of Fuentes de Oñoro a year ago—"

Margaret well knew this. She'd scoured the lists of injured and dead hoping not to find his name.

"He's been somewhat of a recluse ever since. My father called upon him once, but the captain refused to see him. Curious that suddenly he's attending this party." Miss Savard clutched Margaret's arm. "Oh, my goodness. There he is. Not Captain Veall. My sweetheart. I would know him no matter his disguise."

The man who captured her attention wore a simple black domino and looked to Margaret indistinguishable from the others.

"Is he not handsome, my Mr. Kinney?" She gave Margaret an imploring look. "Will you forgive me if I abandon you? I am so eager to see him."

"By all means."

Miss Savard rushed to the man's side.

Margaret lifted her glass to her lips and searched the guests, both hoping and fearing she would see Captain Veall.

She'd been a little girl with hair in plaits and front teeth missing. He'd been a few years older. She had not even given him her name. He would never know her now, even without her mask, but she greatly desired to discover the man he'd become.

Margaret finished her second glass of claret and tried to determine which of the men in black dominoes might be Captain Veall. She walked back to the refreshment table for another claret. The orchestra began to play in the Grove.

Behind her, a man's deep voice spoke. "Miss Leigh?"

She froze, then turned. She'd almost forgotten why she'd come.

The gentleman was tall, so tall he filled her vision. His domino, like his hair, was as black as the night, but he swirled the fabric to show its red lining. His mask, unlike any of the others, covered one side of his face, not just the top half.

She felt robbed of breath. "I am Miss Leigh."

His eyes, a startling blue, appraised her. "I am the gentleman with whom you have corresponded."

"Sir." She curtsied.

Through the eyehole of his mask Margaret could see an angry red scar that the fabric did not entirely cover. Neither did it cover the drooping of one side of his mouth. The unusual mask was meant to cover his scars, she realized.

She lowered her eyes. "What do I call you?" He'd merely signed his letters *A Gentleman*.

"Call me Graham."

Her gaze flew back to his face.

The eyes. She remembered his blue eyes.

That long ago day in the woods when Bob and Hughy Newell threw their sticks and stones at a little girl too small to outrun them, a boy with those blue eyes had come to her rescue. Graham Veall had been her first, nay, her only hero.

"Would you walk with me, Miss Leigh?" His voice seemed to resonate deep in her soul.

It shook her. "You do not wish to stay at the party?"

"I only came for you." He pressed a purse into her hand.

Her payment. She swallowed.

He was letting her know she had already fulfilled their bargain. She could refuse his request if she wished.

But she wanted to be with him. He was Graham Veall.

"My pleasure, sir," she murmured.

His eyes creased at the corners. "Graham."

"Graham," she repeated in a stronger voice.

He led her through the porticos, away from the throngs of people, away from the music. They walked on a gravel path toward trees with fewer lamps and where shadows loomed ahead. Any trepidation Margaret felt about this meeting had vanished. This was Graham Veall walking at her side. She held his arm and savored the warmth of his skin beneath the silk domino.

"I thought it very likely you would not come, Miss Leigh." His voice sounded rusty from disuse.

"I needed the money." No use to pretend otherwise, she thought.

It crossed her mind to tell him of their prior connection, but she was too proud to reveal how poorly her father had provided for her.

His expression turned sympathetic. "Are you so in need of money?"

She lifted the purse. "This will pay to keep my younger brother in school one more year." She could not bear to think beyond that one year.

"It is for your brother?" Graham looked surprised. "How old is he?"

"Fourteen."

"Is his schooling so important?" He sounded incredulous.

Education was Andrew's joy; it was all he lived for. Even before Andrew was out of short coats, his thirst for learning had been evident. They'd been a family of scholars, so Andrew's talent was not surprising. Their grandfather and Henry's father had been schoolmasters. Margaret's parents had run a small boarding school in their home to supplement their father's church living. She and Andrew had always been surrounded by books and lessons and learning.

Until her mother died of influenza and her father could not manage the boarders alone. He'd used every spare penny to send Andrew to a good school, and Margaret had never begrudged the expense.

"My brother has a mind that begs for education. Now I can provide it for him." She squeezed the purse.

Graham touched her arm and the warmth of his touch radiated through her. "I merely was surprised the money was not for yourself."

She returned a steady gaze. "Andrew's schooling is more important."

He tilted his head as if examining her anew.

Threading her arm though his again, he continued their stroll. The paths were now much darker, and from the deep recesses of the shrubbery came sounds of murmuring and laughter. Ever since the Newells had chased her, Margaret had hated walking through woods, but with Graham she would be happy to walk all the way to the hermit who inhabited the farthest reaches of the Gardens.

"Tell me more about your brother," he said.

She complied, telling of Andrew's love of physics, of chemistry and of all things mechanical. Graham asked questions and seemed to listen to her answers. Margaret could almost delude herself that he was a beau, instead of a man who'd paid for her company. Because he was Graham, she wished he was a beau.

As they walked on, two men burst from the shrubbery and stumbled onto the path ahead of them. Margaret jumped back, uttering a cry. Graham wrapped his arms around her and pulled her into the trees, his black domino cloaking them both. The two young men, deep in their cups, staggered by, talking loudly and apparently never noticing them.

Still, Margaret trembled under Graham's embrace.

"I would allow no harm to come to you," he whispered in her ear.

Her trembling came not from feeling again like that little girl clinging to the boy who rescued her, but from an acute awareness that he was a boy no longer. He was a man with a man's needs, and was willing to pay to have those needs met. His arms felt wonderful around her, his strong muscles holding her with such reassuring confidence. Her body was pressed against his, and it seemed that all his power and strength were melding with her.

Her breathing quickened, and sensation flared through her. She felt hungry for more, although she did not know precisely what made her ravenous. She only knew this moment must never end or she would surely perish.

Unfortunately he released her, but slowly, as if as reluctant as she to break the embrace. Still clasping her arms with his strong fingers, he looked down on her, his blue eyes gleaming in the dim light, pleading for something she wanted desperately to give him, but not knowing precisely what it was he desired. He lowered his head and Margaret's excitement grew. She rose onto her toes.

The sounds of more revelers came near. He again enveloped her in his domino. "We will walk back to the supper boxes," he rasped.

Her disappointment was crushing.

They walked in silence, and Margaret searched her mind for a question she could ask him, a question that was not *Why did you release me?*

"Why did you advertise for a mistress?" she finally asked.

She felt him stiffen. "Isn't it obvious?"

Obvious? It was inconceivable that this virile man could not have any woman he wished. He was tall, well-formed, and as darkly handsome as any hero in a Minerva Press novel. What woman would not seek his bed?

"No, it is not obvious."

The path was growing lighter, although their surroundings still seemed leached of color. Only his eyes remained sharply blue. And pained.

He stopped and gestured to his mask. "I am disfigured."

"What could that matter?" She reached up to his mask.

He seized her hand and roughly thrust it aside. "Do not remove it!"

She jerked away, alarmed by his violence.

He lowered himself onto a bench nearby and sunk his head in his hands. Margaret sat next to him and placed the purse in her lap.

She pulled one of his hands into both of hers. "I am sorry."

He straightened, but averted his face.

It was his unhappiness for which she was sorry. Sorry for his shame at his appearance, and so sorry for her foolish boldness.

He glanced at her and away again. "I should not have come." He picked up the purse and gave a dry laugh. "At least you have the money."

"And it will be well spent." She gently squeezed his hand. "On your brother."

She smiled. "On my brother."

He examined her face so intently, it was as if his gaze permeated every part of her. "What else do you want?"

She blinked. "What else?"

His gaze did not waver. "If you could have your heart's desire, I mean. What would you want?"

Her heart pounded. Some hopes were best abandoned, like the hope that he would again put his arms around her.

She said instead, "I should like to send my brother to Cambridge."

He laughed.

She felt wounded. "It is nonsensical, I agree. No lady's companion or governess can afford Cambridge."

"That is not why I laughed. I expected you to want a house or carriage or jewels." He caught her gaze again. "Is there no patron to help your brother?"

"No one." She smiled wanly. "There is only my cousin, but he hardly earns enough to hold himself together. He is an actor. I am staying in the boarding house where he lives, until the actress whose room I'm in returns." A few days from this. "Perhaps you saw my cousin. He is dressed as Puck."

"I did see him," he answered absently. He was silent for a long time before piercing her with another intent gaze. "Miss Leigh, I will send your brother to Cambridge."

She blinked. "Why would you do that?"

He shrugged. "Because I have the wealth to do so."

She did not understand him.

He glanced away and back again. "I will do it. I will pay for Cambridge, but I will also pay you. An annuity for life, if—"

She held her breath.

His eyes bored into her. "If you agree to my original proposition."

Everything around her blurred. "To be your mistress?"

"For at least two months," he added. "Cambridge, an annuity so you will never have to be a lady's companion. All that for two months of your life."

She gaped at him.

"I live very privately. No one will know where you have spent those two months. I give you my word. I will trouble you no further afterward. You will not even know who I am. No one will know. Your reputation will be unsullied."

She must be lost to all propriety, Margaret thought, because it was not her reputation she thought of. She thought only of how short a time two months could be and how very much she owed him already.

He'd saved her life that day when Bob and Hughy were carried away with their mischief. They'd driven her to the ground, their laughter maniacal as their rocks and sticks struck her over and over. Graham had run to her rescue. He'd fought them off. He'd saved her and remained the hero of her heart ever since.

"I will do it," she whispered, thinking now of his arms around her and how his body felt against hers. She made her voice stronger. "I will be your mistress."

Chapter 2

Three days later, Graham Veall tugged at the cuffs of his shirt and tried not to look at his image in the mirror.

"Coward," he said aloud.

He forced his gaze upward.

Even with the mask in place, he looked like a miscreation. He snapped his eyes shut and again heard the sounds of battle, the thundering of horses' hooves, the clang of the Frenchman's sword against his own. Again he smelled the pungent odor of gunpowder, of soldier's sweat, of spilled blood. Again he saw the Frenchman's wild eyes and bared teeth and the sight of the gleaming sword right before it sliced into his face.

Breathing hard, Graham opened his eyes and pressed his palm against his masked cheek. The mask was a cleverly tailored bit of silk and batting that fit snugly against his skin and covered all but a peek of the carnage the Frenchman's sword wrought.

Graham pressed his lips together.

Below stairs a woman waited, a woman any honorable man would send back to London. Any honorable man would forget this insane, impulsive idea that had overtaken him one lonely afternoon.

But he would not send her home.

He might be robbed of a face, but he'd be damned if he'd forego every pleasure in life because of it. He wanted company. He wanted conversation. He wanted to hear a woman laugh, to smell her hair, to feel her bare legs wrapped around his. He wanted the pleasure of plunging into her body, of feeling her release, of spilling his seed inside her.

Even if he must pay for it.

Miss Leigh was more than he'd dared hope. She certainly possessed all the charm her letters promised. Old enough not to be *missish*, obviously intelligent, she'd appeared to have more to converse upon than society gossip from *The Morning Post.* He knew little else of her except that the eyes beneath her mask had been a warm brown and her lips invitingly full. She'd not jumped at the chance to take his money and, in his opinion, her hesitation showed a discernment that gave her credit. But she also had not shirked when he cast out the lure that secured her agreement.

A younger brother in need. Admirable indeed.

This enticement alone would have been sufficient to secure her agreement, he'd have wagered, but adding the annuity assuaged his conscience. The least he could offer a respectable young woman was a comfortable income for life. It would pose him no hardship. He could well afford both Cambridge and an annuity.

While still in leading strings Graham had inherited a vast amount from an uncle who'd made a fortune in the East India Company. Unlike most younger sons, Graham's desire to purchase a commission in His Majesty's army had not been made for financial reasons, but for the vainglorious notion that his country needed *him* to vanquish Napoleon.

Well, he must leave victory to Lord Wellington now. All Graham had done was lose half his face and all of his idyllic future.

He twisted away from the mirror and strode out of his bed-chamber down the stairs to the drawing room where he'd kept Miss Leigh waiting for nearly half an hour.

Through the cracked door, he saw her looking out the window, hands clasped in front of her.

He entered.

She turned and curtsied. "Sir," she said, her voice breathless.

"It is Graham," he corrected, remaining just inside the doorway.

Light from the window illuminated half her face, leaving half in shadow. Nature's cruel mockery, no doubt, of the image he'd just seen in the mirror. Unmasked, she was prettier than he'd imagined. Her eyes were large for her face, and her nose strong. Both seemed perfectly balanced by those lush pink lips. He liked that her hair was the color of nutmeg and that she was taller than most women he knew.

What will it be like to bed a woman as tall as she?

He released a breath. Curse him for thinking such thoughts within moments of their reacquaintance. Even a woman whose company he purchased deserved better.

He glanced around the room. "Did not Coombs bring you tea?"

"Coombs. He was the man who brought me your letters." She gazed at him. "He offered tea. I declined."

Graham took a step forward and gestured to the area near the fireplace "Do sit, Miss Leigh."

She obediently crossed the room and sat on the couch, leaving enough room for him to sit next to her if he so chose. He almost smiled. No, she was not missish, but he sensed she was not entirely at ease either, no matter how much she might wish he'd think so.

He walked over to a cabinet. "Would you prefer something stronger than tea? Sherry, perhaps?"

Her tense mouth seemed to relax. "Yes, thank you. Sherry will do nicely."

Graham poured her sherry and a brandy for himself. Handing her the glass, he chose the nearby chair.

She took a sip. "I did not expect you to be wearing your mask."

By reflex he touched it. "Did you fear I would inflict the horror upon you?"

A tiny line appeared between her eyes. "I thought the mask was merely for the masquerade."

He twirled his brandy glass. "I am in a perpetual masquerade." Downing its contents, he leveled his gaze at her. "The mask remains."

She waved her fingers in a gesture of unconcern and more calmly sipped her drink. "This house seems quite comfortable."

It was a hunting lodge within easy riding distance of London, borrowed from the Duke of Manning with the promise that His Grace would never call. His Grace had only broken the promise once, and Graham surmised his father had sent his friend to check on his welfare.

"It is suitable." He rose and poured himself more brandy. "Have you seen its rooms?"

She shook her head. "Coombs gave me a moment to refresh myself in my bedchamber and then showed me to this room."

He downed his second glass of brandy and extended his hand to her. "Come. I'll give you a tour."

She placed her bare hand in his, skin against skin, and his

body flared in response. By God, he was desperate for a woman. He felt like ravaging her on the drawing room carpet.

His eyes met hers for a moment, and he fancied she'd read his thoughts.

"I will show you the library first." He forced his voice through a suddenly constricted throat. "I added some books I thought you might enjoy."

Her brows rose. "You did? What sort of books?"

He shrugged. "Novels mostly. *The Wild Irish Girl. A Tale of Youth. Self-Control.*"

Her eyelashes fluttered, and amusement tugged at those moist kissable lips. "Oh, dear, where shall I start? With *The Wild Irish Girl*? Perhaps not with *Self-Control.*"

He frowned. "I meant no message. The titles were recommended to me as ones a lady might enjoy."

Her smile wavered. "I was merely jesting."

They entered the library, and he pointed out the new editions.

She ran her finger along one of the shelves. "If I finish the novels, I shall delve into *The Gentleman's Magazine* or *The Sportsman's Dictionary.*"

This time he recognized her humor. "I fear this is a rather masculine residence." He gestured to the door. "Allow me to show you the drawing room. There is a pianoforte there, which might have more feminine appeal."

After a peek at the drawing room, he showed her the dining room and led her down to the kitchen.

As they approached, he heard the banging of pots and pans. "Did you bring a maid with you?"

She laughed. "I have no maid."

"Mrs. Coombs will be available to you, then. She is both cook and housekeeper, so our meals will be simple fare. She and Coombs are the only servants in the house, and their rooms are on this level." In other words, they would have plenty of privacy above stairs.

"I am accustomed to simple fare," she replied. "And to tending to myself."

Mrs. Coombs, busy preparing dinner, greeted Miss Leigh in a friendly tone. "I will be at your service, miss."

Graham appreciated Mrs. Coombs's tolerance of his unusual plan. He'd known her for years and had expected her to have a different view of propriety from a typical London servant.

He explained to Miss Leigh, "Coombs was my batman in the army. Mrs. Coombs followed the drum."

Margaret gave the older woman a respectful look. "How very brave of you, Mrs. Coombs."

"'Twas an adventure, that much I will admit," she answered.

Indeed. Mrs. Coombs had seen things no woman should see, including a man with half his face sliced away.

"I will show you above stairs," he said.

Graham offered his arm and escorted Miss Leigh back to the hall and up another flight of stairs to the bedchambers.

There were four, and some attic rooms above those. He showed her the two smaller bedchambers first, before leading her to the room connected with his.

He stopped by her door. "You have already seen your room. I hope it is to your liking."

She looked into his eyes. "It is perfectly comfortable." Her gaze shifted to the next door.

He walked over and opened it. "This is the room I use."

She merely nodded. Their gazes connected in a moment that stretched far too long, a moment that left him too much time to think carnal thoughts, such as how he might drag her into his bedchamber and urge her to fulfill the implied part of the bargain.

But if bedding had been all he wanted he could have purchased a woman for as many nights as he desired. He'd always found the idea of going to a brothel distasteful, however. He desired so much more than mere physical release.

Graham glanced toward the door to her bedchamber. "Shall I leave you until time for dinner?"

"Leave me?" She sounded surprised. "Here?"

He lowered his brow. "Well, not here if you do not wish it. You may go to any room you desire."

She glanced away as if in thought, then faced him again, looking directly into his eyes. "Then I should like to see your bedchamber."

Chapter 3

Margaret's heart pounded at an alarming rate, although she had no wish to let it show. "Your bedchamber is the only room I have not seen."

He opened the door and extended his hand for her to enter. She crossed in front of him, and that flash of awareness she'd felt at Vauxhall swept through her, fueling her excitement.

His bedchamber was neat and orderly, with few personal items in view. It made her sad that so little of *him* possessed the space. Her eyes riveted on the bed, so neatly made it looked as if he had never slept in it.

"It is the least interesting room in the house," he remarked.

His self-deprecating tone gave her pain. "Perhaps it interests me. I am to spend time with you here, am I not?" Her pert words surprised her, and she finally understood her cousin Henry's choices. To forego propriety and do what one wished was liberating. "That is our bargain, if I understood correctly."

He leaned against the doorjamb, his arms crossed over his chest. "You understood perfectly."

She forced herself to walk over to the bed, where she wrapped her fingers around the mahogany bedpost and leaned her cheek against the cool wood. "I have thought a great deal of this, sir."

He walked toward her. "Call me Graham."

She blinked and averted her gaze. "I seem to have difficulty using your name." She'd always thought of him as Graham, since she'd been a little girl. To speak his name now felt like revealing who she was.

His eyes penetrated as he came closer, so close his scent surrounded her, all soap and bergamot. "Would it help if I called you Margaret?"

She'd signed her name to her letters Miss Margaret Leigh. Her name on his lips felt intimate. "I should like that."

His gaze drifted from her face to the bed.

She gripped the bedpost tighter. "I am not sorry for my decision…Graham. I have no expectation of marriage in my situation, so this may be my only opportunity to—to—" She was not yet so bold that the words came easy. "To bed a man."

He took a step back. "Your only opportunity?"

She felt her face flush and she lowered her head. "Well, I am a vicar's daughter and—"

His voice rose. "A vicar's daughter?"

Her gaze flew back to his face. Had she revealed too much? Would he recall that the vicar that summer had been Reverend Leigh? "He died, so there is no worry."

He scraped a hand through his hair. "Good God. A vicar's daughter and a virgin."

Her brow furrowed. "What did you think I was?"

He shook his head. "I did not think you devoid of experience. I did not expect a virginal vicar's daughter to accept my proposition."

She felt her cheeks burn. "Why does this matter to you?"

His eyes flashed. "Do you think I wish to deflower a vicar's daughter?"

He might as well have torn Andrew's academic gown off his back, but even worse, he dashed her hopes, her romantic dreams.

She placed her hands on her hips. "I have no idea whom you wish to deflower, but if you had such specific requirements, you should have listed them in your advertisement." She pretended to read. *"Seeking an educated lady of genteel birth for companionship. No virgins or vicar's daughters need apply."*

"Very humorous." His face, the half of it she could see, had turned red and his voice was angry. "This changes everything."

She advanced on him. "Why? Why does this change everything? Am I not still the woman who would share your bed so her brother might have a bright future? How has being a virgin and a vicar's daughter changed me?"

He leaned down to her, his face only inches from hers. Even in the emotion of the moment, she glimpsed the scarring visible from a gap in his mask and even through her fury, her heart lurched. She wanted to soothe his injured cheek.

She wanted to slap him across the other one. She was shaking with anger, but very much alive.

With an audible release of breath, he moved away and turned his back to her.

She pressed her fingers against her temple. "I ask only that I might stay the night." The emotion was drained from her voice. "The room in my cousin's boarding house is no longer available to me. I must make other arrangements." She'd already sent the money given her at Vauxhall to Andrew's school. She had precious little coin left.

He spun around to face her. "Do you think I would toss you out in the street?"

"You advertise for a mistress, do you not?" She glared at him. "How do I know what else you might do?"

He took a menacing step forward, but she stood her ground. At least she would not let him see how desolated she felt.

He was so close she felt the warmth of his breath on her face. He placed his fingers on the tender skin of her neck, his thumb caressing. "A test, Margaret." His voice dropped to a whisper.

He slowly brought his lips to hers in a gentle kiss, then his arms wrapped around her and the kiss deepened into something more, something unexpected. Her mouth parted in surprise and he took advantage. She felt his tongue against hers and suddenly she was crushed against him, his hands now at her hips pressing him against her.

She wound her arms around his neck and slipped her fingers through his hair. She'd never known a kiss could feel like this, so all-consuming, so glorious.

He widened his stance and held her even closer. His hands moved over her back, her waist and, wantonly, her derriere. She sighed. Her fingers played in his hair and caressed his neck. His lips broke away and then captured hers again every bit as hungrily. She did not wish him to break off this kiss. She put her hands on both sides of his face to hold him there.

He pushed her away, looking as alarmed as she felt.

"Did I hurt you?" she asked.

He was breathing hard. "I dislike being touched on my face."

He had not minded where her fingers touched him otherwise.

He took another step away from her. "You needn't dress for dinner, unless you desire it."

The change of subject was jarring. "Am I to stay for dinner?"

His blue eyes seemed to pierce into her again. "For dinner

and more. You have convinced me that this arrangement may indeed suit us both."

Her irritation fled. "The kiss was the test?"

"Yes." His gaze was warm.

Dinner was a pleasant affair, more pleasant than any meal Graham could recall since he'd returned from Portugal. Those first dinners with his family were ones of pitying glances and oversolicitousness. They'd nearly driven him mad.

In spite of his abominable behavior earlier, Margaret conversed easily, with apparently a great deal less discomfort than his own. She displayed a curious mind and a brave one. She asked him if he had been in the war in Portugal, a backhanded way of asking how he'd been injured, no doubt. No one else had dared ask about Portugal.

He avoided speaking of the battle, confining his discourse to the people, the land, the architecture. Before he knew it, Coombs had brought in dishes of strawberries and cream for dessert.

When Coombs returned to remove this final course, Graham told him, "We will have tea in the drawing room." He stood, but looked down on Margaret. "If that pleases you."

"Of course." She took the hand he extended to her.

The warmth of her skin threatened to unleash the passion he so carefully kept at bay. The sky outside was only beginning to fade into dusk. Alone, he might have sat in the library with a bottle of brandy waiting for darkness to fall, but he could not merely drink his way to bedtime while she watched.

They entered the drawing room where the sofa and chairs were so cozily placed that knees could touch. She chose the sofa; Graham, a chair. He did not trust himself next to her.

Coombs entered with the tea tray, and when he left, Margaret poured.

She handed Graham a cup. "How long have you stayed at this house?"

He'd spent about three months at the family's estate, first feverish and in bed, later driven to distraction by his mother and sisters fawning over him, and his father and brother laboring to cheer him up. None of them had been able to look him in the face, even though he kept his disfigurement covered.

"About nine months," he replied.

"Nine months!" Her eyes widened. "That is a long time. Have you been alone all that time?"

"With Coombs and his wife."

She shook her head in disbelief. "That is a long time to remain in such solitude."

He gave a wry smile. "Hence my hatching of the plot to solicit companionship."

She nodded. "I quite see now. You were lonely."

His laugh was mirthless. "That is wrapping it in a pretty package." He sipped his tea and searched for something besides his loneliness to discuss. "The letters I received were quite diverting."

She lowered her eyes, showing long, thick lashes. "Was I the only one to think you were seeking a lady's companion?"

"The only one." Hers had also been the only letter that had not overtly addressed both seduction and remuneration, the only letter that piqued his interest.

She looked thoughtful.

He gazed at her. "I could not resist clarifying the matter for you. To my surprise, you wrote again."

Sympathy seemed to pass through her eyes, gone so fast he was uncertain he'd seen it. He finished his tea and pined for brandy. "I am afraid your refusals only increased my determination."

She smiled. "Until you discovered what would win me."

He glanced away. He had exploited her unselfish spirit.

She leaned forward and put her hand on his knee. "Do not be cross. As I said before, I do not regret my decision."

Her touch roused thoughts of sharing her bed and the delights they could create beneath the covers.

She put her hand back in her lap. "Even a spinster wishes to experience life."

"A spinster?" It seemed the wrong term to describe her, especially when his body ached for her.

She blushed. "I am three and twenty and have no prospects for marriage. As I said, this might be my only chance."

Graham slanted a glance toward her. "Are you certain you are a vicar's daughter?"

She laughed. "Yes. I am afraid I am."

"There is something of this that makes no sense." Mere curiosity did not explain it, nor sacrifice for a brother.

She looked down at her tea.

There was something she was not telling him, he was certain of it.

"Shall I play the pianoforte for you?" she asked.

"Only if you wish to." He thought of pressing her for the whole truth. He, however, had no intention of explaining himself to her. He would not tell her he was the younger son of Baron Veall, nor what his regiment had been, nor how his face had been slashed nor how he'd almost died of fever. Better they not truly know each other. Better that this interlude feel like a dream, allowed to fade upon wakening.

She cleared her throat. "Shall I read to you?"

"No." His mind could not attend a book.

She glanced away and back. "Would you desire to play cards?"

"No, please." He could not concentrate on cards. His mind was filled with thoughts of bedding her.

She averted her gaze again and sipped her tea. The silence between them stretched on.

He forced himself to speak. "Forgive me." He could not tell her what consumed him—the thought of undressing her, of running his hands along her bare skin, of plunging inside her and at last feeling release. "I am unused to entertaining."

"I thought I was to entertain you." She peered at him. "What did you do in the evenings when you were alone?"

Besides drink? he wanted to say. "I sometimes took walks outside. When it became dark, that is."

"You walked in the dark?" Her lovely brown eyes widened.

He frowned. "I do not go out in daylight."

"For fear you will be seen?" She put down her teacup. "That is nonsensical, Graham. Is it not an injury you have, nothing more? It cannot be so dreadful that you must hide in the dark."

"I will not speak about my injury," he said through clenched teeth.

"I am persuaded that you ought to talk about it, Graham," she spoke earnestly. "You have altered your whole life around it."

"Out of necessity," he snapped. "Do not presume to advise me on what you know nothing about."

Her eyes were full of concern. "I want to know of it, Graham," she said in a quiet voice.

He stiffened. "You want me to remove my mask."

She nodded. "How else am I to understand?"

"I do not require your understanding," he roared. "I will not show you the monster beneath the mask. There will be no display of horror here, and if you intend to harp upon this subject, you may return to London in the morning." He stood.

"Play the pianoforte. Read. Do as you wish. I am retiring for the night."

Graham stormed out of the room without looking back. He did not head for his bedchamber, however. Instead, he strode to the door at the rear of the lodge and out into the cool evening air. It was not quite dark, but he hardly cared who saw him.

Except the young woman standing at the drawing room window watching his retreat.

Chapter 4

Graham walked until he returned to his senses. By that time, night had fallen and only a sliver of a moon lit his path back to the lodge.

His disfigurement set him apart from other people. He well knew that, but he ought not to have vented his spleen at Margaret. She had never heard the gasps of horror when people saw his face. She'd never seen the disgust on their faces and how they quickly turned away. Graham could not bear for Margaret to turn away.

He groaned. This cabbage-headed plan of his to alleviate the dreariness of his life was nothing more than a sordid manipulation. He wanted her in bed and he'd figured out what to offer her that she could not refuse. How dishonorable of him.

Setting his chin, he resolved to give Margaret the funds for Cambridge and the annuity, then set her free.

Such altruism did not lift his foul mood as he walked back in the house and up the stairs to his bedchamber.

He closed the door, peeled off his coat and kicked off his shoes and stockings. Coombs had turned down the bed and left a lamp burning. Graham caught his image in the mirror as he untied the lacings of his mask and pulled it off so he could splash cool water on his face.

He'd just put the towel down when the door opened. Clapping his hand over his scars, he spun around.

Margaret stood in the doorway that connected their two rooms, looking like an angel come to earth in her white muslin nightdress with her hair loose about her shoulders.

He turned away from her and grabbed his mask. As he fumbled for the laces, he heard the swish of her skirts and felt her fingers take the laces and tie them.

"Have I positioned it correctly?" she asked.

He adjusted it. "Yes." He turned to her more slowly. "You did not have to come. I will require nothing of you, Margaret."

She looked up at him. "I had to apologize once more." She lifted her fingers to his mask, but lowered them again. "It is your right to hide beneath your mask if you wish."

He checked the laces to make certain they were tight enough.

She licked her lips, and he felt desire pulse through him once more. It must have taken a great deal of boldness for a virginal vicar's daughter to agree to bed a disfigured stranger.

"I came here to make you happy," she said. "Not to cause you distress." The rapid rise and fall of her chest, distracting in itself, suggested she was not as calm as she sounded. She touched the cloth of his shirtsleeve, and he felt it as if she'd caressed his skin. "May we not simply…proceed?"

He gazed down at her inviting lips. "Are you certain of this?"

"Yes," she breathed.

"Do you know how to take care of yourself? To prevent a child?" He would not compound the cost to her by creating this complication.

She lowered her head. "The actresses in my cousin's boarding house taught me what to do."

He still hesitated.

She took a step back and untied the ribbons of her night-dress. She pushed the white fabric over her shoulders and let the gown slip down her body to the floor. His gaze wandered over her, slow and savoring. Her skin glowed like candlelight on silk. From her luxuriantly full breasts to her narrow waist and long slim legs, she reminded Graham of the painting he'd seen in Florence when on his grand tour.

Venus Rising from the Sea.

He gazed into her face, and her eyes pleaded. "Do I please you, Graham?"

"You please me," he said, his voice so low he hoped she'd heard.

Her eyes darkened, and she stepped forward to undo his shirt's buttons and lift it over his head. Her eyes flickered with pain when she saw the marks on his chest, more of the French-man's handiwork.

"As you can see," he rasped. "I am not pleasing."

She glanced into his eyes. "You must have been terribly injured."

He stroked her unmarked cheek. "Not enough to kill me."

He'd often cursed the fate that spared him, but at this moment he was glad to be alive, to be with her.

He lifted her into his arms and carried her to the bed, his muscles trembling, not with the effort, but with a struggle for restraint.

He laid her carefully on the bed and climbed in beside her. "I will be gentle with you, Margaret. I promise you."

She smiled and combed his hair with her fingers. "You said you would allow no harm to come to me."

His words at Vauxhall. "I meant it."

He pulled her towards him, kissing her with all the pent-up need inside him. She melted into him, putting her arms around him, holding him against her. His hand slid down her back and her skin was as smoothly perfect as he'd anticipated.

His arousal pressed painfully against his trousers. He reached down to unbutton them. She helped him pull them off, his drawers with them. He saw her gaze at his male organ, so hard with desire, he felt as if he would burst. She did not shy away, and it made him inexplicably proud of her. She had more courage than he. She'd had the courage to enter his room.

He was determined to take her slowly, to make this first time one of pleasure for her, not pain.

"This is new to me," she whispered.

"You make it feel new to me as well," he murmured back.

His lips captured hers again. He stroked her gently with his fingertips, fearing that contact with his whole hand might loosen the binds he kept tight on his passion. She gasped as his fingers explored her breasts, and he gently rubbed their tips over her nipples. Then his fingers slid down to between her legs.

"I will make you ready," he murmured to her.

"Yes," she responded, her voice thick.

She was warm and moist for his touch, and his fingers easily eased inside her. A low moan escaped her lips, and she arched her back, but never pulled away.

There was a pounding in his head that told him to simply mount her and seek his release, but he fought it and focused on pleasuring her, determined she should not regret the decision she had made to come to him.

Margaret gasped at the sensations his fingers created. She knew so little of lovemaking; she'd never imagined a man could touch her so and bring such exquisite pleasure. The sensations grew more intense—not painful, but something akin to demanding.

She clasped his hand, stilling it. "Wait, Graham."

He withdrew his fingers. "Did I hurt you?"

She shook her head. "Not hurt. Not precisely. I—I do not know how to explain."

He held her close. "No need to explain."

She wished she could put it into words, but it was all so new, so profound. One thing she knew, she needed his arms around her at this moment, needed to calm herself, to assimilate the experience.

"Do you wish me to stop?" he asked.

She could tell he was trying to keep his tone mild. "No, do not stop." She thought she might perish if she did not have the yearning growing inside her fulfilled.

He lay on his side, the masked part of his face pressed against the bed linens. She could almost envision how he might have appeared without the injury. His dark good looks took on a rakish appearance with the shadow of a beard on his face. Lifting a finger, she drew it from his cheek to his chin, careful not to touch the mask, lest he become angry again.

He lay still while she explored the contours of his muscles with eager fingers. She slid her hand over his shoulders and down his chest, thrilling at the feel of his skin, the wiry hair that peppered his chest. The scars beneath her fingers made her wish to weep. Battle must be a terrible thing to so mar his body. She felt his muscles tense as she traced the scars. She did not want to distress him.

She moved her hand lower, wondering if she dared touch the male part of him.

She dared.

He groaned when her fingers closed around him.

The actresses had explained how a man's male member

grew hard when desire overtook him. Margaret felt a surge of power knowing she had caused his arousal.

His own hand closed around hers and she felt as if she'd made another misstep, but he said, "My turn now."

He touched her body like she'd touched his, this time caressing her with a firm touch, not mere fingertips. He eased her onto her back and rose above her, both hands kneading her breasts.

The sensation shot all the way to the apex of her legs and she heard an urgent cry escape her lips. The need she did not quite understand grew stronger. Then he did something equally as wondrous. He placed his lips upon her nipple and tasted it with his warm tongue.

Her back arched and she dug her fingers into his skin.

She'd had no idea a man would want to do such a thing, nor want to touch her so intimately. She wanted to cry out with joy, so glad she'd given herself this chance to be loved by Graham, even if only temporarily. The memory of his touch— his tongue—would last for a lifetime.

"I think it is time, Margaret."

She would also remember the sound of her name on his lips.

"Yes." She almost laughed, more than ready for the grandest mystery of all.

He gently spread her legs. With a mixture of fear and need, she forced herself to relax. He began to ease himself inside her, stopping suddenly to whisper in her ear, "This may give you some pain."

He pushed, one hard thrust that made it seem like something tore open inside her. She felt a sharp pain and cried out.

He held her in his arms. "I am sorry."

She stopped him from withdrawing, pressing her hands against his buttocks. "Don't stop."

It seemed all the permission he needed. He began a rhythm with which her body seemed already familiar, meeting his every thrust, growing her excitement until she could not think. She was lost in the sensation, in the pleasure, in the delicious need. She heard their excited breaths, felt their bodies moving against each other. She saw him above her, as lost in the moment as she. They were joined. They were one, sharing the need and sensation and pleasure. It was exhilarating. It was unforgettable.

Faster and faster they moved, until something changed for both of them; she could feel it. Pleasure burst through her, waves and waves of pleasure that washed over her. His muscles tensed, and she realized he'd spilled his seed.

Coming down from the intensity of that shared moment reminded Margaret of a feather floating to earth, slow and languorous.

Graham slid from her. The break from their joining was jarring, a loss from which she could not imagine recovering. Unbidden tears rolled down her cheeks.

He rose on one elbow. "By God, I did hurt you."

She shook her head. How was she to explain it to him, all that she felt, all that seemed now altered inside her? "I am not hurt. Far from it—" She squeezed her eyes closed for a moment, before gazing back at him, so handsome, even if half shrouded. "I did not expect it to feel like that."

She was no longer merely Margaret, because he was now a part of her. Two become one.

He stroked a stray lock of hair off her face. "I swear I will make it better for you next time."

She snuggled next to him, laying her head against his heart. "You cannot possibly make it better."

He held her tight. "There was pain, I know it. There will not be pain again."

The pain had been fleeting. It marked the moment of change in her. She was forever altered, forever a part of him. "It was a mere trifle."

He stroked her hair again and looked so concerned that she searched for a way to reassure him that to worry was misguided. Celebration seemed more in order.

He rose from the bed and walked over to the tallboy that held his washbasin and pitcher. He poured some clean water on a cloth and brought it over to her.

"The linens can be laundered," he said. "There will be fresh ones tomorrow."

She clasped his hand and pulled him back on the bed so that she was underneath him again. "Do not bring me too much reality," she whispered. "I want nothing to spoil this lovely dream."

She reached up to kiss him, and soon the dream was alive again and the changes inside her were etched even deeper.

Chapter 5

The dream lasted into the morning and through the next days and weeks. Margaret tried not to think that it would come to an end when the two months were done.

Their nights were filled with loving. Margaret had not believed anything could bring more pleasure and happiness than that first coupling, but each night Graham proved her wrong. He was a generous lover, this hero of her childhood, this man she adored.

Their daylight hours were an idyll of another sort, consisting of long conversation, of reading to each other, playing savage games of piquet, or singing the silliest songs they could think of, while she played the pianoforte.

They took long walks. She'd even coaxed him out into the sunshine and fresh air. They walked through the garden and the wooded area nearby. The rare person they encountered took Graham's appearance in their stride, probably hearing of his injuries and mask and not being surprised by them. He was not as fearsome as he thought; Margaret was pleased she'd been right about that.

A crack in the fragile shell of their dream-like existence

occurred when Graham's man of business called with the papers that set up a trust to pay her brother's expenses to Cambridge and her annuity. She'd gasped at the amount Graham had given her. She would be able to live in comfort wherever she wished. Neither the trust nor the annuity could be rescinded, even if Graham changed his mind. Andrew's education and her future were secure.

Seeing the papers, however, reminded Margaret that the bargain she'd made with Graham was for a period of two months. And the end was rapidly approaching. The thought cast her in the dismals the whole day, and she could not explain her mood to Graham.

On the morning after the man of business had called, Margaret woke at dawn with a very unsettled stomach. Not wanting to rouse Graham, she slipped out of bed, wrapped herself in a robe, and made her way down to the kitchen where the indefatigable Mrs. Coombs was already busy preparing breakfast. The smells, usually intoxicating, made her retch.

"You are up early, miss," Mrs. Coombs said cheerily.

"Will you check if I am feverish?" Margaret asked. "I feel unwell."

Mrs. Coombs placed her palm against Margaret's forehead and then against her neck. "No fever. What is troubling you?"

"I feel nauseous."

Mrs. Coombs's brows rose. "Indeed?" She lowered them again to peer at Margaret. "Tell me, miss. When did you last have your courses?"

Margaret's mouth dropped open in sudden understanding. "Before I came here."

"I suspected as much." The woman crossed her arms over her chest. "I'd say you are not ill."

She blinked. "I am not ill." Warmth spread throughout her and she pressed her hand to her belly. "I am with child."

"My guess," said Mrs. Coombs.

Margaret hugged the idea around herself. "A child," she whispered. She shook her head. "No, it is impossible. I was taught how to prevent it."

Mrs. Coombs leveled a look at her. "There's no preventing a baby that wants to be born."

"A child," she whispered again. *Graham's child.* What could be more wonderful? A child to watch grow. A child to love, to help against the desolate loneliness of losing Graham.

Mrs. Coombs cut her a slice of bread. "Here. Eat this. It helps to have something in your stomach. Chew it slowly."

Margaret chewed very slowly. "I feel better," she said as she finished the bread. Indeed, she felt joyous. "Thank you so much."

Mrs. Coombs nodded in satisfaction and turned back to her work.

Margaret paused before walking out the door. "Mrs. Coombs, do not tell Graham of this."

The older woman looked up. "I do not keep secrets from him."

Margaret walked over to her. "Please, I beg you. Do not say a word to him of this. It—it is my news to tell." *Or not tell.*

Mrs. Coombs put her hands on her hips. "Very well. I'll not volunteer a word." She shook a finger at Margaret. "But if he asks me, I'll not lie to him."

"That is enough." Margaret gave the woman a hug. "Thank you." She again started for the door.

Mrs. Coombs called after her. "I'll leave a tin of biscuits in your bedchamber. Let me know if that does not do the trick."

Margaret smiled. "You are an angel."

Keeping the secret was not as easy for Margaret as she supposed it would be. She tried to hide her queasiness and her sheer preoccupation with the fact that Graham's child was growing inside her. She was quieter, and the change in her took away some of the ease between her and Graham.

This morning, Margaret had been fighting nausea when Graham reached for her to make love with her as he had so many mornings before.

He broke off abruptly. "What is this, Margaret?"

She sat up. "I do not know what you mean."

"Do not play the innocent with me." He pulled on his shirt. "Something has changed."

She seized his hand and held it against her cheek. "Nothing has changed, Graham. I—I merely feel a little unwell this morning and I did not wish to trouble you."

"Unwell?" He felt her forehead.

"Not feverish," she said. "Unwell."

He gave her an intent gaze. "Have you felt unwell the last few days?"

She could not meet his eye. "A little."

"Then why not tell me before?"

"I did not wish to ruin things."

He took his hand away. "Hiding it was meant to improve matters?"

A child had not been part of the bargain he'd made with her. She was afraid to tell him of it.

"Graham, I have felt a bit queasy in the stomach. I presume it came from something I ate."

He peered at her. "Queasy in the stomach."

She made herself return his gaze. "It is nothing."

He gave her a skeptical look and turned away to dress. She watched him remove his mask, his back carefully to her and the mirror angled so his reflection did not show. After washing and shaving, the mask went back in place and he put on his clothes, all the while avoiding looking at her or speaking to her.

Margaret held her breath as a wave of nausea hit her. At the moment, all she could think of was her tin of biscuits. She found her nightdress and crossed the room to her bedchamber and the bed she never used.

And her tin of biscuits.

He appeared in her doorway. "I'll be down in the dining room."

She quickly hid the tin. "Will you tie my stays first?" It was the one part of dressing she was unable to do on her own and it had been part of their morning ritual for him to help her.

Unlike other days, he did not enter her room. Instead he remained in the doorway as she hurriedly put on a clean shift. She stepped into her stays and positioned the garment, then she walked over and presented her back to him.

When he'd performed this little task for her before, it had been a lovely, intimate moment between them. Not this day. His hands were efficient at tightening the laces, but there were no lingering caresses, no murmured words in her ear. She felt his fingers tying the laces in a bow, but instead of a fond sweep of her shoulders, he merely stepped away and was gone.

She leaned on the doorjamb as another wave of nausea washed over her—and an encroaching fear that the idyll's end had already arrived.

Graham sat across the table from her, watching her nibble on a piece of toast. His appetite was no better than hers, but that only convinced him that matters had indeed changed between them.

Only two weeks were left of the two months they had agreed upon. He had hoped to ask her to stay longer, but now he wondered if he'd been blind to how things stood between them. Now he felt she might at any moment ask if she could leave early.

He could stand the silence between them no longer. "I have matters to attend to in the library."

He did not wait for her response, but strode out of the dining room to the library, where he drew the curtains to block out the light. He found a bottle of brandy and a glass and sat behind the desk in the dark. He had finished half the bottle before the door opened.

She was silhouetted in the doorway. "What is this, Graham? You are sitting in the dark?" She marched over to the windows and opened the curtains. The sunlight he'd blocked out came flooding back like a triumphant army.

She turned to him and saw the bottle. "You are drinking? It is only nine-thirty in the morning."

He lifted his glass. "In the dark, it might be any hour."

She walked up to the desk and picked up the bottle, measuring how little remained. "This is nonsensical. You are succumbing to a fit of depression merely because I felt a little unwell this morning."

He defiantly drained the contents of his glass. "Do not turn tables on me. You are the changed one, Margaret. You have been different ever since the money I promised you came into your control."

Her chin shot up. "The money? You think I changed because of the money?"

He let his eyes bore into her. "Possibly. I cannot undo it now. The money is yours."

She returned his gaze with a wounded expression that was quite effective. He almost believed in it.

"Oh, Graham." She twisted away from him, walked back

to the window and gazed out on the garden where she had taught him he need not hide in darkness. She turned back to him. "I admit reading the papers and recalling that I would receive money for—for our time together did sober me." Her arm swept the expanse of the nearly floor-to-ceiling window. "It was a bit like opening the curtains. It let the outside world back in, the reality. I did not much like being reminded of it. The money itself was not the cause."

He poured more brandy, not because he wanted it, but because he needed to be numbed. "If not the money, then what has changed you?"

She turned away again.

"You are hiding something from me, Margaret. I am convinced of it."

She looked over her shoulder at him. "Are you the only one who is allowed to hide, Graham?"

He gave a dry laugh. "Me? I have been honest with you from the beginning. Have you been honest with me?"

She swung around to him. "Honest? Perhaps. But you have hidden yourself from me just the same. I am not to know who you are. I am not allowed to see what you look like."

He stood. "Back to my face again, are we? I ought to have known. You will not be satisfied until you unmask me."

She took a deep breath, as if attempting to muster courage. "I will make another bargain with you. Reveal yourself to me, and I will tell you what I have kept hidden."

He met her gaze and held it, like one cat staring down another before lashing out with its claws.

It would serve her right to see him as he really was. She would finally understand the choices he made. There would be no chance she would stay, but he'd always known that.

Without any warning, he pulled off the mask.

He heard her swift intake of breath. Saw her eyes widen. But she did not flinch. She did not turn away. Instead she walked closer to him, so close they were inches apart. She raised her hand and touched the jagged scars that criss-crossed his cheek. With her finger, she traced the scar that caused the drooping of his eye and the one that pulled at the corner of his mouth.

He forced himself to endure her touch. The sunlight was bright enough to illuminate every detail. None of it was hidden from her now.

He braced himself for platitudes. *It is not so bad, Graham. Perhaps the scars will shrink, Graham.*

She was silent.

Finally she stepped back. He realized he was still gripping his mask in his fist. He lifted it to put it back in place.

She seized his hand. "Leave it off, Graham. Sit with me." She led him over to the sofa, also bathed in sunlight.

He did not mind that the light made her skin glow and her hair, worn tied back in a ribbon, shine with gold, but that same light revealed the monster he had become.

She still did not look away from him when she sat with him. She continued to grasp his hand.

"Now my secrets," she whispered.

She told a story of her childhood, of being chased through the woods by two boys, of falling and being pummeled with sticks and stones until another boy came to her rescue.

"By God," he said. "I remember it. It was me. I had my father see that the boys were given a severe dressing down." He gazed at her. "You were that little girl."

She nodded. "I needed you that day and you needed me when we met at Vauxhall. That is why I agreed to your proposition."

"You knew who I was all along? Did someone put you up

to this? The duke?" That he could not tolerate. It bore too close a resemblance to pity.

She squeezed his hand. "Not at all. I discovered by accident that Captain Veall would also be a guest at the party. When you gave me your first name, I knew you were Graham Veall."

He frowned and averted his gaze.

"Do not worry," she said. "I will keep our association as secret as if I never knew you. I give you my word."

He sat back and rubbed his forehead. She had known all along who he was.

His eyes shot open and he leaned towards her. "This is not the cause of your withdrawal from me. You have known this from the beginning."

She glanced away.

He took her chin in his hand and made her face him. "You are hiding something else."

Tears glistened in her brown eyes, making them appear even more luminous. "Oh, Graham," she gasped. "I think I might be carrying a child."

He gaped at her, speech failing him. This he did not expect. A child. *His* child, growing inside her.

"I—I do not know for certain, so I did not want to tell you. You must not be concerned, though, because you have given me more than enough to support a child. And I am happy about it." A tear rolled down her cheek. "Very happy."

She was carrying his child inside her.

She took a shuddering breath. "I did what I was taught to prevent it, but it didn't work. But I am content. This will most probably be my only chance to have a baby, but I need not burden you with any of it."

"Burden me?" he managed to utter. "I am not that sort of monster, Margaret."

"I know you do not want a child. But I do so very much want one. Want *this* one."

He scraped a hand through his hair. "Good God. I did not want to walk outside in the daytime. Or to remove my mask. I've done those things." He took her face in both his hands. "I did not want a woman to love, merely a woman to make love to, but you changed everything."

"I do not understand."

He released her and looked away, covering his scars with his hand. "It is no use. There's no chance. I cannot be a husband. A father. What woman would want to look upon this the rest of her life?" He pointed to his scars. "I'd frighten my own children."

She stared at him. "Graham, what are you saying to me?"

He gazed upon her. "I'm saying if I were not some monstrosity best reserved for a display of oddities, if I had met you before, I would marry you and consider myself the most fortunate of men. I would adore any child you bore."

She gaped. "Are you proposing marriage, Graham?"

He turned away. "How can I propose marriage to you?"

She laughed softly. "Place an advertisement in *The Times. Seeking a once-virginal vicar's daughter for marriage. Gentleman of good character offers happiness and a great deal of pleasure.*"

She touched the mangled side of his face and brought her lips to his.

Epilogue

London, February, 1818

Graham walked in the door of his London town house, shaking the rain from his topcoat. Coombs helped him with the garment and took his hat and gloves.

"Thank you, Coombs." Graham headed up the stairs. As he neared the top step, he pulled off the mask. "Anyone at home?"

"Papa!" came an excited squeal.

A little girl with nutmeg-colored hair and brown eyes ran into the hallway. Behind her was a blue-eyed little boy still in a short coat. "Papa," he cried, mimicking his sister's exact tone.

Graham crouched down to catch them both in his arms, these perfect children of his. His daughter flung her chubby little arms around his neck and kissed his cheek—his scarred cheek.

"I missed you so much, Papa!" she cried.

"I missed you, too," his son said.

He laughed. "I missed you the most." He kissed them both on their smooth, unmarred little faces. Still holding them, he glanced at the doorway to the drawing room.

His wife stood there.

Even after nearly six years, Margaret's beauty still took his breath. Carrying their children, he walked over to her and leaned down for a long lingering kiss that made him wish it were time for the children to be tucked in bed.

As his lips left hers, she whispered. "I missed you the most."

He smiled, but knew she was wrong. Everything worth possessing was here in his arms now. His wife. His son. His daughter. This was life itself.

And he'd almost missed it all.

* * * * *

Harlequin Intrigue top author
Delores Fossen presents
a brand-new series of
breathtaking romantic suspense!
TEXAS MATERNITY: HOSTAGES
The first installment available May 2010:
THE BABY'S GUARDIAN

Shaw cursed and hooked his arm around Sabrina.

Despite the urgency that the deadly gunfire created, he tried to be careful with her, and he took the brunt of the fall when he pulled her to the ground. His shoulder hit hard, but he held on tight to his gun so that it wouldn't be jarred from his hand.

Shaw didn't stop there. He crawled over Sabrina, sheltering her pregnant belly with his body, and he came up ready to return fire.

This was obviously a situation he'd wanted to avoid at all cost. He didn't want his baby in the middle of a fight with these armed fugitives, but when they fired that shot, they'd left him no choice. Now, the trick was to get Sabrina safely out of there.

"Get down," someone on the SWAT team yelled from the roof of the adjacent building.

Shaw did. He dropped lower, covering Sabrina as best he could.

There was another shot, but this one came from a rifleman on the SWAT team. Shaw didn't look up, but he heard the sound of glass being blown apart.

The shots continued, all coming from his men, which

meant it might be time to try to get Sabrina to better cover. Shaw glanced at the front of the building.

So that Sabrina's pregnant belly wouldn't be smashed against the ground, Shaw eased off her and moved her to a sitting position so that her back was against the brick wall. They were close. Too close. And face-to-face.

He found himself staring right into those sea-green eyes.

How will Shaw get Sabrina out?
Follow the daring rescue and the heartbreaking
aftermath in THE BABY'S GUARDIAN
by Delores Fossen,
available May 2010 from Harlequin Intrigue.

Copyright © 2010 by Delores Fossen

Bestselling Harlequin Presents® author

Lynne Graham

introduces

VIRGIN ON HER WEDDING NIGHT

Valente Lorenzatto never forgave Caroline Hales's abandonment of him at the altar. But now he's made millions and claimed his aristocratic Venetian birthright—and he's poised to get his revenge. He'll ruin Caroline's family by buying out their company and throwing them out of their mansion... unless she agrees to give him the wedding night she denied him five years ago....

**Available May 2010
from Harlequin Presents!**

www.eHarlequin.com

HPI2915

Former bad boy Sloan Hawkins is back in Redemption, Oklahoma, to help keep his aunt's cherished garden thriving and to reconnect with the girl he left behind, Annie Markham. But when he discovers his secret child—and that single mother Annie never stopped loving him—he's determined that a wedding will take place in the garden nurtured by faith and love.

Where healing flows...

Look for

The Wedding Garden
by Linda Goodnight

Available May 2010
wherever you buy books.

Steeple
Hill®
LI87595

www.SteepleHill.com

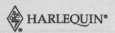
INTRIGUE

BESTSELLING
HARLEQUIN INTRIGUE® AUTHOR

DELORES FOSSEN

PRESENTS AN ALL-NEW
THRILLING TRILOGY

TEXAS MATERNITY: HOSTAGES

When masked gunmen take over the maternity ward at a San Antonio hospital, local cops, FBI and the scared mothers can't figure out any possible motive. Before long, secrets are revealed, and a city that has been on edge since the siege began learns the truth behind the negotiations and must deal with the fallout.

LOOK FOR

THE BABY'S GUARDIAN, *May*
DEVASTATING DADDY, *June*
THE MOMMY MYSTERY, *July*

www.eHarlequin.com

HI69472

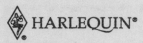

LAURA MARIE ALTOM

The Baby Twins

Stephanie Olmstead has her hands full raising her twin baby girls on her own. When she runs into old friend Brady Flynn, she's shocked to find herself suddenly attracted to the handsome airline pilot! Will this flyboy be the perfect daddy—or will he crash and burn?

"LOVE, HOME & HAPPINESS"

www.eHarlequin.com

HAR75309

REQUEST YOUR FREE BOOKS!

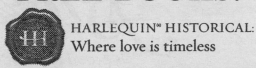

HARLEQUIN® HISTORICAL:
Where love is timeless

2 FREE NOVELS PLUS 2 FREE GIFTS!

YES! Please send me 2 FREE Harlequin® Historical novels and my 2 FREE gifts (gifts are worth about $10). After receiving them, if I don't wish to receive any more books, I can return the shipping statement marked "cancel." If I don't cancel, I will receive 6 brand-new novels every month and be billed just $4.94 per book in the U.S. or $5.49 per book in Canada. That's a saving of 20% off the cover price! It's quite a bargain! Shipping and handling is just 50¢ per book.* I understand that accepting the 2 free books and gifts places me under no obligation to buy anything. I can always return a shipment and cancel at any time. Even if I never buy another book from Harlequin, the two free books and gifts are mine to keep forever.

246/349 HDN E5L4

Name _____ (PLEASE PRINT) _____

Address _____ Apt. # _____

City _____ State/Prov. _____ Zip/Postal Code _____

Signature (if under 18, a parent or guardian must sign)

Mail to the Harlequin Reader Service:
IN U.S.A.: P.O. Box 1867, Buffalo, NY 14240-1867
IN CANADA: P.O. Box 609, Fort Erie, Ontario L2A 5X3

Not valid for current subscribers to Harlequin Historical books.

Want to try two free books from another line?
Call 1-800-873-8635 or visit www.morefreebooks.com.

* Terms and prices subject to change without notice. Prices do not include applicable taxes. N.Y. residents add applicable sales tax. Canadian residents will be charged applicable provincial taxes and GST. Offer not valid in Quebec. This offer is limited to one order per household. All orders subject to approval. Credit or debit balances in a customer's account(s) may be offset by any other outstanding balance owed by or to the customer. Please allow 4 to 6 weeks for delivery. Offer available while quantities last.

Your Privacy: Harlequin Books is committed to protecting your privacy. Our Privacy Policy is available online at www.eHarlequin.com or upon request from the Reader Service. From time to time we make our lists of customers available to reputable third parties who may have a product or service of interest to you. If you would prefer we not share your name and address, please check here. ☐

Help us get it right—We strive for accurate, respectful and relevant communications. To clarify or modify your communication preferences, visit us at www.ReaderService.com/consumerschoice.

HH10R

HARLEQUIN® *Blaze*™

is proud to introduce...

New York Times bestselling author

Brenda Jackson

with
SPONTANEOUS

Kim Cannon and Duan Jeffries have a great thing going. Whenever they meet up, the passion between them is hot, intense…spontaneous. And things really heat up when Duan agrees to accompany her to her mother's wedding. Too bad there's something he's not telling her.…

Don't miss the fireworks!

Available in May 2010
wherever Harlequin Blaze books are sold.

———————————————

red-hot reads

www.eHarlequin.com

HB79542